Richard Newsome lives in Brisbane with his family. He won the inaugural Text Prize for Young Adult and Children's Writing for *The Billionaire's Curse*, the first book in The Billionaire Series.

richardnewsome.com

THE
CRYSTAL CODE

BOOK IV *of*
THE BILLIONAIRE SERIES

RICHARD NEWSOME

TEXT PUBLISHING MELBOURNE AUSTRALIA

textpublishing.com.au
richardnewsome.com

The Text Publishing Company
Swann House
22 William Street
Melbourne Victoria 3000
Australia

First published in Australia by The Text Publishing Company, 2012
First published in the United States by The Text Publishing Company, 2013

Cover and page design by WH Chong
Cover illustration by Sebastian Ciaffaglione
Typeset by J & M Typesetting

ISBN: 9781922079039 (pbk.)
ISBN: 9781921961281 (ebook)

Printed and bound in the United States by Edwards Brothers Malloy.

For Bruce Waite, Ron Morse,
Tom Weidenman, 'Creepy' Crowther,
and all great English teachers everywhere.

Prologue

The man propped his motor scooter against a gravestone and dusted the snow from his jacket. He patted his pockets. Good. Everything was in place. He tossed his leather satchel over a shoulder and tramped along the avenue of bare trees that led out of the Grove Street cemetery.

Twice he almost lost his footing as he shuffled along icy paths into the campus of Yale University. Alphonse hated winter. Sure, he had natural insulation to fend off the chill, but his joints were no longer up to it. From November to February, he creaked. He had promised himself a holiday in Fiji: two weeks of sun and sand, a hammock under a palm tree, cocktails with tiny paper parasols. But then he received the phone call. And he was yet to say 'no' to the person on the other end of the line.

Alphonse huffed a plume of steam into the morning air as his boots scuffed and skated across the courtyard outside the rare-books-and-manuscripts library. The Yale campus, in America's north-east, sat under a fresh dump of snow.

Alphonse paused in front of the large box-like building with its sides designed like an albino checkerboard. He adjusted his beret and leaned on the revolving door. He greeted the woman at the information counter cheerily, but her manner held all the warmth of the courtyard outside.

'Professor Peregrine, you say?'

'That's right,' Alphonse said with a wry smile. 'Just like the falcon.'

The woman ran a finger down a list of visiting academics. 'You don't seem to be here. Which university are you from?'

'The Van Den Hoofdakker Institute,' he said with a mild accent. 'In the Netherlands.'

The woman looked up through over-sized glasses, then back down to the list. 'Mm-hmm,' she said. 'And you're here for the Voynich Manuscript?'

Alphonse ran a hand across his round belly. This was going to be too easy.

'You'll need to check your bag in at the cloakroom,' the woman said.

Alphonse's heart skipped a beat. 'I have to check

my satchel?' he said. 'That is most inconvenient. My notebooks. My pencils.' He raised a corner of his mouth and gave his head a cocky wobble. 'Surely some exception can be made'—he looked at a nametag pinned to the woman's cardigan—'Patricia. *Such a pretty name.* Can't we bend the rules, just this one time? Patricia?'

The receptionist didn't blink. 'No.'

Alphonse's brow wrinkled. This one was troublesome. But he had made a career of sweet-talking his way past the Patricias of this world.

'Perhaps, Patricia, you and I could have coffee sometime?' His eyes sparkled as he leaned an elbow on the counter. 'I assume you don't have a boyfriend?'

The receptionist glared at him through feline eyes. 'Professor Peregrine,' she said. 'You can either check that bag in or you can go back to the Van Den Hooffendacken—'

'It's Van Den Hoofdakker,' Alphonse corrected. 'In the Netherlands.'

The receptionist gave him a look that said she really did not care.

'Uh—I'll check my bag in,' Alphonse said. 'Could you tell me where the nearest men's room might be?'

Without shifting her gaze, the woman pointed a pencil towards the far end of the library.

Five minutes later, Alphonse was back at the counter, a notebook and pen in his hand.

'I've checked my bag in, Patricia,' he said brightly.

The receptionist considered him with a wary eye. 'But not your coat?'

Alphonse ran a hand across his belly, which appeared to be somewhat larger than it had been when he entered the library. 'I feel the cold,' he said.

'Mm-hmm.' The receptionist pushed herself to her feet. 'This way.'

Alphonse followed her down a spiral staircase to a vast open-plan study area. Academics and students, their heads bowed over ancient texts, occupied banks of study cubicles. The receptionist led Alphonse to a large glass-walled room and opened the door. On a desk in the middle of the floor was a roughly bound nest of papers, about the size of a school scrapbook. It appeared to be extremely old.

'No smoking, no eating, no drinking,' the receptionist said. 'And wear these at all times.' She held out a pair of white cotton gloves. 'The Voynich Manuscript is at least five hundred years old and is one of a kind. It is very fragile.' She pointed to a row of archive boxes that lined the floor along one of the glass walls. 'All these documents are extremely rare. They're waiting to go back to the stacks.' She leaned down until her nose was a bare centimetre from Alphonse's face. 'Do not touch them.'

'Of course, my dear Patricia,' Alphonse said, with a tiny bow. 'You can rely on me.' He glanced at the walls of glass that allowed an uninterrupted view of the library and coughed into his hand. 'It is somewhat like the bowl

4

for the goldfish, yes? I prefer to do my research without distraction. Is there somewhere more...private?'

The receptionist looked at Alphonse as if he was an untrustworthy ten-year-old in a lolly shop. She flicked a switch by the door. A tiny electric motor whirred and a bank of navy curtains was drawn around the walls. As the final pane was blocked off, she said, 'It's double-glazed. Soundproof. Satisfied?'

'Only one thing could make me happier,' Alphonse said with a wink.

The woman narrowed her eyes. 'No smoking. No eating. No drinking.' She closed the door, leaving Alphonse to himself.

The moment the door clicked shut, the smile left Alphonse's face. He tossed his notebook into a corner, pulled on the white gloves and settled onto a desk chair. He cracked his knuckles and took a deep breath.

Gently, he opened the manuscript cover. The pages were thick between his fingers, more like pressed cloth than paper. They were covered with an array of shapes and patterns. It was an alphabet in a language the likes of which Alphonse had never seen. Page after page was filled with intricate symbols. Hand-painted illustrations showed a curious mix of dancing maidens and bizarre plants. There were pictures of odd-shaped vegetables and trees with root systems like clutching skeleton fingers.

Alphonse closed the manuscript with the greatest of care, and ran a finger along a wire cable that tethered it to a metal ring clamped to the desktop. The manuscript itself was attached to a thick Kevlar board—it would be impossible to remove the document without destroying it.

Alphonse studied the security set-up. 'Titanium,' he mumbled to himself. He unbuttoned his coat and shrugged it from his shoulders. Underneath he wore a false belly strapped to his stomach like a kangaroo's pouch. He tore open a velcro fastening and fished inside, removing a thick roll of cloth tied at the middle.

Nimble fingers untied the bundle. What appeared to be a can of lemonade was nestled inside.

Alphonse picked up the can and unscrewed a concealed top. It popped off with a hiss. Inside was a tiny valve and tap handle. He took a mechanical pencil from his pocket and bit off one end to reveal a long needle-like point. He jabbed it into the valve to form a nozzle and opened the gas tap. A blue flame ignited, sharp as a scalpel.

Alphonse laid the cloth across the manuscript as a fire blanket, taking care to ensure the ancient masterpiece was completely covered. Then, pulling dark glasses over his eyes, he directed the flame onto the cable.

A shower of sparks sprayed across the desk. After a moment, the cable glowed red. Alphonse flicked off the gas tap and pulled out a tiny silver chisel and hammer from his pouch. A gentle blow from his lips flared the hottest point of the cable. He placed the edge of the chisel onto the hot spot and struck it with the hammer. The cable broke neatly in two with a *ping* like the sound of a crystal glass being flicked with a fingernail. Alphonse smiled to himself.

Then he looked up. The room was on fire.

Sparks had ignited the archive boxes, turning the ancient documents into a million-dollar bonfire. Alphonse's eyes popped at the sight of the wall of flame just metres away.

'Eep!' he cried.

Smoke rose up the curtains. Alphonse's gaze shot to the ceiling above the door. The red eye of a smoke detector blinked back at him.

'Eep!'

The grey haze climbed higher. An archive box exploded in flames. Alphonse heaved the desk chair across the carpet and jumped onto the seat, riding it like a high-rise skateboard. He took a leap and flung out his hands as far as his stubby arms would allow and managed to wrap his fingers around the smoke detector just as the first piercing *PEEP* sounded. For a second he hung there, suspended from the little white box on the ceiling. The smoke rose higher.

PEEP!

Alphonse swung his legs furiously, trying to wrench the alarm from its moorings. In mid-swing, it gave way. Alphonse landed on his back with an *oomph*. He looked with satisfaction at the alarm in his hand. Then it let forth with a stabbing *PEEP-PEEP-PEEP*.

Alphonse clambered to his feet, hurled the alarm to the floor and stomped on it again and again. Each blow forced out another piercing *PEEP*. Smoke choked the room. Alphonse doubled his efforts to kick the alarm to death. Finally the little white box gave out its last, feeble squawk, and Alphonse stumbled across to the desk, hands wafting smoke from his eyes. He sighed with relief.

The Voynich Manuscript lay safe beneath the fire blanket. But smoke still billowed from the archive boxes. Alphonse rummaged in his kangaroo pouch and pulled out another soft-drink can. He fumbled with the false end and out popped a short hose. He shook the can and let loose a torrent of foam towards the burning boxes. But the surge shot the can from Alphonse's grip and he stumbled back. His foot landed in a pool of white froth, sending him reeling to the floor. As he landed, for the second time, he was suddenly aware of two things: his mini fire extinguisher was spinning wildly on the table, coating the curtains with a blanket of expanding foam; and the room was growing lighter. Then he noticed the whirr of a tiny electric motor.

The curtains were opening.

Alphonse stared in horror as the glass walls were slowly laid bare. He clawed himself upright and cast a panicked eye to the room beyond. He was surrounded by scores of students at their desks. Behind him, the archive boxes continued to belch smoke like factory stacks. The fire extinguisher farted out the last of its foam with sufficient force to shoot it across the room. It ricocheted off the side of Alphonse's head.

The curtains completed their journey.

The fishbowl was fully exposed.

Alphonse stared for a manic second at the acres of academia around him. Pens scratched on paper; fingers tapped on computers. No one raised an eye.

There followed a frenzied beating of the switch box as Alphonse tried to get the curtains moving again. After a flurry of swearing, the electric motor sparked into life, sending the drapes on a torturously slow path back around the room.

Alphonse dived towards the table and whipped off the fire blanket. He yanked a protective sleeve from his pouch and slid the manuscript inside. Shoving the package down the front of his trousers, he searched for his coat and found it on the floor. In seconds he had the coat on, and the oxy torch, the fire extinguisher and the gloves stuffed into his fake belly. He took a deep breath and buttoned himself into place. Apart from the thick smear of foamy ash across his face and clothes, he looked mostly unremarkable.

Alphonse took a step towards the door. His foot slid in a mush of foam and parchment and he landed bottom-first in the stack of smouldering archive boxes.

'*Eeep*!'

He bounced to his feet and was out the door. He

scuttled across to the spiral stairs just as the first fingers of smoke curled into the main study area. He threw a casual 'Thank you, Patricia,' over his shoulder as he breezed past the information desk and out through the revolving doors.

It was brisk outside—far colder than when he had arrived. He lowered his head and charged across the courtyard, past a cluster of wide-eyed college girls who stared after him as he disappeared around a corner in the direction of the graveyard.

'The Falcon has swooped again,' Alphonse said to himself with a grin of triumph.

It was only after he threw his leg over his scooter and plopped into the saddle that he realised the backside had burned out of his trousers. In an instant, the soft skin of his buttocks froze to the ice-covered seat.

Witnesses would later tell police that the fire alarm that sounded from the library was extraordinarily loud. But it was nothing compared to the screams that came from the stout man on the motor scooter as he shot past them and out of the campus.

Chapter 1

Farnborough Airport on London's south-western outskirts is basic by international standards. It's not very big or very attractive. But it is where the filthy rich land their private jets when they fly into London.

On this particular December afternoon, the airport was abuzz. The world's youngest billionaire, thirteen-year-old Gerald Wilkins, craned his neck, trying to spot his friends in the crowd that milled around the terminal concourse. It wasn't like Sam and Ruby Valentine to be late. Especially Sam, who regarded any trip on Gerald's private Airbus A380 Flying Palace as an event not to be missed.

Gerald's butler, Mr Fry, manoeuvred a train of trolleys, piled high with baggage, up to the check-in counter. Gerald's mother hovered by the butler's elbow.

'Take care, Mr Fry,' Vi Wilkins said. 'I had those suitcases custom-made by Birkin. I don't want a scratch on them.'

Mr Fry muttered as he unloaded the mountain of bags. 'Perhaps madam should have packed them into something.'

'Pack a suitcase into another suitcase?' Vi arched an eyebrow. 'Whatever are you talking about, Mr Fry? Honestly, I wonder whether you're looking forward to this holiday at all.'

The butler hefted a trunk the size of a small wardrobe from the cart. It landed on the floor with a thud. He leaned on it to catch his breath. 'Forty house guests, two dozen staff, three tons of ski gear and a Christmas banquet to organise,' he said. 'What's not to look forward to?'

'Oh, Mr Fry, you do carry on.' Vi pulled out a diamond-encrusted compact and re-applied her lipstick. 'Anybody would think you're not enjoying yourself. Oh, *squee*! There's Frannie and Jacinta. Yoo-hoo! Girls! Over here!'

Vi flapped her hands over her head, rattling her jewellery. She darted into the crowd, abandoning Mr Fry to his duties and charged across to two women who had just walked into the terminal. She threw her arms around them. Squeals of excitement sounded above the buzz of the crowd.

Gerald shook his head. It was going to be a long two weeks. Again, he scoured the concourse for his friends. He hadn't seen them for three months—not since the start of term at his new school. St Cuthbert's wasn't the most famous school in Winchester, or even the best school, but it was the most expensive. That made it the boarding school of choice for the sons of wealth and privilege from around the world. Sam and Ruby had been at school in London, and Gerald was keen to catch up with them. He was particularly anxious to see Ruby again. To explain what had happened over the past months.

But there was no sign of the Valentine twins.

The noise inside the terminal intensified. It was like the last day of school, except all the students were overweight and in their forties. Gerald recognised a few of his parents' friends—the ones who had been to their Chelsea townhouse for dinner. But there were many others now hanging around Vi and Eddie Wilkins, clapping them on the shoulders and thanking them for their hospitality.

A few weeks earlier, Vi had called Gerald at St Cuthbert's and informed him of her plans for Christmas.

'Just a few close friends of your father's and mine, dear,' she had trilled down the phone line. 'And you can invite some pals as well. The Valentines, of course. Aren't you and that gorgeous Ruby special friends now? And how about your friend Oswald from Sydney? You haven't seen him in such an age. Won't it be delicious, Gerald? Just imagine: a white Christmas at your great aunt's private ski field in the Sierra Nevada mountains in California! But of course, it's *your* ski field now, my darling boy.'

Gerald gazed at the crowded airport terminal. A few close friends? He was feeling distinctly outnumbered.

Then a pair of soft hands wrapped themselves over his eyes.

And a silken voice cooed in his ear, 'Guess who?'

Gerald's heart skipped. He reached up and pulled the hands from his face.

'Ruby!' He spun around. 'It's so good to—'

He stopped mid-sentence. Gerald had expected to find the smiling face of Ruby Valentine, but instead found himself staring into a pair of hazel brown eyes.

'Oh,' he said. 'Felicity.' He paused for a long second. 'You came, then.'

A tall slender girl of fourteen, her face framed by long chestnut plaits, beamed back at him. 'Of course I came, silly! What a *curious* boy you are.' She rocked up onto her toes and squeezed Gerald's fingers. 'This is going to be the best Christmas holiday *ever*!'

Gerald arranged his face into something resembling a smile. 'Yeah,' he said. 'The best. Ever.'

Felicity bounced up and down on the balls of her feet. 'The Colonel was ever so pleased when I told him you'd invited me for the hols, Gerald. Got him out of a real jam. He's stuck in Afghanistan with the regiment for, like, ever. And Mother's not back from her ashram in Nepal till the end of January. Dire. So it would have been Christmas turkey for one in the dining hall at St Hilda's for poor Flicka if you hadn't come to the rescue. The Colonel said he never thought he'd see the day when he'd be grateful to an Australian. Hilarious. But there you are. My knight in shining armour, Gerald. Whatever would I have done without you?'

All this was said without pause for breath and at a speed that made Gerald's head bob. Before he could open his mouth to respond, Felicity launched forth again. 'I'm ever so lucky, and skiing is just my most favourite thing in the world. Not counting riding, of course. You don't ride, do you Gerald? We'll fix that. Are there stables on the mountain? I bet there are. Because wouldn't that just be the best thing. The best thing *ever*. A ride in the snow! Oh, how lovely would that be? I could teach you, Gerald. Miss Urquhart says I've the best seat in my year. Maybe even the whole school. And she should know. Three Olympics and three silver medals. She's ever so good. Really knows her horseflesh. Oh look! Is that your friends Ruby and Sam over there?'

Gerald, exhausted from nodding along to Felicity's breakneck monologue, followed the direction of her pointed finger.

His heart lurched in his chest. 'Yeah,' he said, his voice catching. 'That's them.' He waved a hand above his head.

Sam reached Gerald first. Looking as fit as ever, and

maybe a bit taller, he threw an arm around Gerald's shoulders. 'Look at you, pasty face!' Sam said. 'You've got a real English tan now.' Gerald laughed. Three months of a British autumn had stolen away any sign of their wild summer together in Europe.

'Good to see you too, Ugly,' Gerald said through a broad grin.

'How's the new school?' Sam asked. 'Gold taps in the bathrooms and posh beyond belief? You still talking to commoners like us?'

Gerald shrugged. 'It's a school.'

'Fair enough,' Sam said. 'Now, this flight to San Francisco—do we get fed? Coz I'm starving.'

Gerald could not believe how good it was to see his friend again.

Then Ruby walked up.

Gerald stopped breathing.

Ruby wore a pair of blue jeans, and a leather jacket over a plain T-shirt. A simple scarf was knotted loosely at her neck. Her hair, longer than he remembered, was tied to the side with a dark ribbon. A remnant of summer freckles dusted her cheeks. She crinkled her nose and smiled, her face alight. Her blue eyes scanned Gerald's face, taking in the changes after so long apart. They stared at each other for a silent half-second, time seemingly frozen. She took a half-step forward, spread her arms, and—

'Ruby!' Felicity bounced in front of Gerald, straight

into Ruby's embrace, squeezing her tight around the middle. 'Hi! Hi! I'm Felicity. Felicity Upham. But do call me Flicka. All my friends do. Gerald has told me ever so much about you. And Sam as well.'

Felicity flashed Sam a brilliant smile, then directed her full attention back onto Ruby, clutching her hands. 'I'm so looking forward to this trip, and getting to know you. Last holiday my father, the Colonel, took me on a tour of the Lake District. We did brass rubbings at all the churchyards. It was okay, but it wasn't as good as skiing. I'm babbling, aren't I? I do that when I'm excited. My father says he should have named me Brooke! Ha! Isn't that too funny? Oh, I just know we're going to be best friends. Do you ride? I bet you're brilliant. I love your shoes. And your hair! Oh God, I'm so jealous. I saw some amazing hair bands and charms in the gift shop over there. Come on. I'll show you.'

With an effort, Ruby managed to free herself from Felicity's clutches. She shot a confused look at Gerald.

'I'm sorry,' Ruby said, shaking her head as if she hadn't heard right. 'Who did you say you were?'

Felicity let out a laugh like a china bell. 'Oh, Ruby,' she said. 'I'm Felicity. You know. Gerald's girlfriend.'

Ruby stared open mouthed at Gerald. For some reason, Gerald couldn't think of anything sensible to say. He shrugged and managed a tight smile.

'Surprise,' he said.

Chapter 2

There wasn't just a gap in the conversation—it fell into an abyss. Felicity took full advantage. She held tight onto Ruby's hand. 'Come on. This gift shop is the best thing *ever*.' Then she dragged Ruby towards the far end of the terminal building.

Sam turned to Gerald. 'Who is that?'

'That,' Gerald said, 'is Felicity.'

'Bit of a force of nature, isn't she.'

'Yep,' Gerald said. 'Cyclonic.'

'And where do we know her from?'

Gerald took a deep breath. 'She goes to a girls' boarding school across town from mine—St Hilda's. We met at the annual Hilda's versus Cuthbert's dance.'

'Sounds more like a rugby match,' Sam said.

'It is a bit. Both schools line up on either side of the hall and wait for the whistle.'

'Whistle?'

'Well, music. Then it's non-stop dancing till a nun blows full time and everyone goes home.'

'I see.'

'Felicity likes dancing.'

'I can imagine. And brass rubbings too. Quite the catch.'

'She's nice. You know, lots of fun. We've been to the movies together. School lets us out on Saturday nights and we go into town.'

'Time off for some bad behaviour, eh? Are you two boyfriend-girlfriend then?'

'Well, sort of,' Gerald said, shaking his head. 'At least, not fully. We're just—'

'Good friends?' Sam suggested.

'Yeah, that's it,' Gerald said. 'Just...good friends.'

'Uh-huh,' Sam said. He looked across to the gift shop window, where Felicity was urging an unenthusiastic Ruby to try on some necklaces. 'Just a friend, who you invite aboard your private jet for an all-expenses-paid Christmas holiday in the California snow.'

'So?' Gerald said. 'What's so unusual about that?'

Sam shrugged. 'Bit of a step up from Saturday night at the movies.'

Gerald's heart sank into the pit of his gut. 'I asked her along because she's fun. And she would've been alone at Christmas otherwise.' He bit his bottom lip. 'Do you think Ruby will mind?'

Sam let rip with a snort. 'Let's see. It's been, what, four months since we've seen you? Ruby has mentioned your name about five times every day. That increased to twenty times once your mum phoned up to ask us along on this trip.' Sam did some quick calculations on his fingers. 'That'd be about a thousand times I've had to hear her utter the word 'Gerald' since the start of September.' He stared at Gerald's face. 'What do you think?'

Gerald held Sam's gaze for a moment, then slid into a seat. He cupped his head in his hands. 'What have I done?'

Sam sat next to his friend and nudged him with his elbow. 'Don't worry about it. Girls go crazy for this sort of drama. Gives them something to talk about when they go to the loo together. The thing is, I thought you were keen on Ruby.'

'I am. Or at least, I was,' Gerald said. 'I think.'

'Then why did you invite Felicity?'

Gerald looked across to Sam. It was a good question. A really good question. Unfortunately, Gerald did not have a good answer. 'I think I like her too,' Gerald said.

'Oh yeah, that type of thing always ends well,' Sam said. 'Don't sweat it. The truth is, I'm glad.'

'You are?'

'Sure. You and Ruby moping around like a couple

of love-sick puppies was really boring. This way at least we can enjoy ourselves.'

'Even with Ruby hating my guts?'

'Especially with her hating your guts. She's more fun when she's ticked off at something. The last four months have been a colossal bore. I've never seen her so happy.' He placed a hand on Gerald's shoulder. 'The argument that you two are about to have could well save this holiday.'

Gerald snuffled out a mirthless laugh. 'So you think there's going to be an argument?'

They both looked across to the gift shop, in time to see Ruby glaring back at them with a face that would freeze the fairy from the top of a Christmas tree.

'Oh yes,' Sam said. 'There will be an argument. And then some.'

Gerald swallowed. It wasn't the start to the holiday he had hoped for.

'So, what's with all these people?' Sam asked, indicating the throng around Gerald's parents with a tilt of his head. 'Are they all coming to America with us?'

'I think so,' Gerald said. 'Mum wants a big traditional Christmas. You know—turkeys under the mistletoe, that kind of thing. Apparently my great aunt's private ski field is pretty awesome. And we've never had a white Christmas before. It's usually boiling hot and you're sweating into your lunch.'

'I forgot you Australians do everything upside down,'

Sam said. 'Mum said there's been some heavy snowfalls in California so the skiing should be good.'

They looked up to the sound of another burst of excited squealing from Gerald's mother. She was racing towards a couple that had just stepped from an Aston Martin One-77.

'Alisha is joining us in San Francisco,' Gerald said. 'And you'll get to meet Ox. He's flying in from Sydney with his folks. You'll like him—he's hilarious.' Gerald suddenly raised his head and looked about. 'Are your parents here? I didn't see them.'

'Yeah, they're in the middle of the mob down there somewhere,' Sam said. 'It was a good idea of your mum's to invite all of us.'

'Why's that?'

'Because every time Ruby and I go on a trip with you, someone ends up dead. I don't think Mum would have let us come if she wasn't invited too.'

Gerald gave a grim nod. His holidays with the Valentine twins did tend towards the dramatic.

'Oh, wait,' Gerald said, shoving his hand into his back pocket. 'I've got something to show you two.' He pulled out his wallet and flipped it open.

Sam gagged at the thick fold of US hundred dollar notes stuffed inside. 'You don't need to show off, you know,' Sam said. 'I get it. You're a billionaire.'

Gerald gave him a quizzical smile. 'Not the cash, dummy,' he said. 'This.' From a sleeve in the wallet, just behind the black American Express card, Gerald removed a square of buff-coloured cardboard.

'What is it?' Sam asked.

'Ruby needs to be here as well.'

They looked back to the gift shop. Felicity had Ruby swathed in colourful scarves.

'Good luck getting her out of there anytime soon,' Sam said. 'Come on. What've you got?'

Gerald frowned—he had wanted to share it with both Valentine twins. But his reunion with Ruby hadn't gone exactly to plan. 'Okay,' Gerald said. 'This was in the box of stuff that Inspector Parrott dropped round to the house at the end of the summer holidays. The bits and pieces from Mason Green's room at the Rattigan Club. Remember?'

'That's right. We were playing cards. What is it?'

Gerald held up the square of cardboard between his fingers. 'It's a dry-cleaning ticket.'

'Hmmm,' said Sam. 'On the face of it, not very interesting.'

'It's a ticket for a dry cleaners in San Francisco.'

'Still not interesting, really.'

Gerald waved the ticket under Sam's nose. 'Don't you see what this means?'

'You have a perspiration problem?'

'I'm beginning to see why Ruby gets frustrated with you. It's not my ticket. It's Mason Green's.'

'So he's the one with the perspiration problem,'

Sam said. 'Brilliant. The case of the sweaty billionaire is solved. Holmes, you astound me.'

'No, you idiot. If Green had a dry-cleaning ticket it means he must have left something there to be cleaned.'

Sam nodded slowly. 'Yes. Yes, I think I follow you.'

'Don't be a pain,' Gerald said. 'We're about to fly to San Francisco. The dry cleaner is in San Francisco. It's the perfect opportunity.'

Sam's expression didn't change. 'To do what? See some of Mason Green's underwear?'

Gerald was about to clip Sam over the ear when a voice interrupted them.

'What are you two talking about?' Felicity appeared over Gerald's shoulder. She was beaming, like she'd been given a puppy on her birthday. Gerald looked up to find her holding Ruby's hand. Ruby's head was festooned in ribbons and bands. The look on her face did not reflect the party that was going on in her hair.

'You two seem to be having fun, then,' Sam said. He swallowed down the giggle that was trying to scale his windpipe.

'We certainly are,' Felicity said. Then she snatched the ticket from Gerald's fingers. 'What have you got there?'

Gerald tried to grab it back, but missed. 'It's a dry-cleaning ticket,' he said, irritated. 'It's nothing.'

'Then why were you making out it was the discovery of the century?' Sam said, oblivious to the glare Gerald shot at him.

'Yes, Gerald. Why?' Felicity asked.

Gerald took in a slow breath. 'Because of the address of the dry cleaners.'

Felicity looked at the ticket. 'It's in San Francisco,' she said. 'On the corner of Mason and Green streets.'

'Where did you say?' Ruby almost choked on the words. She took the ticket from Felicity. 'Bay City Cleaning, on Mason and Green.' She turned to Gerald. 'What's going on?'

They were the first words Ruby had said to him. Not 'Hi,' or 'How are you?' Not 'I've missed you,' or 'So good to see you.' But a blunt, 'What's going on?'

It was like they'd never met before.

'It was on Mason Green's desk at the Rattigan Club,' Gerald said, trying not to sound disappointed. 'With all that stuff he'd stolen from my place.' He was painfully aware that Felicity was sitting right next to him. 'Don't you think it's a bit odd that Green would use a cleaner at that particular address.'

'That Mason Green would use a cleaner at the corner of Mason and Green?' Sam said. 'Getting clean at Mason and Green. Maybe he has a strange sense of humour.'

'I don't recall him being a bundle of laughs,' Gerald said. The memory of Green's murder of Gerald's great aunt was still fresh in his mind.

'What are you saying?' Ruby asked Gerald.

'Maybe Mason Green isn't his real name,' Gerald said.

Ruby stared at him blankly. 'And he used the address of some random dry cleaner in San Francisco as an alias? That's absurd.'

'It's a possibility,' Gerald said.

'So is the question of your sanity,' Ruby said.

Sam looked puzzled. 'So it's not just about his undies then.'

Felicity tugged on Gerald's elbow. 'Isn't that the man who tried to kill you, Gerald? How perfectly sick-making.'

Gerald ignored the looks of disbelief from Sam and Ruby. 'I'm just curious to see the place, so here's what I think we should do,' he said. 'The plane gets into San Francisco about two o'clock this afternoon. We don't leave for the ski field till tomorrow. What say we go for a visit to the corner of Mason and Green and see what this ticket gets us.'

'So instead of seeing the Golden Gate Bridge or Alcatraz, you want to see some of Green's dirty clothes?' Sam said.

'No,' Gerald said, 'I think they should be clean by now.'

Chapter 3

The circus train of limousines pulled into the forecourt of the Fairmont Hotel in San Francisco. From the warmth of the backseat of his Lincoln Town Car, Gerald saw his mother was already out of the lead vehicle and directing operations. A team of porters was jumping at her orders, hauling luggage from the back of a van. Mr Fry, wrapped in a thick overcoat, was at her elbow, checking items from a list on a clipboard. The rigours of an eleven-hour aeroplane flight were not apparent on Vi Wilkins as she snapped her fingers at anyone not moving fast enough.

'I think my mother would have made a fair army general,' Gerald said, his breath fogging the inside of the car window.

'The Colonel would be impressed,' Felicity said.

'She certainly likes to take charge,' Ruby said.

Ruby had barely spoken during the flight. She seemed content to curl up in an armchair and read her book. While Felicity and Sam played marathon sessions of computer games, laughing themselves silly over the action in *Zombie Cookout IV*, Ruby had quietly turned pages, her legs tucked in under herself. Gerald had tried to strike up a conversation but he didn't get very far.

'So what've you been up to?'

Ruby didn't look up from her book. 'Not much. School. You know. Stuff.'

'Uh-huh,' Gerald said. 'I'm really looking forward to this ski trip. I've got a new snowboard I'm dying to try out.'

Ruby turned a page. 'That's nice.'

'Yeah. Yeah, really nice.' Gerald wracked his brain for a way to get a conversation going. 'Uh, Felicity likes you.'

'Mm-hmm.'

'She's a lot of fun.'

'Yes, I suppose so,' Ruby said. 'Not at all sick-making.'

Gerald pressed his lips together. 'Are you going to be like this the whole holiday?'

Ruby held up a finger as she finished reading a paragraph. She placed a bookmark between the pages, closed the book and stared hard at Gerald. 'I'm sorry,' she said. 'Like what, exactly?'

Ruby's expression was painted on like a china doll's. They looked at each other for what seemed an age.

Gerald finally broke his gaze and jumped up. 'I'm going to play *Mutant Unicorn Rangers* with Sam and Felicity,' he grumbled.

Ruby returned to her book. 'That's nice,' she said to Gerald's back as he slouched off. 'That sounds really nice.'

That was as far as Gerald had got with Ruby. Now that they had landed, things were just as bad. The rear door of the car was hauled open and Gerald stepped out into the freezing San Francisco afternoon. A uniformed doorman saluted with a finger to the brim of his cap as Sam, Felicity and Ruby followed Gerald into the cold. They gathered in a tight cluster under the hotel canopy. A convoy of cars pulled up and disgorged a stream of well-dressed occupants. There was Gerald's father and his golfing buddies, guffawing at some inappropriate joke. And Vi's giggling tennis friends—six women spray-tanned a deep mahogany in defiance of the season. Then there was the entire membership of the Chelsea Mahjong Club, still clutching champagne glasses from the aeroplane and lost in a fog of gossip.

Servants from Gerald's country estate in Somerset arrived in the final limo and headed straight to Mr Fry to help him and the porters with the luggage.

All around him, Gerald could see people thrilled

about the prospect of Christmas on the ski slopes—it was hard not to get swept up in all the excitement. Then his eyes fell on Ruby, who stood to one side, her coat pulled tight across her chest, her chin braced against the collar.

Gerald was about to try talking to her again when he was distracted by a cry of delight.

'Master Gerald!'

A stout woman with a loose bun of white hair grabbed hold of his hands and squeezed them tight. Then she held Gerald at arm's length for inspection.

'Goodness, but you've grown!' she said. 'But, have they been feeding you? Boarding school dining halls are no fit place to raise a young gentleman, pardon me for saying so.'

'Mrs Rutherford!' The cry came from Gerald, Sam and Ruby at the same instant. They crowded in for a hug. It was the first time Gerald had seen his housekeeper since leaving for St Cuthbert's at the end of the summer. She seemed as happily batty as ever.

'Master Sam and Miss Ruby!' She held them tight. 'So very good to see you again. And this must be Miss Felicity. How marvellous to meet you at last. Mrs Wilkins has told me so much about you.' Gerald glanced at Ruby—her face was inscrutable.

For the first time that day, Felicity couldn't get a word in. 'You must catch me up on all your news,' Mrs Rutherford said as she conducted them into the hotel lobby. 'I've been here a few days already, getting things ready and I've taken the liberty of preparing a little snack for your arrival. I'll leave Mr Fry to attend to the adults.' She looked both ways and dropped her voice to a conspiratorial whisper. 'The better grub is through this way.' She led them to a private dining room at the far end of the lobby and threw open the doors. Gerald, Sam, Ruby and Felicity crowded the entryway and peered inside.

'Oh, Mrs Rutherford…' Sam said.

Set out before them, on a huge round table in the centre of the room, was a feast of truly epic proportions. Platters were piled with steaming pies and sausage rolls. A roast turkey with a mountain of stuffing lay carved and succulent and waiting. Bowls of mashed potatoes and mint peas and honeyed carrots and fresh salad were crammed next to plates of lamb, duck and beef. A carved ham, decorated with sprigs of holly, sat at one end of the table. A cooked goose, glazed in brandy butter, sat at the other. Gravy boats brimmed to the gunwales with juice-laden yumminess, steam curling up in siren fingers beckoned their easily tempted taste buds.

A crackling log fire filled a stone fireplace in one corner, and a colossal spruce, bedecked with tinsel and twinkling lights, filled another. Across from the mantle stood a dessert trolley, covered with pudding bowls of trifle, cake, mince pies, ice cream, custard and other sugary delights.

It was as if they'd stumbled into Santa's dining hall.

Sam pulled up a seat at the table. A waiter stepped forward to lay a linen napkin across his lap and start to load up his plate.

'I must say the Americans are very fond of their food,' Mrs Rutherford said, filling glasses with home-made lemonade. 'Even by my standards. Still, this should fuel you up after such a long flight.'

Sam bit into a turkey leg and glanced across to Felicity's plate. She was alternating slices of tomato and slices of goat's cheese across a bed of lettuce and baby spinach leaves. 'You not having any food, then?' Sam said through a mouthful.

Felicity stabbed a carrot julienne with her fork and took a nibble. 'Nothing in excess, Sam,' Felicity said. She sipped an iced tea, no sugar. 'Gluttony is just filling a void in your life with food. I avoid voids.'

Sam pondered this and took another mouthful of turkey. 'What's the opposite of void?' he asked Gerald.

Ruby took a look at Felicity's plate and then at her own. She put back two sausage rolls and added some salad. 'So what's been happening, Mrs Rutherford?' she asked. 'Anything interesting going on?'

The housekeeper was busy topping up Sam's glass when the pitcher slipped and spilled over the tablecloth. Sam leapt clear as lemonade cascaded onto his chair.

'Oh, will you look at that,' Mrs Rutherford said. 'What a muddle I've made.'

Gerald had never seen his housekeeper drop so much

as a pea during a dinner service. He looked at her closely as the waiter helped mop up the mess. 'Are you okay, Mrs Rutherford?' he said.

Mrs Rutherford brushed aside a wisp of hair that had fallen across her face. She looked up at the young billionaire and her veneer of unflappable calm dropped away. She slumped into a spare seat at the table and let out an enormous sob.

'What is it, Mrs Rutherford?' Ruby asked. 'Is everything all right?'

'No, Miss Ruby,' the housekeeper said. 'Everything is most decidedly not all right.'

'Is it all the preparations for Christmas?' Ruby asked. 'It must be a lot to organise for all those guests.'

'Should Mr Fry be helping more?' Gerald asked. 'I'll have a word with him.'

Mrs Rutherford sat back and fanned herself with a napkin. 'Thank you for your concern, Master Gerald, but Mr Fry is doing quite enough. You don't need to take my word for it. He'll tell you that himself. And Miss Ruby, I could prepare Christmas dinner for the Coldstream Guards without raising a sweat. That's not what's weighing on my mind.'

'Then what is it?' Sam asked, still clutching a turkey leg in his hand.

'You can't have heard,' Mrs Rutherford said. 'And it's not really my place to be telling you.'

'Telling us what?' Gerald asked.

The housekeeper took in a deep breath. 'Sir Mason Green has escaped from the prison in Athens,' she said. 'It was on the news last night.'

'*What?*' Gerald couldn't believe what he was hearing.

The man who had ordered the murder of his great aunt, who had tried to kill Gerald and the Valentine twins on more than one occasion, was free?

'They're saying he had outside help. They have no idea where he is,' Mrs Rutherford sobbed. 'I am so sorry, Master Gerald.'

Gerald stared at the plate of food in front of him. He put his fork down beside it. His appetite had suddenly deserted him.

Mason Green.

Free from jail.

Gerald pulled the dry-cleaning ticket from his pocket and stared at it.

'Anyone feel like a walk?' he asked.

Chapter 4

The cable car strained up the hill in the grey afternoon. It was still an hour until sunset, but the day had slipped into the slow decline towards a winter's evening.

Gerald stood on the runner boards at the rear of the cable car, clutching a pole for support as the pavement slid away beneath his feet. Sam and Felicity had run to jump aboard at the last minute and were squeezed inside at the front. Ruby was standing next to Gerald, her gloved hands wrapped around the pole between them. She stared out at the buildings as the cable car climbed the hill. The clickety-clack of the cable running under the street played a wistful serenade.

Gerald shivered. There were only a few stops until

they reached the dry cleaners. He decided to have another attempt at making peace with Ruby.

'What's the matter?' Gerald asked in as polite a tone as possible. 'What have I done wrong?'

Ruby pulled her gaze away from the streetscape to look at Gerald. Her eyes were red. From the cold, Gerald thought. Or not.

'It's different now,' she said, simply. The words floated in the air for a moment before the wind swept them down the street, along with the litter and leaves.

The brake man pulled back on the long metal handle. The cable car juddered forward, jostling Gerald into Ruby's shoulder.

'Is it Felicity?' Gerald asked. 'Is that the problem?'

Ruby blinked against the wind. 'That's not a bad place to start,' she said. She pressed her lips together.

'I don't understand.'

'I know you don't. I wrote to you every week during term. Every week at that fancy-pants school of yours. I told you what I'd been doing, what Sam had been up to.' She paused for a breath. 'How I missed you…'

Gerald looked on, silent.

'And you didn't respond. Not once.' She shook her head. 'After everything we said to each other after Delphi. Nothing, for four months.'

Gerald swallowed. He struggled to think of what to say. 'I was…uh…busy,' he mumbled. 'New school. And all that.'

'Nothing to do with the fact you'd found yourself a new girlfriend?' Ruby glared at him. 'You must think the sun shines out of your backside, Gerald.'

Gerald shifted uncomfortably as the cable car broached the hill and started down. He shot a glance inside to Felicity—she was laughing at something Sam had said. 'We just saw a couple of movies together,' Gerald said in a flat voice. 'She's not really my girlfriend.'

'Oh really?' Ruby said. 'Well you better let her know that, because that's exactly what she thinks she is.' Ruby flared her nostrils and moved in closer. 'I don't get it, Gerald. Is it a billionaire thing? Why settle with having one girlfriend when you can have two?'

'That's not fair,' Gerald mumbled.

'Or is it like all those houses you own? One for the country and one for town? Well, guess what, Mister Billionaire, Felicity is a really nice person. I like her, despite you and everything you've done. And neither of us is some piece of property that you can jet between on holidays.' She jabbed a finger into Gerald's chest. 'You need to sort this before Felicity finds out the type of person you really are. I don't want her thinking I'm so shallow that I once had someone like you as a friend.'

The cable car hauled to a stop.

'Mason and Green!' the brakeman called.

Gerald's fist slid down the pole and brushed Ruby's glove. She snatched her hand away. 'This is where we get off,' she said. She jumped onto the road and jogged to the opposite footpath.

Gerald sighed. How had he managed to stuff things up so royally? He was tempted to stay onboard and ride the cable car into the sunset. Or, preferably, the bay. He looked up to see that Felicity was already by Ruby's side and was beckoning him across. He stepped off as the cable car lurched down the hill.

They stood at the crossroads.

A street sign showed Mason and Green.

'So our man is on the loose again,' Sam said. 'Do you really think Mason Green is a fake name?'

Gerald had lost all enthusiasm for the expedition. He looked across the intersection to a green shopfront with 'Dry Cleaner' painted above the door. 'Come on,' he said. 'Let's see what dirty laundry we can find.'

A fug of cleaning fumes assaulted them as they walked inside. Suits and dresses in clear plastic bags hung from a conveyor system that disappeared into a dark back room. Price lists, yellowed with age, were pinned to the walls. A woman sat at a counter, sewing a button onto a shirt.

'Hello,' Gerald said, holding out the dry-cleaning ticket. 'I'm just collecting this.' He was surprised to find that his hand was shaking. What if the cleaner knew Green by sight? How would Gerald explain his way around that? Or worse, the woman knew where Green was hiding and alerted him that Gerald was trying to steal his cleaning. He wished he'd thought it through properly, but the whole Ruby disaster meant he couldn't think straight.

The woman looked closely at the four faces on the other side of the counter, and took the ticket. 'This has been a long time,' she said. 'Another week and I would have sent it to charity.'

She turned in her seat and flicked a switch, sending the racks of garments along the track suspended from the ceiling. She switched the conveyor off and removed a black dinner jacket covered in its thin plastic bag. She laid it across the counter and nodded at the hanger. 'Some things were left in the pockets. They're in that envelope.'

Gerald went to pick up the jacket. The woman clamped a heavy hand over his, pinning it to the counter.

'I think you've forgotten something,' she said, staring hard into Gerald's eyes.

Gerald's pulse tripled. What was she talking about? Was there some sort of code word?

'Uh, Mason Green,' Gerald babbled. 'Oracle. Delphi. Rattigan.'

The woman's face creased into a scowl. 'What are you talking about? Twenty-five dollars.'

'Huh?'

'Twenty-five dollars. For the cleaning.'

'Oh, right. Of course.' Gerald pulled out his wallet. The woman's eyes bulged at the bankroll.

'Can you change a hundred?' asked Gerald.

On the footpath outside, Gerald tore off the plastic wrap and pulled a bespoke Saville Row dinner jacket off the hanger. It was lined in a deep-purple silk.

'What's in the envelope?' Sam asked.

'Ooh, let me,' Felicity said. She took the envelope from Gerald and tore it open. She pulled out a set of keys on a large silver fob. There was ornate engraving on one side.

'The Palladium Apartments,' Felicity read. She tossed the keys to Gerald.

Ruby clicked her tongue. 'An old jacket and some house keys. Well, that's cracked the case wide open.'

Gerald held the jacket up and looked at Ruby. She glared back at him.

'Here, Felicity,' he said. 'Try it on for size.'

Felicity slid her arms inside the sleeves and wrapped the pure merino warmth around her. 'Oh, this is so cosy,' she said, smiling brightly. She folded up the cuffs to above her wrists. 'Thank you, Gerald.'

Ruby narrowed her eyes.

Gerald glared straight back at her. 'The least I could do,' he said. 'For my girlfriend.'

If the temperature around Ruby had dropped any lower it would have started to snow.

Chapter 5

The moment Gerald walked into the Fairmont Hotel lounge, he spied his old school friend from Sydney.

'Ox!' Gerald threw his arms around a stout lad of about fourteen and wrapped him in an enormous hug. 'How're you going?'

Ox stood there for an awkward moment, his arms by his side. 'Uh, this is all very European,' he said, squirming to free himself. 'You do this to all the boys you know?'

Gerald laughed. 'Only the ugly ones,' he said. He looked at Ox for a few seconds, studying him. He hadn't seen him in six months. Then he gathered him up in another bear hug. 'The *really* ugly ones!'

Ox raised his eyes to the ceiling. 'Gerald,' he said.

'I would like you to release me as this is making me uncomfortable.'

Gerald looked at his friend in surprise. 'Excuse me?'

Ox cleared his throat and spoke a little louder. 'You are invading my personal space and I would like you to respect my wishes please.'

Gerald released his grip and took a step backwards. 'Are you serious?' he asked.

Ox's face broke into a broad grin. 'See! It works. How amazing is that?'

'What are you talking about?'

'My assertiveness training,' Ox said. 'People in the know call it A.T.'

'Do they?'

'Oh yes. My mum booked me into some self-confidence classes so I can be more comfortable around girls. You remember how hopeless I was trying to talk to them.'

Gerald remembered. Even by his own rubbish standards when it came to dealing with girls, Ox brought new meaning to the word 'useless'.

'The classes have been fantastic,' Ox said. 'It turns out I was rude to girls because I was nervous around them. But the instructor has taught me a bunch of ways to relax and act natural whenever they're around. I can talk to girls now like they're normal people. You remember Madeleine from our history class?'

Gerald's eyes bulged. He once had a major crush

on Madeleine. But she hadn't responded all that well to his drawing of him rescuing her from a fire-breathing dragon.

'You didn't ask Madeleine out, did you?' Gerald stared at Ox in awe.

'Of course I did,' Ox said, with a smug grin.

'What did she say?'

'She said she wouldn't be seen dead with me unless I was the last human being on earth.'

'Oh.'

'But that's good,' Ox said.

'How is that good?'

'When I asked her the time before that she gave me a flat "no". So there's some progress.'

Gerald shook his head. Ox hadn't changed at all.

Just then, Felicity, Ruby and Sam wandered into the lounge. Gerald waved them over.

'I'll introduce you,' he said to Ox. 'Hey everyone, this is Ox—'

Ox silenced Gerald with a flick of his hand. 'I've got this,' he said with a confident nod. 'A.T.'

Ox walked up to Ruby and took her by both hands. 'I'm Ox,' he said, his voice clear and strong. 'You must be Felicity. Gerald wrote to tell me all about you.'

Ruby's face looked like it had been soaked in vinegar for a week. 'Did he?' she said.

'Oh yes. It sounds like you two get up to all sorts of fun on weekends. But that's Gerald. He's always been one for the ladies.'

Ruby whipped her hands free and turned on Gerald. 'So you managed to write a letter to this boy but not to me,' she said. 'You truly are unbelievable.'

Gerald closed his eyes and muttered, 'Ox, this is Ruby, a very good friend. Ruby this is Ox, a blundering idiot.'

Ox looked to Ruby and then to Felicity. 'Ohhh,' he said. 'So *you're* Felicity.' He paused to look at her for a second. 'That makes sense. Gerald said you were really pretty.'

Felicity blushed.

Ruby's mouth dropped open.

Gerald tried to fill the painful gap in the conversation. 'How about we get some hot chocolates, eh?'

Ox clapped his hands. 'Great idea, Gerald. I'll do it.' He looked around and his eyes fell on a young woman dressed in a smart black suit as she walked into the lounge. Ox beckoned her across.

'Excuse me, Miss,' he said. 'Can we order five hot chocolates, please?'

Alisha Gupta glared at Ox like she had just stepped in something foul on the footpath.

'I beg your pardon?' she said.

'Five hot chocolates. And if you could hurry it up. My friends are thirsty.'

Alisha's eyebrows peaked into an incredulous arch.

Ox tapped his foot. 'Come along. Time's wasting.'

Then a light went on in his eyes. 'Oh! You're wanting a tip first.'

Alisha watched with growing fascination (and Gerald with growing horror) as Ox reached into his pocket and pulled out a crumpled dollar note. He flattened it out and held it up. 'There's another one of these for you if you're quick,' he said.

Alisha stared at Ox then down at the money in his hand. She plucked the dollar from his fingers, balled it up and flicked it against his forehead.

'Hey!' Ox said.

Alisha brushed past him and leaned into Gerald, kissing him lightly on each cheek. 'Thank you for inviting me, Gerald. Tell me, is this a friend of yours?' she said, indicating Ox with a nod of her head. 'If so, you're a better person than I am.'

'This is Ox,' Gerald said.

Alisha looked at Ox through half-closed eyes. 'Mm-hmm,' she said. 'So he is.'

Ruby rushed to Alisha with an excited cry and grabbed her by the hands. 'Alisha, thank goodness you've come,' she said. She shot a poisonous glance at Gerald. 'I've got so much I need to tell you.'

Alisha smiled broadly, and gave Ruby a warm hug. 'Hello Sam,' she said, giving him a wink. Sam's face glowed red and he let out a goofy laugh.

Then Alisha's eyes came to Felicity. 'And who is this?'

Felicity stepped into the circle and held out her hand.

'I'm Felicity. Felicity Upham. But please call me Flicka. All my friends do.'

Alisha's eyes barely moved but Gerald knew she was conducting an instant top-to-bottom laser scan, taking in every detail of Felicity's hair, her makeup, her clothing, her shoes, her poise. The whole process took less than half a second. Then Alisha smiled—and Gerald let out his breath.

'I love your jacket, Flicka,' Alisha said. 'Where did you get it?'

The girls settled onto a cluster of chairs and ordered hot chocolates from a waitress.

Ox introduced himself to Sam, then sighed. 'That could have gone a bit better,' he said, looking across to where Alisha was holding court with Ruby and Felicity.

'Yep,' said Gerald. 'Just like the *Titanic* could have gone a bit better. Why did you say that stuff to Ruby?'

'I don't know,' Ox said. 'When I get nervous all girls start to look the same.'

'Don't worry about Ruby,' Sam said. 'She's saving all her hatred for Gerald at the moment. And Alisha just comes across as a bit of a toff. She's fine once you get to know her.'

'I don't think that's going to happen any time soon,' Ox said. He rubbed his belly. 'It feels like someone's tied my intestines in knots. Speaking of which, I'm starving. Is there any food about?'

Sam patted Ox on the shoulder. 'Come with me,' he

said and he led his new friend towards the rear of the lobby. 'I want you to meet the most amazing person in the world.'

The day dawned under a clear winter's sky. The fleet of helicopters spread across the heavens like a flight of mechanical geese. But rather than heading south to escape the winter, this flock was going east, straight towards the snow of the Sierra Nevada.

Gerald peered out the window to the white-capped mountains below. Massive forests of conifers spread as far as he could see, like a never-ending plantation of Christmas trees. The glare from the empty blue sky made his eyes ache. He fumbled for his sunglasses, then adjusted the headphones over his ears and moved the microphone in front of his mouth.

'How much further is it, Mr Fry?'

Seated in front of him at the joystick, his butler studied the flight plan clipped to a board by his elbow. 'Our ETA is thirteen-thirty Pacific.'

Gerald shook his head. 'Normal human language, please.'

Mr Fry cleared his throat. 'Our expected time of arrival at Mt Archer is 1.30 p.m., about another twenty minutes.'

'Thanks, Ace.'

'Roger that.'

Mr Fry's transformation whenever he was behind the stick in a helicopter never ceased to amaze Gerald. But it was nothing compared with the change that came over him when Alisha's governess Miss Turner was around. And as she was now sitting next to Mr Fry in the front of the helicopter, the butler was at his most cheery.

A squadron of twenty helicopters fanned across the skies, carrying houseguests, ski gear and supplies.

'I can't believe it's Christmas Eve already,' Felicity said. 'And we get to have Christmas at our own private ski resort. It's going to be such fun. Epic.'

'Won't it be strange, though,' Ruby said, 'being away from your family?'

Felicity reached out and took Alisha by the hand. 'Alisha and I were talking about that,' she said. 'We're boarding-school brats—we're used to fending for ourselves.'

Alisha nodded. 'I'm a corporate orphan. When work calls, my father responds. He'll be in Delhi all winter. But there's always Miss Turner to keep me company.'

Ox puffed out his chest and nudged Alisha with his shoulder. 'I can keep you company if you like.'

Alisha's eyes dropped to where Ox's shoulder was pressed against hers. 'Are you always like this?' she said. 'Or are you making a special effort at being unpleasant just for me?'

Ox's ears turned pink and he leaned the other way.

Gerald glanced at the back of Miss Turner's head. Her hair was pulled into a fierce riding-school ponytail. 'If she keeps Mr Fry happy,' Gerald said, 'that'll be the best Christmas present I could get.'

Felicity looped her arm through Gerald's and flashed him a smile. 'I can't wait to see what Santa brings me.'

Gerald let out a nervous laugh. 'Oh yeah,' he said. 'Good ol' Santa.'

He caught Ruby looking at him. The arrival of Alisha had tempered Ruby's attitude. But things were still frosty.

Then Mr Fry's voice crackled through the headphones. 'Welcome to Mt Archer.'

They swept over a ridge and there was a collective gasp from the back of the helicopter.

A winter playground was laid out beneath them. A ski field sat ready, complete with lifts and a dozen runs that wound through stands of redwoods down the mountainside, like an unopened gift waiting for someone to tug on the ribbon. At the base, on the shore of a frozen lake, was a magnificent chalet, built from red stone. It looked large enough to host a small army. Smoke curled up from the cluster of chimneys that poked through the snow-covered roof. The lake reflected the winter blue sky like a mirror. It was the sort of place that postcard photographers could only conjure in their most elaborate dreams.

'Mate?' Ox said to Gerald as they all drank in the view below.

49

'Yeah?'

'I love you.'

Not for the first time, Gerald could only marvel at the fortune his great aunt Geraldine had left him. An island in the Caribbean, a luxury yacht and a country estate in England were something, but a private ski resort was on another level altogether.

'And we have this whole place to ourselves?' Felicity asked, squeezing Gerald by the arm.

'Yep. Apart from our folks and my parent's closest thousand friends, this is our private playground for the next two weeks. Nothing to do but ski, snowboard, skate and eat.'

Mr Fry and Miss Turner cringed at the cheer that sounded out from behind them.

Mr Fry swept the helicopter through a broad arc and brought them down onto a helipad at the end of a row of identical choppers, all bearing the blue and gold insignia of the Archer Corporation. They had landed by a large hangar in a natural bowl in the hillside, out of sight of the main house.

Gerald jumped out, followed by the others. As the rotors wound down, a roar like a turbo-charged lawnmower came from over the rise. A snowmobile emerged over the lip and pulled a tight circle to come to a halt in front of them. A figure in a bright-yellow ski suit straddled the machine. He pulled a pair of designer sunglasses from his tanned face.

'Hey there,' he said. 'Welcome to Mt Archer.' He was about eighteen years old with blond hair, and he looked like he would be more at home riding waves at Maui. Gerald noticed that Ruby and Alisha were staring. Even Felicity's eyes had widened a touch.

'Howdy everybody. I'm Travis. I'm helping out here over the winter. Now, you guys are the last to arrive and since you're about a hundred years younger than everyone else staying here, I figured you might like some fun on the way to the chalet.'

'Sounds good to me,' Gerald said. 'What kind of fun?'

'You Gerald?' Travis asked, thrusting his hand into Gerald's. 'Good to meet you, sir. Fun, as in these little beauties.' He pointed to a row of five gleaming snow-mobiles beside the hangar. Each had a red sled attached to the rear. 'It's a bit of a hike to the house, so you may as well go in style.'

The next five minutes consisted of a quick tutorial. Sam managed to roll his snowmobile twice.

Travis led the way towards the house, followed by Ruby, then Alisha, Sam and Ox. As there was only one snowmobile left, Gerald pointed Felicity to the driver's seat and he climbed onto the sled. The ride to the house took them alongside the frozen lake. They crossed a covered bridge and, in the final turn to the front of the chalet, Felicity gunned the engine, flinging Gerald from the sled and sending him airborne into a snow bank. He emerged laughing and covered in snow.

Felicity smiled at him. 'That's what happens if you're too slow to get to the driver's seat,' she said.

Mrs Rutherford was there to greet them at the front entryway. 'Miss Felicity, I've put you in with Miss Alisha and Miss Ruby. I hope you don't mind sharing. And Master Oswald—I can't bring myself to call you Ox, dear, no matter how I try—you'll be sharing with Master Sam. Master Gerald, your suite is across from your parents. There's a buffet lunch in the dining hall, and if you need anything, there's a service button in each room. Press one and we'll be there to help you with anything you require.'

A chorus of 'Thanks, Mrs Rutherford!' rang out. Gerald was on his way with the others to get something to eat when a large hand fell on his shoulder. He looked up to see his father.

'This way, Gerald,' Eddie Wilkins said. 'A word.'

Gerald waved his friends on and followed his father into a large library. A tall bank of windows looked onto the slopes outside. Eddie directed his son to a chair near a log fire that crackled and popped in the grate.

'Having fun so far, son?'

'You bet, Dad,' Gerald said. 'We're all going skiing after lunch. The snow looks perfect.'

'And your friends? They're all having fun too?'

Gerald eyed his father curiously. 'Uh, yeah. Like I said, we're going skiing after lunch.'

Eddie stared out the window, his hands clasped

behind his back. 'Good. Good. You should go skiing this afternoon,' he said. 'The snow looks perfect.'

'Dad?'

'Yes, Gerald?'

'Is something the matter?'

Gerald's father picked at some flecks on his trousers and flicked them into the fire. 'Matter? No. Not really.'

Gerald was not convinced. 'Dad.'

Eddie looked across at his son. 'Well, there are a couple of things.'

'Yes?'

'We've had some phone calls. The first was from Mr Prisk.'

Gerald braced himself. His family's corporate lawyer loved to pile Gerald with as much eye-glazing paperwork as he could. The last thing Gerald wanted to worry about during his holiday was the inner workings of the Archer Corporation.

'It was about some business leaders' association called the Billionaires' Club,' his father continued. 'They've invited you to join.'

Gerald shrugged. 'Do I have to do anything during the holidays?'

'No.'

Gerald shrugged again. 'Fine. Sounds good to me.' He went to get up.

Eddie placed a hand on his son's shoulder, pushing him back into his chair. 'There is one other little thing.'

But before Eddie could finish there was a cry from behind them. Gerald swung around to see his mother, leaning against the doorframe, as if about to fall into a deep swoon.

'You've found him,' she cried. 'Thank goodness.' She swept into the room like a silent-movie starlet appearing on screen, only louder. 'My darling boy. You're safe.' She wrapped a fur-lined arm around Gerald's neck.

Gerald struggled to get air. 'Of course I'm safe,' he said through a mouthful of fake ocelot. 'Why wouldn't I be?'

'Oh, Gerald. My little soldier. We've just had a call from Inspector Parrott. It's the most terrible news.'

Gerald was still spitting out fur. 'What? That Mason Green has escaped?'

His mother took in a sharp breath. 'You know?'

'It's no big deal,' Gerald said. 'It's not like Green is going to come all the way out here. We're a million miles from anywhere.'

'But he was so cruel to you,' Vi said. 'Not to mention poor Aunt Geraldine.'

'Mum, he's just escaped from prison. He'll be lying low somewhere.'

Vi cupped Gerald's cheeks in her hands. 'I so want us to have a nice family Christmas together.'

'Gerald's on the right ticket,' Eddie said, ruffling his son's hair. 'The main road is snowed out for the season. The only way in is by helicopter or snow plough.

We're as safe here as anywhere.'

Gerald wasn't entirely sure of that but he wasn't too concerned about Sir Mason Green. Green was a fugitive—he'd be keeping well out of view.

Vi gave Gerald's cheeks a squeeze and planted a moist kiss on his forehead. 'You are my brave little trooper, aren't you.' She glanced at the grandfather clock in the corner. 'Good Lord! Is that the time? Come along Eddie. We must find Mrs Rutherford and see about preparations for the Christmas Eve feast. Have fun, my dear.' Gerald's mother gave him one last squeeze on the shoulder then hurried Eddie out the door, brushing past Ruby on the way.

Gerald slumped back into his chair and Ruby dropped into the one opposite.

'Are they worried about Mason Green?' she asked.

'Not as much as about tonight's menu, apparently.'

Ruby leaned forward and put a hand on Gerald's knee. 'Don't even think about that horrible man. Greece is on the other side of the world, and there's no way he'd be able to sneak into the US. You've got nothing to worry about.' She thought for a second. 'At least not from Mason Green, anyway.'

Gerald grunted a half-laugh. They were the first civil words he and Ruby had exchanged since the start of the holiday. 'Look, about Felicity—' he started to say.

'Don't talk about it, Gerald,' Ruby said, taking her hand back. 'What you did was hurtful. Really awful. You made me feel so small.' She paused, and blinked back a tear. 'And that's not a nice thing to do to anybody. Especially a friend.'

'I'm so sorry,' Gerald said.

'And look at the horrible position you put Felicity in,' Ruby said. 'Inviting her along on a holiday when you've invited me as well. How embarrassing for her.'

'I didn't think—'

'No. You didn't think, did you? But lucky for you, Flicka and I get along really well.'

Gerald paused for a beat. 'You do?'

'Yes. We had a really good talk last night at the hotel. I filled her in on some of your more annoying personality faults.'

Gerald sensed a slight thawing in the iceberg that had been Ruby. 'Only some of them?' he asked.

'Well, it is a long list. But I think between the two of us we identified most of them. She's now aware that "loyalty" and "commitment" might be a touch flaky. And "openness" and "communication skills" could do with some work.'

'You were very thorough.'

'I could have filled a notebook.' Ruby said. 'But for some reason, Felicity still seems to like you. It's beyond me why she does, but at least now she's fully informed.'

Gerald narrowed his eyes. 'How can I ever thank you?'

'You can promise that you won't break Felicity's

heart,' Ruby said. 'Because no one should have to go through that.' Gerald looked away to the fire in the grate. 'Flicka is lovely,' Ruby said. 'She has promised to take me riding when we get back to London. Lucky for you, after the embarrassing position you put her in, she's a forgiving person.'

Gerald bit his bottom lip. 'But we're still friends? Even if the sun does shine out of my backside?'

Ruby pressed a knuckle to her eye. 'That's where Felicity and I differ. I am not a forgiving person. So don't think for a second that I won't make your life a living hell.'

'Fair enough,' Gerald said, trying to hold back a grin. Relief flooded through him. In her own way, it looked like Ruby was moving on.

'It's better like this anyway,' Ruby said.

'What do you mean?'

'I never liked you that much.'

Gerald wasn't completely sure that Ruby was joking.

Ruby leaned forward. 'There's a half-dozen ski slopes out there with no queues at the lifts. Mrs Rutherford has fixed a lunch fit for royalty. There's nothing to stop us from having a good time. Come on, before Sam and Ox scoff the lot.'

They set off in search of the dining hall. Gerald knew Ruby was right about one thing. Mason Green had better things to do than risk coming after him. Green wasn't into revenge—that wasn't his style. And what did Gerald have that Green could possibly want?

Chapter 6

Gerald stood in fresh snow as fine as talcum powder and adjusted his boots. Lined up beside him like a centre spread in a sports equipment catalogue were Felicity, Ox, Sam, Ruby and Alisha, making final tweaks to skis and poles, goggles and gloves. Mr Fry and Travis were behind them by the helicopter. Its rotors turned slow circles in the clear afternoon air.

Gerald shifted his sunglasses on his nose. The ski run below them had not been touched that day—it was clean snow all the way down.

'Just take a care past that stand of redwoods,' Travis said to them. 'It gets icy close in. Otherwise it's all plain sailing. We've had a heap of snow the past two weeks, and there's more forecast for tonight. If you fall, it'll be a soft landing.'

'Aren't you coming with us, Travis?' Ruby asked. She was dressed in a pale-blue one-piece ski suit and matching ear warmers. Gerald found himself thinking the colour matched her eyes.

Travis shot back a smile straight from the 'after' photo in an orthodontist's waiting room. 'Not this run. Old Fry and I have to do some avalanche prevention over in Cooper's Bowl. We're going to drop a few explosive charges from the chopper to break up the snow banks. Don't want them to build up too much.'

Gerald tried not to smile at his butler's reaction to being called 'Old Fry'.

Sam clapped Ox on the shoulder and nodded at the clear run below. 'Come on, Ox. Let's show them how it's done.' They snapped their boots onto their snowboards and took off. 'See you girls at the bottom,' Ox called back. 'That includes you, Gerald!'

Gerald watched as his friends swooped down the slope, carving swathes across the white blanket of snow, hooting and laughing as they went. He wanted to try out his new snowboard as well, but he'd agreed to go skiing with Felicity instead. He muttered under his breath.

Alisha settled her goggles over her eyes. 'Ruby and I are going this way,' she called, pointing to a run with her ski pole. 'Don't be too far behind us, lovebirds.' Then she whispered something to Ruby and they both set off, giggling. Gerald stared after the pale-blue ski suit as it disappeared around a bend.

He muttered again.

'Don't mind them, Gerald,' Felicity said, breezy as ever. 'They're just jealous. Tragic.' She heaved on her poles. 'Race you to the tree line,' she said, and was gone.

Gerald watched as Felicity swept across the slope, elegance in motion. She was an excellent skier. With a grunt, he pushed his poles into the snow and took off in pursuit.

Felicity was a good eighty metres in front of him, making long, graceful arcs. Gerald set a more direct path towards the trees. If he was stuck skiing with Felicity instead of snowboarding with his mates, he wasn't about to be shown up.

Tucked into a ball, his poles under his arms, Gerald cannoned down the mountainside, skis carving through the powder. His legs juddered and bounced but he was gaining. Crisp wind slapped his cheeks as the sheer exhilaration of downhill skiing spread through his body like a rampaging virus. Then his head filled with a mountain-sized sense of horror as he realised he was going way too fast and the trees were getting close. He leaned hard to the side, trying to lift his skis for a hockey stop. But the powder was too deep. He was flying too fast.

He skidded under the first of the trees. It was like stepping onto an ice rink. Gerald shot forward, one ski in the air, his poles dangling at crazy angles. Branches whipped at him on both sides as he leaned left then right to avoid the massive trunks. His trailing ski snapped free, victim to a stump hidden in the snow. And then Gerald saw it: the biggest redwood in the world. It stood like a chimneystack in a clearing right in front of him. Girth the size of an elephant. As ancient as creation. He couldn't take his eyes off it. And he was speeding right towards it. It was like he was plummeting into a black hole and there was no sense in resisting.

This was it.

His head.

A mighty redwood.

And nothing more.

He closed his eyes.

Felicity swooped. Like an arrow, she shot into the clearing from the side and took Gerald out at the ankles. Skis and poles exploded as they bundled and rolled and careened through the snow in a blur of multi-coloured nylon and ice.

Gerald landed on his back. When he opened his eyes his sunglasses were gone. It was only when his vision cleared that he realised Felicity was on top of him, her pink beanie askew across her face. She looked like an exuberant bank robbery gone wrong.

Gerald blinked up at her.

'What'd you do that for?' It was all he could think of saying.

Felicity grinned wide. 'Because that tree wasn't about

to step aside for you,' she said. A large dollop of snow toppled from her beanie and splotted across Gerald's forehead. 'And how would I get my Christmas present with you in traction?'

Gerald considered this for a second. Felicity made a very good point. He thanked her and, as they righted themselves and went searching for lost skis and poles, Gerald thought how close he had come to death. And, considering he hadn't actually bought a present for Felicity, how close to death he would be on Christmas morning.

They spent the rest of the afternoon on the slopes. After a hectic few hours, Gerald found himself sharing a chairlift with Alisha as it took them high into the mountains. It was good to sit back, dangle in the air and take in the view.

'Flicka is lovely,' Alisha said, breaking the silence.

Gerald pulled his gaze from the sweep of the hillside beneath them and looked across to Alisha. 'Yeah, she's pretty cool.' He paused. 'So is Ruby.'

Alisha laughed.

'What is it?' Gerald asked.

'You are such a boy, Gerald Wilkins.'

'Well, yeah. Obviously.'

'What is it with boys and how they treat girls? You expect us all to worship you like gods, like we're all mini versions of your mothers—'

Gerald screwed up his nose. 'Eww.'

'But you don't put in any effort yourself. Ruby thinks the world of you. She really, *really* likes you. And so does Felicity. But you treat them like they're no different from your new snowboard—something fun to play with until the next fun thing comes along. Girls aren't possessions to be collected, you know.'

Gerald shifted in his seat. 'I never said they were.'

'Where's the consideration for how others might feel?' Alisha said. 'Of course, it's nice to have people like you. Everyone likes to be liked. But you need to treat people with respect, Gerald. Just because you can buy whatever you want, doesn't mean you can have it all.'

Gerald couldn't believe what he was hearing. 'What about you?' he said, turning on Alisha. 'You must realise that you're an absolute knockout. Just look how Sam and Ox act when they're around you. They can barely string two words together.'

Alisha gave him a knowing smile. 'I can't help who I am, Gerald. But the difference between you and me is I'm not leading anyone on. I like Sam. He's my friend. And I value that. But I'm not looking for a boyfriend.'

'Well, how about Ox?' Gerald said. 'He really likes you.'

'Yes. I'm his favourite waitress,' Alisha said, grinning.

'That was an honest mistake.'

'Yes, so much better than the dishonest ones, don't you think?' Alisha gave the tip of Gerald's nose a gentle poke with her finger. 'It may come as a surprise to you,

63

Gerald Wilkins, but just because a boy likes me doesn't mean I have to like him back.'

Gerald stared into the vacant sky. He wondered where Sam and Ox were. Life with them was so much easier.

The Christmas Eve feast promised to be a triumph. Mrs Rutherford had excelled herself. She and the kitchen staff had laboured all day to prepare a banquet befiting the luxurious setting. Mr Fry had overseen the decorations and there wasn't a surface or hanging space that hadn't been tinselled, candled or mistletoed. An enormous fir tree brushed the ceiling in the baronial dining chamber. It was covered in ornaments that would put to shame anything in a department store in Oxford Street or Fifth Avenue. The enormous stone fireplace was ablaze and, as if on cue, snow started tumbling outside to greet the first course.

Everyone had dressed for the occasion. Vi was encased in a silk creation from Paris with matching champagne flute, and even Eddie had scrubbed up in a dinner suit.

Gerald, Sam and Ox were milling around just inside the dining room when the girls arrived.

'Holy cow!' Gerald said.

Felicity walked in first. She was wearing Mason

Green's dinner jacket, the sleeves rolled fashionably to the elbows, over a pair of chalk-striped pants. Her hair was pinned up and she wore a simple crystal pendant on a silver chain.

As usual, Alisha was elegance personified, wrapped in a silk sari, a wash of gold, lavender and orange.

Ruby was the last to arrive.

She wore a floor-length off-the-shoulder evening gown of the palest lemon. Her blonde hair was plaited and pinned with a matching flower. She brushed past the boys as if on her way to the dance floor. 'Nice to see you fellows put in the effort,' she said.

Ox, Gerald and Sam had managed to find clean jeans and matching socks.

Gerald made sure to sit between Sam and Ox for the meal. After an afternoon of having his personality dissected, he needed a break. He comforted himself with seconds of peach trifle for dessert and an extra large hot chocolate with four marshmallows.

'Feeling a bit hungry, are we?' Sam said, noting Gerald's intake.

Gerald let his spoon drop into the empty bowl, then emitted a belch that sparked cries of disgust from around the table.

'Condemned man,' Gerald muttered into his napkin. 'Last meal.'

'What are you talking about?' Ox said.

With a tip of his head, Gerald beckoned Sam and

Ox to lean in close. He glanced ruefully towards Felicity, then whispered, 'I haven't got her a Christmas present.'

'No present!' Ox said, way too loud. He shut up when Gerald grabbed him by the collar and yanked his head in closer.

'No present,' Gerald whispered. 'And on top of that I've had the benefit of a free character appraisal from Ruby and Alisha, so pardon me if I'm not in the best of moods.'

'How could you not get her a present?' Sam asked. 'I got one for Ruby. And she's my sister.'

Gerald held his head in his hands. 'I know. I meant to get her one. I thought about it every day for a week before we left. But the more I thought about it, the more I couldn't do anything.'

'Target fixation,' Ox said, nodding wisely. 'Classic case.'

'What?'

'I learnt about it in Assertiveness Training. It's when you get so absorbed in a problem that you feel power-less to do anything about it,' Ox said. 'You were so concerned about how bad it would be if you didn't get Felicity a present that you didn't do the simple thing and get her one.'

Gerald thought about what Ox had said. 'Like me and that massive tree this afternoon,' he said. 'I couldn't take my eyes off it. I knew I was going to hit it but I couldn't do anything about it.'

'The brain's a strange thing,' Ox said. He helped himself to more apple pie and cream. 'Sometimes it gets so obsessed with stuff that all sense and reason goes out the door.'

Gerald glanced at the other side of the table, where the girls were chatting happily. Felicity caught his eye and gave him a cheeky wink. She was in the middle of a story that had the others in stitches. Ruby had her chin cupped in a hand, her face brushed with the warm light that flickered from the fireplace behind them. Almost in slow motion, her eyes wandered across to meet Gerald's, and she gave him a smile that had him questioning everything he'd done since the end of summer.

After coffee was served, the dinner guests started to break into groups. Eddie led a bunch of buddies to the billiards room, while Vi gathered a gaggle of friends in the lounge for more champagne and chocolate. The staff descended on the dining room for the monumental clean up. Mrs Rutherford guided Gerald and his friends down a long corridor into the east wing. At the end, she flung open double doors to a wood-panelled games parlour filled with pinball machines, arcade-style video games and even an old carnival shooting gallery with moving ducks and air pistols.

They crowded the doorway, mouths agape.

'Gerald?' Ox said, his eyes still bulging.

'Yes, mate?'

'I love you.'

For the next two hours there was non-stop play. They cranked the music up and Sam established himself as the best shot in the group, pinging ducks with ease. At one point, Gerald snuck out and ransacked the house in search of something that would make do as a present for Felicity. As always, Mrs Rutherford came through. She found a pair of vintage emerald earrings that had belonged to his great aunt. 'They'll look beautiful on her, Master Gerald,' she said, her eyes misting up.

Gerald snuck back into the games parlour just as Sam shot a duck from clear across the room, sparking howls of disbelief from the others. Ox gave Gerald a 'where have you been?' look, but Gerald just patted his pocket and gave a quick thumbs up.

The fire in the grate had burned down to embers and Ruby was leading the tally in an epic pinball challenge when Gerald crossed to the windows.

Alisha joined him and hooked an arm through his. 'It's really tumbling down out there,' she said. 'Plenty of snow for a white Christmas in the morning.'

Gerald watched the plump snowflakes as they trailed in from above. Alisha gave his arm a squeeze. 'Thank you again for inviting me, Gerald. It's been such fun.'

'No worries,' he said. 'And thanks for setting me straight on a few things. You've given me a bit to think about.'

Alisha smiled, then tried her best Australian accent, 'No worries, mate.'

A clock on the mantelpiece struck the hour with Westminster chimes.

'Oh my goodness!' Felicity cried. 'It's midnight! Happy Christmas everybody!'

As the chimes continued towards twelve, embraces and kisses were exchanged. Felicity gave Gerald an enormous hug and kissed him on the cheek.

Just as the final strike for midnight sounded, Gerald found himself standing beside Ruby.

'Happy Christmas, Gerald.' Ruby smiled up at him.

Gerald smiled back. 'Thanks,' he said. 'You, too.'

Then the lights went out.

There were cries of surprise as the room plunged into darkness. The music and the video machines cut out. A faint red glow came from the embers in the fireplace, but it was not enough to see by.

'All the outside lights have gone as well,' Alisha said. 'The snow must have brought down the power lines.'

'We'd be on generator power all the way out here,' Sam said. His voice came from by the pinball machines. 'Something must have broken.'

'I think I saw an emergency torch on the wall,' Ox said. 'There should be a blinking red light somewhere.'

'I see it,' said Felicity. 'Hold on. I'll get it.'

There was some shuffling and a muffled yelp as Felicity bumped into a low table in the dark. 'There, that's got it,' she said. A torch flicked on. It provided just enough light for everyone to see Gerald and Ruby, their eyes closed and blissful looks on their faces, holding each other in the most tender embrace.

'Gerald?' Felicity said. 'What are you doing?'

Gerald and Ruby broke apart. Busted.

But before anyone could speak, a series of sharp explosions sounded from the front of the house.

'Are we having fireworks?' Ox said. 'That's a nice way to bring in Christmas.'

A fresh volley of bangs rattled the windows.

'I'm not sure those are fireworks,' Alisha said as she peered out into the snow.

Then a high-pitched scream came from deep within the house.

'What was that?' Felicity asked.

The double doors burst open. Mr Fry and Miss Turner barged into the room.

'Is everyone here?' Miss Turner demanded. Fry bolted the doors behind them.

'Yes,' Gerald said. 'What's going on?'

'The house is under attack,' Fry said. 'Men. With guns. They're coming this way.'

Chapter 7

There was no time to think. No time to plan. Mr Fry crossed to the windows and pressed on a panel in the wall. It popped open to reveal a narrow door. The butler fumbled with a ring of keys and had it unlocked in seconds.

'In here,' he said. 'This passage leads to the kitchen. There's a drying room at the far end with jackets and boots. You need to rug up and get out into the kitchen garden.'

There was a stunned silence.

They were under attack?

'Is it Mason Green?' Gerald asked.

'Don't talk,' Miss Turner said. 'Listen and act. The power has been cut but once you're in the garden you'll see the covered bridge. The one we crossed when we arrived this afternoon. Go over it and follow the roadway to the left for about two miles. There's a caretaker's cottage.'

'Lock yourselves in and stay there,' Fry said. 'We'll come and get you when it's safe.'

'But our parents,' Ruby said.

Another scream echoed from the front of the house, followed by the sound of breaking glass.

Fry bundled them to the passage doorway. 'Go! Now!'

Ruby pushed Alisha and Felicity ahead of her. Gerald was last through, behind Sam and Ox. He looked back to see Mr Fry, grim-faced, closing the door behind them. And he heard the key turn in the lock.

They were in a narrow corridor that snaked off into the distance. Felicity switched off the torch.

'What did you do that for?' Sam hissed. 'I can't see a thing.'

Felicity shushed him. 'This will be a service passage,' she said. 'It will pass behind every major room in the house on the way to the kitchen. That means we need to be totally quiet. No noise. No torch. Look, further down there.'

As their eyes adjusted to the gloom they could make out ribbons of light at floor level, marking a path.

'The power must have come back on,' Felicity said. 'That light is shining under the doors of every room we have to pass.'

'Felicity's right,' Gerald said. 'We can't let anyone know we're here.'

'How do you know all this stuff, Flicka?' Ox asked.

Felicity took a tentative step down the corridor. 'Boarding school brats in old buildings learn a lot.'

They picked their way along the passage. Ruby kicked off her shoes and continued in bare feet. They'd been going for a minute when voices sounded from the room they were passing.

'All jewellery! Everything in your pockets! Put it on the table.'

Felicity froze. Everyone behind her stopped in the narrow walkway, banked up like a traffic jam.

Gerald looked down at the strip of light beneath the door.

'Hurry up!' The voice was rough and urgent.

'Listen, we're doing everything you ask.' It was the voice of Francis Valentine. Calm. Rational. 'There's no need to—'

The sound of a slap sliced through the door, followed by a chorus of shocked cries.

Ruby clung to Gerald's arm. A gasp caught in her throat. It was just light enough for Gerald to see Sam's jaw tighten. Sam was reaching for the door handle when Ox grabbed him by the wrist and whispered a single word.

'Guns.'

Sam allowed his hand to be lowered to his side, but his face glowed red in the gloom.

None of them dared move.

Then Gerald noticed the peephole in the door. A tight pencil of light poked through it into the passageway. The hole must have been there so servants could check that it was appropriate to enter the room.

Gerald pressed his eye to the opening. What he saw on the other side made him sick to his stomach.

At least ten guests were huddled in one of the chalet's many drawing rooms. Gerald could make out Francis and Alice Valentine as well as Ox's parents. But he couldn't see his own mother and father. Francis Valentine was holding a hand to his jaw.

There were three intruders—thick-set, dressed in black, wearing balaclavas. Each had a rifle slung over a shoulder and a handgun at the ready. They looked like heavily armed bears. Gerald could see a low coffee table near the guests. It was covered in necklaces and rings and strings of pearls and watches and wallets. But still the bandits were demanding more.

'Everything!' one of them yelled. 'Earrings, pinkie rings. The lot.' He held his pistol at one woman's face. Her hands shook uncontrollably as she tried to remove a diamond brooch from her gown.

Then the main door to the room was thrown open and another man stepped in. He was enormous—broad-shouldered and hulking. Coarse whiskers from a dark beard poked through his balaclava. Judging by the reaction from the other bandits, this man was in charge.

'Well?' he demanded. His voice was like a roll of thunder across the plains just before a twister touches down.

The bandits pointed to the haul of diamonds, silver and gold on the coffee table. The man swept a gloved hand through the trove.

'It's not here,' he rumbled. 'Radio the others to search the bedrooms. Turn the place upside down. The Falcon came through with one side of the deal. I'm not leaving here without the other.'

The thug coughed heavily into his fist and swore. He moved across to Francis Valentine. 'Where are the children?'

Francis stood tall and stared the man directly in the eye. 'You can leave the children alone. Whatever it is you're looking for, they don't have it.'

Gerald could feel Ruby tensing at the sound of her father's voice. He kept his eye to the peephole.

The bandit pulled his fist back—gasps came from the others—but he didn't strike. 'We'll see,' he said.

Gerald swallowed. Felicity was still at the head of their group. Gerald pulled himself away from the peephole and leaned forward to tap her on the shoulder. He pointed further up the corridor and she nodded. They moved off, painfully aware of the sound of their feet on the floor.

They gathered at the end of the passage, inside a set of swinging doors. 'This must be the kitchen,' Gerald whispered. 'Stick close.'

He eased one of the doors open and poked his head through. It was just as Mr Fry had described. The door to the drying room was open at the far end: jackets and ski suits hung on pegs, and boots were lined up on racks.

'Come on,' Gerald said over his shoulder. 'Grab some gear and let's get to this cottage.' He channelled everyone into the drying room, and pulled the door shut behind them.

Gerald, Sam, Ox and Felicity quickly had jackets, snow pants and boots on. But Ruby and Alisha's gowns were causing a problem. 'We can't just pull pants over these,' Ruby said.

Gerald was peeking through a crack in the door back into the kitchen. 'Then take them off,' he whispered back.

Ruby glared at the back of his head. 'There is no way I am getting undressed in front of you.' She turned to look at Alisha and found that she had already unwound her sari into a bundle on the floor and was pulling a ski suit over the thermal shorts and T-shirt that she had been wearing underneath.

Alisha glanced up at her. 'I always wear these in winter,' she shrugged. 'I'd freeze my butt off otherwise.'

'Great,' Ruby muttered.

'Oh, get on with it, Ruby,' Sam hissed. 'No one cares

about your undies.'

'Look the other way,' Ruby said. Gerald rolled his eyes and turned back to peek into the kitchen. Sam and Ox readied themselves by the door to the garden.

Gerald heard the sound of a zip, followed by the rustling of material. After a moment Ruby breathed, 'Okay, I'm done.' He turned to find her dressed in a red ski jacket, and lacing on rugged hiking boots. Alisha had folded her sari into a neat parcel that she slipped inside her ski suit.

'Can't we just phone someone?' Felicity asked, pulling ear warmers onto her head. 'Call 911 or something.'

'There aren't any phones here,' Gerald said. 'It's too remote. Mr Fry said something about a satellite phone for emergencies but I have no idea where it is.'

'The helicopter!' said Alisha. Everyone turned to her. 'We could use the chopper.'

'And you're going to fly it, are you?' Ox said.

Alisha shot him a filthy look. 'There's a radio in it,' she said. 'Foolish boy.'

'Actually, I've been taking flying lessons through my school's aero club,' Gerald said, 'but I wouldn't know where to start in a helicopter.'

Sam looked at him. 'Your school has an aero club? Just how posh is that place?'

'Pretty posh, I guess. But Alisha is right. We could radio for help from the hangar. I should be able to do that.'

Ox zipped his jacket to the chin and led the way outside. Gerald and Alisha were last through the door.

'Ruby's cost us some time,' Gerald grumbled as they ducked into the night. 'Was it really so shocking to see her in her undies?'

'Girls should be modest,' Alisha said. 'You never know when someone is going to grab you for a sly squeeze especially when the lights go out.'

Gerald almost throttled himself on a low hanging clothesline at the edge of the garden.

It was blowing a blizzard outside. A frigid wind sliced through them like a razor, driving snow in thick flurries before it. Gerald pulled a beanie from his pocket and yanked it over his ears. Ox had his head down, leading Felicity, Sam, Ruby, Alisha and Gerald—a family of frozen ducklings making for safety.

Gerald could barely see. The snow, falling thick and relentless, was halfway up to his knees. Ox ploughed onwards, and finally they gathered in the shelter of the covered bridge.

'I'm freezing,' Felicity said, clapping her arms across her chest. 'This snow is ridiculous.'

Gerald glanced back at the chalet. The front was decorated with blinking coloured lights and warmth shone from the windows. On any other night, it would have been a Yuletide delight. But Gerald shivered at the thought of what was going on inside.

'We've got to move on,' he said. 'The snow will cover

our tracks but those thugs will figure out we've made a run for it soon enough.'

'What did you see through that door, Gerald?' Ruby asked. 'Is Dad okay?'

Gerald pulled his beanie lower. 'He's okay.' He refused to catch Ruby's eye. 'But we need to get help.'

Ruby turned to Sam. 'Can't we do something?' she said.

For a moment, Gerald thought Sam was about to dash back to the house and take on the intruders by himself. But he zipped his jacket to his chin. 'They've got guns,' Sam said. 'We need the police.'

They set off further into the white night. Down by the hangar the snow had banked almost up to the windows, blocking the main entry. But in the lee of the building, sheltered from the wind, they found an unlocked door and poured inside.

It was still cold but better than trudging through the snow.

'Felicity,' Gerald said. 'Do you still have that torch?'

He clamped his hand over the end and flicked it on. The light glowed red between his fingers, giving some dull illumination to the darkened hangar. There were two helicopters inside, sleek and spotless.

'The other choppers must have been flown back to San Francisco,' Gerald said. He clambered up to the door of the closest one and pulled on the handle to the cockpit. 'Let's see what we can do in here.'

Ox climbed in after him. Ruby and Felicity crowded the doorway, and Sam and Alisha kept watch through the front windows of the hangar.

Gerald pulled on the pilot's headgear and gazed at the dark panel of switches, dials and screens in front of him.

'Wish I'd paid more attention when Fry was flying this thing,' Gerald said. He flicked a few switches. Nothing happened.

'Do you need to get some power going?' Ox said. 'What about that red button there?' He pressed a large disk. Immediately, the control panel flickered to life, blinking red, green and yellow.

'Ox!' Gerald said. 'You're a legend.'

'Yeah, I'm a bit of a natural,' Ox said. 'A.T.' His knee brushed against a bank of switches, and a low whine could be heard in the cabin.

'What's that?' Gerald asked. The whine grew louder.

'Beats me?' Ox said, looking left and right.

Ruby provided the answer. 'You've started the chopper, you morons!' she yelled.

Gerald and Ox looked up through the perspex canopy to see the huge rotors turning slow circles. They were gathering speed.

'Turn it off!' they yelled at each other.

'I don't know how!' they screamed back.

The rotors spun faster and faster. Ruby and Felicity abandoned Gerald and Ox, rushing heads down to the front of the hangar.

'Which button did you push?' Gerald frantically flicked switches and turned dials. The chopper started to bobble up and down on its landing gear.

'Dunno!' Ox cried. He screwed up his eyes and poked a finger at random. The whir of the rotors gained intensity. The helicopter started to move across the floor.

'Not that one!'

The chopper tilted to one side and set off across the hangar, kangaroo hopping on its skids.

'Shut it down!' Ox screamed. In the confined space of the hanger, the roar of the engine was incredible.

Gerald scanned the dash of flashing lights. Then his eye fell on the big red button that Ox had first pushed. He said a silent prayer and jabbed at it. The power cut out. The lights died. And the roar of the rotors abated. But they were still bouncing across the floor. A second later there was a sickening jolt and the screech of bending metal as they collided with the second chopper.

They came to a sudden halt. Silence returned to the hangar.

Gerald let out a long breath. 'Maybe the radio isn't such a great idea after all,' he said.

They jumped down from the cockpit to find the two helicopters locked in a tangled embrace. 'I don't think these two are flying anywhere for a while,' Ox said.

Ruby hurried across to them. 'Could you two make any more noise?' She had a daypack slung over her shoulder. 'I've emptied the snack tray from the office into here and we've got some cans of soft drink. But unless you can get that radio to work we should get out of here.'

Gerald reached back inside the cockpit and pulled out an emergency kit with a big red cross on the front. He tossed it to Ox. 'This could come in handy,' he said. But before they could make a move, Alisha's voice cut through the air. 'Someone's coming!'

Gerald, Ox and Ruby dropped to the floor and scurried across to where Alisha and Sam were squatting by the window. 'I think there's only one,' Alisha whispered. 'I saw the flash of a torch.'

Gerald was about to poke his head up to look outside when he heard the crunch of boots in the dry snow. Then a beam of light shone through the window.

The man was right above them.

Gerald pressed in close to the wall. The beam swept left then right across the floor. It played across the front of the closest chopper. But was it bright enough to see the wreckage beyond?

The torchlight flicked off and they could hear boot steps tracing around the side of the building. Gerald's stomach jolted. He hadn't locked the door after they came in.

'Hide!' he hissed, and threw himself towards the door at the rear of the building. He skidded across the floor like he was sliding into home plate. The door was the type with four small windowpanes set in a square in the top half and he could see the glow from the torch as the man rounded the corner outside. Gerald came to a stop just centimetres from the wall. He shot his hand up to the door handle and jabbed the button, locking it.

A split second later, the handle rattled. The intruder was trying to get in.

Gerald lay on the floor, making himself as small as possible. A ribbon of cold air blew onto his back from the gap under the door. He tilted his head to look up. A face was pressed to the window.

A balaclava.

A dark set of eyes.

And a gun.

Gerald held his breath. The torch beam shone through the glass, casting a dim light across the floor. Everything looked deserted. His friends had hidden themselves well. He let out a silent sigh of relief—only to see a puff of vapour escape his mouth and float slowly into the beam of light.

A second later, the world exploded around him. The thug's kick demolished the door in a shower of timber and glass shards. Gerald tried to roll clear, but he took the impact hard into his ribs. Then the man was straddling him, grabbing his collar, snatching at his hair.

'They're in the hangar!' the man yelled into a walkie-talkie clipped to his shoulder. 'I've got Wilkins!'

Gerald writhed and kicked. But the man was strong. Then Gerald heard two things in quick succession: Felicity yelling 'Oi!' And then a whipping *thwack* as she swatted the man across the face with a ski pole, breaking his nose instantly. The impact sent him reeling. His legs tangled in Gerald's. He toppled and landed heavily, cracking his skull on the concrete floor.

Gerald freed himself from the mess of limbs and scrambled to his feet.

'You've knocked him out,' he said to Felicity with undisguised awe. 'Where'd you learn to do that?'

Felicity stood over the prone shape of the man and planted a boot on his chest like a big game hunter. 'The Colonel taught his little girl some self-defence,' she said. 'Are you okay?'

Gerald clutched at his right side where his ribs had taken the force of the shattering door. He pressed gingerly, and winced. 'I'll survive,' he said.

Ruby, Sam and Alisha emerged from the shadows. 'What do we do now?' Alisha asked.

The walkie-talkie on the man's shoulder crackled. 'Hold them there—we're on the way.'

'We get away from here as fast as possible,' Gerald said. He looked around. 'Where's Ox?'

He was answered by the rattle of a metal roller door opening. At the far end of the hangar Ox was pulling on a chain. Beside him were three brand new snowmobiles.

'Nice one, Ox,' Gerald said. He jumped onto the closest one, wincing at the pain in his side. Felicity clambered on behind him.

Ruby pointed Sam to the pillion seat of the next snowmobile. 'I've seen you drive,' she said, silencing his protests.

Ox was already holding the handlebars of the third machine and grinning at Alisha by the time she arrived. She glared at him but climbed in behind without saying a word.

'We split up,' Gerald said, pulling goggles over his eyes and handing a pair to Felicity. 'Don't go straight to the cottage.'

'Take this,' Ox said, and tossed something to Sam and Gerald.

Gerald looked down at his hands. 'An air pistol?' he said.

'I took them from the shooting gallery,' Ox said. 'Hope you don't mind.'

'They're not much use against real guns,' Sam said. He tucked it into his jacket pocket.

Ox shrugged. 'Yeah, but the bad guys don't know they're not real.'

Gerald pressed the starter and revved the engine. 'Go fast,' he called. 'And good luck.'

He powered through the door, at the same moment as a black-clad man stepped into his path. It was impossible to tell who was the more surprised. Gerald hit the throttle and cannoned into the intruder, belting into his ribs and spinning him through the air. Felicity tightened her grip around Gerald's waist as they thundered into the night. She craned her neck back to see the gunman sprawled in the snow.

Ruby and Sam were next out of the hangar. They banked right and disappeared over a rise towards the lake. Ox and Alisha emerged a second later. The gunman managed to raise himself to his knees, just in time for Alisha to stamp the sole of her boot square into his chest, hurling him back into the snow.

'Faster, Gerald!' Felicity shouted into his ear above the roar of the snowmobile. 'There's more of them coming.'

Gerald didn't look back. Ruby and Sam? Ox and Alisha? They were on their own now.

Chapter 8

The snowmobile's headlight pierced the night, jigging wildly as Gerald struggled to keep control. He couldn't slow down or they would risk sinking into the carpet of fresh powder.

He aimed between two stands of redwoods and shot through the gap. The engine screamed with the strain. They bounced into an open field, ploughing a furrow through the snow. Gerald thought the cottage must be two or three kilometres to their left but he didn't want to turn yet.

Then Felicity was yelling into his ear. 'There's two of them,' she cried. 'Right behind us.'

No sooner had the wind whipped her words away than Gerald heard the twin drones of two snowmobiles.

He shot a look over his shoulder. There they were, about fifty metres away. Two headlights, bobbing across the field. It had stopped snowing and a full moon burst through a break in the clouds, flooding the mountainside with light. Gerald could plainly see the black-clad men urging their machines on, riding them like thoroughbreds towards the finish line.

And they were gaining.

'They're too fast,' Gerald yelled to Felicity. 'We're going to have to out-manoeuvre them.'

They hit a snow bank and took to the air, soaring over the top.

'Hold on!' Gerald yelled.

Felicity squeezed the last word out of him. Pain shot from Gerald's ribs. They landed with a crunch and the snowmobile roared on. Gerald chanced another look behind. Both pursuers were still there. Thirty metres.

Gerald knew he had to take extreme measures. He gunned the machine and set a new path.

'Isn't this taking us back to the house?' Felicity yelled in his ear.

Gerald didn't respond. His ribs were killing him and a screaming match wasn't going to help. Felicity would just have to hold on for the ride.

The three snowmobiles skimmed across the ground in an arrow-shaped blur, spraying muck in their wake. Gerald had a vague plan. He guessed the men had sent out every snowmobile they had for the chase. So the area around the house should be reasonably safe. And there were possibilities there.

In the distance Gerald could see the covered bridge, and the chimneys from the chalet. He wondered what was going on inside. Were his parents okay? And why did trouble always seem to find him, no matter how far away he ventured?

Then Felicity was yelling at him. 'Hurry up!'

Gerald glanced over his shoulder—ten metres.

They flew straight through the covered bridge without slowing down. Gerald steered towards the rear of the house, towards the kitchen garden.

'When I yell "duck",' he screamed to Felicity, pain creasing through his side, 'duck!'

'What?'

'When I yell "duck", duck.'

They were hurtling back along the path they'd walked earlier in the evening, straight along the trench that Ox had ploughed from the house.

'*What?*'

They were less than twenty metres from the kitchen garden. The snowmobiles behind them had closed in to five metres. Gerald could see the men as plain as day.

'When I say—'

'*What?*'

Gerald looked up in panic. They'd got there quicker than he'd expected. He reached around and grabbed Felicity by the collar, yanking down hard. 'DUCK!'

They shot under the low drooping clothesline like a bolt from a crossbow. The cords brushed the back of Felicity's jacket. Gerald looked back at the sound of a loud *twoing!* The line took the front rider clean across the throat. It was like a giant invisible hand had taken him by the neck and plucked him from his snowmobile. The man seemed to hang in midair as his machine soared on without him and plunged deep into a snow bank, burying itself to the back tracks. The rider fell to the ground and the other man ran clear over the top of him. He tore after Gerald and Felicity without a backward glance.

'Brilliant!' Felicity was bouncing with glee behind Gerald. 'One down. One to go. Where now, Gerald?'

Gerald pressed his lips together. 'The lake.'

Felicity's eyes grew wide behind her goggles. 'Are you sure that's a good idea?'

'No.'

The snowmobile shot around the chalet and headed down the slope towards the frozen lake.

'What if the ice isn't thick enough?' Felicity cried.

'Can you swim?'

'Yes.'

'Good.'

Gerald urged the machine straight at the shoreline. They hit the ice at full speed, hurtling off the snow and skewing out onto the lake. The rider in pursuit didn't slow down.

'Move it, Gerald!' Felicity was pounding on his back. 'He's getting closer!'

Gerald had the throttle fully open. It was at least another hundred and fifty metres to the opposite shore.

Felicity was in his ear again. 'Gerald? Is the ice breaking?' She pointed ahead of the front skis. A spider's web of fine lines was fanning out before them, as if being pushed along on a wave. A loud *crack*, followed by another, sounded out like rifle shots above the howl of the snowmobiles. The lake was breaking apart.

They careened past a sign stuck in the lake's surface. Felicity looked back over her shoulder. 'It says *Thin Ice*,' she cried.

'Terrific,' Gerald muttered. Then the back of the snowmobile lurched down, like someone had whipped the ground from beneath it. They'd driven straight into a quagmire of broken ice and water, the world's biggest slushie. Gerald's hands fell from the controls. For a second, the snowmobile bobbed about like a lifeboat from the *Titanic*. Then they started sinking. Water washed up to their hips. The cold pierced their clothing like a million tiny ice needles. Gerald opened his mouth in shock but no sound came out. He looked behind them. The man was just twenty metres astern. He'd be on them in seconds. Felicity screeched in Gerald's ear: 'Go!' Gerald looked dumbly at the controls, his actions as frozen as his feet. He couldn't move. Felicity pounded on his back. 'Gerald!' Then she threw her arms over his shoulders and grabbed at the handlebars, pulling the throttle on full. The snowmobile engine roared. But without anything for the tracks to grip in all the slush, they just sank lower. Any moment the engine would be swamped. Gerald saw the man had come to a stop by the *Thin Ice* sign. He was off his snowmobile and pulling a rifle from his shoulder.

'Felicity,' he shivered. 'Do something.'

Then they bumped into a large chunk of ice. Felicity gunned the throttle again. The engine gave a pathetic growl, the snowmobile's tracks spun—and bit into the floe. The machine surged forward and up, gaining traction the further it went. It bounced through the slush like an icebreaker carving a path to shore.

'Woo-hoo!' Gerald cried. 'Go Felicity!'

Felicity was on her feet, leaning over the top of Gerald and driving them onwards. Gerald glanced at the gunman. He was scrambling back to his snowmobile. By the time Felicity charged off the lake and onto land, they'd opened up a fifty-metre lead.

'Just like riding a horse!' she screamed in Gerald's ear. 'Too much fun!'

It was then that the deer bobbed up. It bounded square into their path, stopped and looked at them. Gerald could see the headlights reflected in its eyes.

'Hold on!' Felicity screamed. She jammed the handlebars to the right, sending the snowmobile into a sideways slide and smack into a snow bank that swallowed them whole.

The engine stalled.

The sudden quiet was made even more eerie by the sense they had just been packed in ice like lobsters bound for market.

Gerald would have been content to sit there and gather his thoughts. But a gloved hand stabbed through the snow and grabbed him by the collar. He was yanked out and thrown to the ground. A second later Felicity landed next to him, slumped on her elbows and knees.

Gerald opened his eyes to find a pair of black boots in front of his face. He looked up to take in the full scale of the man standing over them. He was almost two metres tall and had a clean-shaven jaw that looked like it had come straight from a razor blade commercial.

'Are you Gerald Wilkins?' the man asked.

Gerald lay on the ground, hugging his aching ribs. His beanie was gone, his jacket was torn open, and he was hopelessly, miserably cold.

'No.'

The man smiled. He was reaching for the radio on his shoulder when the night sky exploded. A colossal fireball appeared from the far side of the lake, rising up from the hills beyond the chalet. The snow around them was lit in yellow and orange and red. The fireball was followed a second later by a thunderous bang that rolled across the lake. Gerald felt the sound like a percussive punch to his chest.

The gunman swung round to witness the pyrotechnics,

his mouth agape. The fireball mushroomed and faded. The man turned back just in time to receive Felicity's palm jab square on the end of his chin. She drove in hard, twisting at the hips, generating maximum power. In the cold air, the man's jawbone snapped like a dry branch. Felicity followed up by raking her boots down the man's shins, yelling 'No! No! No!' at the top of her lungs.

The gunman howled with pain, and wrapped his hands around his face. Felicity swooped on a broken ski from the wreckage of their snowmobile and whipped it around the back of his legs. The man went down like a felled redwood, howling again. Gerald seized a pair of handcuffs hanging from the man's belt and quickly secured his wrists behind his back. He and Felicity stepped clear to inspect the damage.

'Self-defence lessons?' Gerald asked.

'Yes,' Felicity said, a smug look on her face. 'I topped the class.'

'Clearly.' Gerald leaned down and took the radio from the man's shoulder.

'Yousenustednynee!' The man was slumped on his side and stared up at them through one crazed eye. 'Yousenustednynee!'

Gerald and Felicity stared back at him. 'Sorry?' Gerald said. 'I didn't catch that.'

'Ny nee!' the man protested. 'Nusted ny nee!'

'Oh,' Felicity said, taking Gerald's arm. 'I think he says we've busted his knee.'

'Really?' Gerald looked down at the man on the ground. 'I'm not sorry. You were about to shoot us out on the lake.'

They couldn't make out what the man said next but it was a fair bet it involved a lot of swearing.

Gerald swung himself onto the saddle of the man's snowmobile. Felicity squeezed in behind him. 'Who are you working for?' Gerald asked the man. 'Is it Mason Green?'

'Get stuffed!' the man managed, spitting red into the snow.

'Well that's just rude,' Felicity said. 'Is your mother proud of what you do for a living?'

The man's curses followed Gerald and Felicity as they drove the snowmobile into some woods and away from the lake. The snow had started falling again, thick and plump, but the wind had died away to nothing. It took Gerald and Felicity about half an hour of weaving and winding through snow-packed gullies and copses of firs until they came over a hill and found the caretaker's cottage.

A classic log cabin, it stood dark and mysterious at the bottom of a small clearing in the woods. There was no smoke from the chimney. There were no tracks in the freshly fallen powder. The only sound was the whisper of fat snowflakes piling up around them.

The scene was truly something from a fairy tale.

They left the snowmobile in a clump of trees and hid

it under some fallen pine branches. Then Felicity took Gerald by the hand and they started towards the cottage.

'Come along, Hansel,' she said. 'Let's see if the wicked witch is at home.'

Chapter 9

Gerald stepped up to the porch and peered through a window. Inside was as dark as coal dust. He gave Felicity a 'here goes nothing' shrug and tried the door handle. It was unlocked. He pushed the door open.

Before he could take a step, a flash of movement caught his eye. He ducked, just as a ski pole whipped across the door and slammed into the frame, biting into the wood.

Gerald lost his balance and tumbled into the cottage. As he struggled to get to his feet, he caught sight of Ox winding up to have another swing at him.

Alisha was behind him. She grabbed Ox by the arm. 'It's Gerald, you idiot.'

Ox lowered the pole and gave a sheepish, 'Sorry.'

Felicity closed the door behind them. 'Is everyone here?' she asked. 'Is everyone safe?'

Ruby and Sam emerged from the darkness and there was a quick round of hugs and high fives as everyone tried to be first to tell about their adventures.

Alisha pulled the curtains across the windows and switched on a small table lamp. It supplied just enough light for Gerald to see that she was seething.

'What's the problem?' he asked.

'We made a clean getaway,' Alisha explained. 'I'll give this boy one thing—he can drive a snowmobile. But that's about all he can do.'

Ox opened his mouth to protest but Alisha cut him off with a flick of her hand. 'We got through that redwood forest without anyone following us. We could have come straight here. But we came to a clearing. And there was a helicopter there. Just parked in the snow. It was totally black, no markings.'

'That must be how those men got here,' Gerald said. 'All the roads are closed, so a chopper is the only way in.'

'Exactly,' Alisha said. 'And their only way out.' She jerked a thumb towards Ox. 'So what does Einstein Junior here decide to do?'

Gerald didn't hesitate. 'Blow it up.'

Alisha was astounded. 'You approve of this?'

'Of course,' Gerald said.

Sam nodded. 'I'd do the same thing.'

Alisha tossed her hands in the air. 'Boys,' she said.

'It was the coolest thing,' Ox said to Sam and Gerald. 'I just opened the fuel tank and set it off.'

'But how did you light it without blowing yourself up?' Gerald asked. 'Aviation gas goes off like a bomb.'

'I know,' Ox said. 'I couldn't just strike a match. But remember that emergency kit we took from the hangar? There was a flare gun in it.'

Sam and Gerald's faces lit up. 'Cool,' they chorused.

'So Alisha and I got back a bit and I shot a flare right into the open fuel tank.'

'How many flares?' Alisha said, her eyes sweeping the ceiling.

'Well, three,' Ox said. 'All of them, as it turns out. The first two didn't really hit the target. But when the third one hit? Man! You should have seen it. It blew us right off our feet!'

'We did see it,' Gerald said. 'That's how we got away from our guy. You should have seen Felicity's one-woman war effort.'

Alisha was not impressed. 'Don't you understand?' she said. 'That helicopter was their way out. Now they're stuck here. With us.'

'They might use one of Gerald's choppers,' Ox said, scratching at the floor with a toe.

'Really?' Alisha said. 'I seem to recall some bright spark managed to wreck two of them in the hangar. Now who might that have been?'

Ox was completely crushed. He tried to change the

subject. 'How about you guys,' he said to Sam and Ruby. 'What happened to you?'

Ruby glanced at her brother. 'It was total madness,' she said. 'I can't believe we got here. Not after Sam fell off the snowmobile when we were halfway across the lake.'

'You were on the lake?' Felicity said.

'We headed there straight from the hangar,' Sam said. 'We'd only just got onto the ice when one of those goons was after us on a snowmobile.'

'So how did you fall off?' Felicity asked.

Sam looked to Ruby. 'It was when he started ramming us, wasn't it?'

Ruby thought for a moment. 'That'd be right. Just after you shot him.'

'You shot him!'

They'd all settled onto a cluster of armchairs and sofas as Sam told his tale. 'With the air pistol,' he said. 'He was right on our tail so I figured anything to slow him down would help. I let off a few rounds. I think I got him coz he yelped pretty loud.'

Ox chuckled to himself. 'Nice one,' he said.

Alisha shook her head.

'He got pretty mad,' Sam said. 'That's when he started ramming us. Hard. Ruby did an awesome job just keeping us going.'

Ruby dropped her head onto her brother's shoulder. 'Why, thank you,' she said.

'So this guy is really hitting us hard. Swinging wide and slamming into us. I almost fell off a couple of times.'

'I thought I better take some evasive action,' Ruby said, 'and pulled this huge turn just as he was coming at us again.'

'That's when I fell off,' Sam said.

Gerald laughed hard. 'What? It wasn't even from him hitting you? You just fell off?'

Sam held his head high. 'Ruby pulled a *really* big turn,' he said.

Ruby joined in the laughter. 'It was pretty funny. Sam went flying. Flat on his back across the ice. And then the most amazing thing happened.'

'What's that?' Felicity asked, wiping a tear from her eye. 'This is too hilarious.'

'The guy chasing us on the snowmobile?' Sam said. 'He ran over me.'

'What!' the room chorused.

'Well, "ran over" is a bit of an exaggeration,' Ruby said. 'He went by very, very close.'

'So close,' Sam said, 'that I hitched a ride.'

'You what?' Gerald said.

'Hitched a ride. He was towing one of those red sleds behind him and as he slowed to turn after Ruby, I grabbed on. He must have dragged me across the ice for—how far, Ruby? Fifty metres?'

'At least,' Ruby said. 'Then Sam had the bright idea of actually climbing onto the sled.'

'I got right up behind the creep before he even realised I was onboard,' Sam said.

'What did he do?' Felicity was entranced.

'Well, he stood up, trying to grab me. He was lashing out with one hand and steering with the other. And he got me, right by the collar.'

Felicity gasped, drumming her feet up and down. 'Then what?'

'Have you ever heard the rule: Never stand up on a snowmobile if you're going under a low bridge?'

'No,' Felicity said.

'Well, neither had this guy.'

There was a stunned silence.

'Anyway,' Sam said. 'He let go of me pretty quick after that. Lucky for him he had a helmet on. We left him nursing his head, nicked his snowmobile and came here.'

And then, through the laughter, the radio in Gerald's pocket crackled into life.

Instantly, everyone fell silent. Gerald pulled out the device and dropped it on the floor, as if it were alive.

'*Snow's too thick...*' a tinny voice filled the room. '*No sign of them.*'

A different voice came through the speaker. '*Boss says to come back to the house. That's it for tonight.*'

'*What's the plan for the morning?*'

'*He's considering options. We might be pulling out.*'

'*Good. Coz I've got a splitting headache.*'

Ox slapped Sam on the shoulder with a, 'Nice one.'

Gerald turned down the radio volume and looked at the people in the room. Once again, he'd managed to drag his friends into a disaster. And while they'd all been excited by their close escapes, Gerald knew everyone was worried about what was going on up at the house. He suddenly realised that his legs were soaked. And he was freezing.

'I think it's safe for us to light a fire,' he said. 'That snow's too heavy for anyone to come looking for us tonight. Let's dry off these clothes.'

For the next hour they shared stories about their adventures that night. Alisha found a store of dry clothes in a bedroom and shared them round, although Sam insisted on walking around in his lurid green-and-red striped thermal underwear. Ruby, wearing an oversized Boston University sweatshirt and pants, handed out the snacks she'd taken from the hangar, and Ox and Felicity got the fire going. Sam and Gerald dragged out mattresses and blankets to make a huge bed in front of the grate. Alisha rolled up her sari to form a makeshift clothesline and soon, jackets, pants, boots and children were steaming by the fireplace.

'You should have seen what Felicity did to that guy's jaw!' Gerald said, rolling back onto a nest of pillows. 'It was a massacre. A mandibular massacre.'

'Wasn't he president of South Africa?' Sam asked.

'Who?'

'Nelson Mandibular.'

'Nelson *Mandela*, you goose!' Ruby burst into a laughing fit.

'I knew that!' Sam protested. 'I *knew* that. I was joking.' Everyone was laughing, Sam included. No one believed him. And it didn't matter. One by one, as the embers grew low, they dropped off to sleep, snug and warm, but still with such a long way to go.

Chapter 10

Gerald woke with a snowball to the face.

He had been dreaming quite happily. He was walking along a golden beach dotted with palms, somewhere warm. Alisha was running a beachside kiosk, selling cold drinks and sweets. Gerald had been trying to decide weather to buy an apple muffin or a blueberry muffin. He'd just decided on apple when both the muffins grew mouths, and told him that neither of them wanted anything to do with him.

The snowball came as a relief.

Gerald shook his head and wiped away the powder. The first thing he saw was the evil smile on Sam's face. 'That's your 7 a.m. wake-up call, Mr Wilkins. Breakfast will be served in the main dining room at eight. Today's menu includes half a can of Coke and a stale packet of corn chips. You have a nice day now, y'hear?'

Gerald thought about retaliating but couldn't muster the energy. Sam laughed, adjusted his red-and-green thermals and continued on his way to the bathroom.

Gerald propped onto his elbows and surveyed the bodies strewn around him. Ox was snuffling to himself in deep slumber on one of the couches. Felicity and Ruby were curled up next to each other on a mattress on the floor, sharing a blanket. Alisha was already up, dressed in her snow gear and studying a picture hanging on the wall.

She looked around and saw that Gerald was awake.

'Come see this,' she said. 'It's a map.'

Gerald dragged himself from under his warm blanket and hopped across the cold wooden floor. The fire had burned itself out and the temperature inside the cabin was on the unpleasant side of frosty.

'See?' Alisha said, pointing to a square marked on the chart. 'I think that's the chalet, by the lake. So this would be us here.'

Gerald studied the map through bleary eyes. 'There's nothing much around, is there? No towns. No villages. It's the back of beyond.'

Alisha nodded. 'We have a long walk to get any help.'

'What do you mean walk?' Gerald said. 'We've got three snowmobiles out there.'

'Those snowmobiles are now buried under a metre of snow,' Alisha said. She opened the curtains—the snow was up to the windowsill, and still tumbling down. 'And do you see those lines on the map?'

Gerald looked to where Alisha was pointing. 'They're contour lines. They show how high somewhere is. The closer together the lines are, the steeper the land. Understand?'

'Course I understand,' Gerald said. 'I'm not stupid.'

'So you say.' Alisha said. 'The best way out of this valley is up here. Through Cooper's Bowl.'

'Where the lines are really close together,' Gerald said. 'So not good snowmobile country.'

'Not with all this soft powder about. But there are snowshoes here. We should be able to make decent time on foot. So over the mountain it is.'

Gerald chewed the inside of his cheek. 'Terrific. So now we're mountain climbers.' Then he noticed something in the top corner of the map, along a ridgeline. 'What's that?' He pointed to a symbol that looked like a guard tower from an old war movie.

Alisha dropped her eyes to the map legend. 'It's a fire ranger's lookout tower,' she said. 'But there wouldn't be anyone there this time of year. It's not exactly fire season.'

'Maybe not,' Gerald said. 'But I bet there's a radio.'

Alisha's eyes widened. 'Of course. That's perfect! That's where we're going.'

Felicity had woken and joined them, wrapped in her

blanket. 'That looks a long way,' she yawned. 'Can't we just use the radio that Gerald took last night?'

Ruby appeared over Felicity's shoulder, sleep still in her eyes. 'That little thing is just short range,' she said. 'Couple of miles at best. We use them on camping trips.'

Gerald poked his head up. 'Where is that radio anyway?' he said. He wandered over to the coffee table, making sure to whip Ox's pillow out from under his head on the way.

'Hey!' Ox grumbled. 'I'm not awake.'

'Come on, sleeping beauty,' Gerald said. 'We've got work to do.' He picked up the radio and fumbled with the volume knob. There was a crackle. And then the words, '*I'm going in now. Come straightaway...*'

Gerald looked across to Ox. Before he could say anything the cottage door burst off its hinges and flew into the room. There was snow halfway up the doorframe and a large figure slid through the opening like an Eskimo into an igloo. He landed squarely on his feet—a giant of a man, dressed in a black snowsuit and balaclava, and brandishing a handgun.

He spotted Gerald in an instant.

'Gerald Wilkins,' he said in a voice of deep threat. 'I've been looking for you.'

Strands of a wiry beard poked through the man's balaclava. His eyes narrowed and locked onto Gerald. 'You have put me to a lot of trouble, young fellow.' His breathing was laboured in the thin mountain air. 'You have cost me time that I can ill afford to lose.' The man raised his gun and took a step towards Gerald. But it was as far as he got. Sam's swinging ski pole collected him across the nose. A metallic *dong* reverberated through the cottage. Sam's arms juddered as if he had just hit a fencepost. But the strike had the desired effect. The man stumbled backwards and dropped to the floor, his hands wrapped around his face.

Gerald looked at Sam, his mouth open. Sam held up the ski pole. Gerald could swear there was a nose-shaped dent in the middle of it. For a second, no one moved. Then there was bedlam.

Bodies dived into ski gear. Boots were yanked on. Alisha snatched the map from the wall and tore it from its frame, shoving the paper into her pocket. Gerald climbed out a window, straight into waist-deep snow.

'There's one snowmobile out here,' he called back. 'With a sled. We should all fit.'

Ruby climbed out after him. 'Can't we dig out the other ones?'

Alisha scrambled through the door. 'What about the snowshoes?'

'No time,' Gerald said. 'Laughing boy in there called for back-up, remember. They'll be here any minute.'

Gerald pointed Ruby to the driver's seat. Felicity and Sam squeezed in behind her. Then Gerald, Alisha and Ox clambered onto the sled and held on as well as they could.

'Go, Ruby!' Gerald called. 'Straight up the hill in front of you.'

Ruby pushed the starter and the engine fired. 'How far?' she called over the noise.

'Until you can't go any further,' Alisha called back.

The snowmobile moved off. The going was tough. The tracks struggled to get traction in the soft powder. The engine strained against the passenger load. But somehow they started the long climb out of the valley.

The cottage disappeared behind a hillock and for a moment all Gerald could see was a world of white, where the sky and the horizon melted into one.

Ruby pulled on the throttle and the snowmobile surged on, bouncing the sled behind it. Gerald, Alisha and Ox clung to each other. If they weren't fleeing for their lives they would have been having a ball.

Then Gerald saw them. Two black specks at the bottom of the hill below them. Snowmobiles, each with a single rider.

'Faster, Ruby!' he shouted. 'We've got company!'

Ruby urged the machine on. They topped a low rise onto a narrow saddle. A colossal slope towered over them like a snow-filled amphitheatre.

'Cooper's Bowl,' Alisha said. 'We go straight up here.'

The rise got steadily steeper. The snowmobile lurched on. Great swathes of snow broke away behind them and slid down the slope. At one point they bounced between two ridges, bucking the sled up into the air.

Then Ox fell off.

He went without a sound, tumbling and rolling, carried away in a flowing river of fresh powder. It happened so silently that Gerald didn't register that it had happened at all.

'Oswald!' Alisha called out.

Gerald reached around and pounded Sam on the shoulder with his fist. 'Stop!'

Before the snowmobile could judder to a halt, Alisha had thrown herself off the sled. She landed up to her hips in snow and waded down the hillside towards where Ox had fallen. 'Oswald!' she called again. In the sudden quiet, her voice rang out like a clarion in the mountain air.

Gerald rolled off the sled and started after Alisha, struggling through the deep snow. The pain stabbed into his ribs again and he clutched at his side. He could see no sign of Ox.

Then a sharp *crack* split the silence.

Gerald stopped, breathing hard, and looked to the bottom of the mountain. Their two pursuers were off their snowmobiles. And each held a rifle to his shoulder.

Another *crack* sounded up the slope. Then another.

Instinctively, everyone ducked. But in the middle of the huge natural bowl, there was no place to hide.

Gerald heard one more *crack*—this time from far above them. The sound was deeper, louder and way more frightening than any bullet from a gun. Gerald spun around to face the mountaintop. And in that instant he understood.

The gunmen weren't shooting at them.

They were shooting over them.

Trying to start an avalanche.

An avalanche that was now bearing down on Gerald and his friends as if someone had flung open the gates of hell.

Chapter 11

There was no time to run, and no shelter to run to. What started out as a rumble, like low thunder at the top of the mountain, grew quickly to a roar. Gerald could feel the pressure building in his eardrums. The air being pushed ahead of the wave of snow almost knocked him off his feet.

The crest of the wave picked up Ruby and Felicity. It swallowed Sam and the snowmobile.

And then it hit Gerald.

He was lifted and thrown backwards, headfirst down the hill. His mouth filled with snow and ice, blocking his airways. The outside world disappeared into a grey haze as he was rolled and shaken like a rag doll in a tumble dryer.

Over and over he went, in a gymnastics routine with no end. Gerald threw his arms up, trying to swim to the surface of the surging river of snow and ice. His ribs screamed at the pummelling. And still he couldn't breathe. It was like being caught in a rip at Bondi—the ocean toyed with him, rolling him under the surface like some giant game of tunnel ball.

Then it struck him. It was *just* like being caught in a rip. And the best defence in a rip is not to fight it, but to swim across it and hope to be spat out at the side. He doubled his efforts with his arms, flailing about like a windmill in a cyclone. After what seemed an age, he finally rolled to a stop.

For a moment, Gerald lay encased in the powder, eyes blinking and ears straining to hear anything. But there was total silence. His hand was pressed up against his cheek. He jabbed fingers into his mouth to clear away the snow packed inside. He sucked in air and felt his lungs respond to the sharp cold. He blinked again. All around him was a shroud of blue grey. He had no sense of where was up. It took him a moment to realise the blue light he was seeing was actually the sun through the snow. He must be lying on his back. In one of those moments when the brain spits up a long lost memory from nowhere, he remembered a ski holiday with his parents, when he was just a little kid. The ski instructor had said something about being caught in an avalanche. About how the churned-up snow sets like concrete within minutes. Gerald's eyes shot wide. He had to act.

He clawed at the snow around his face, driving his hands as hard as he could towards the light. He'd lost a glove in the fall but he felt no cold as his bare fingers scratched their way towards the surface. And then in a glorious moment, he broke through. It was like looking out of a tunnel. He could see the sky and the tops of some fir trees. He pushed with all his might and managed to clear a hole large enough so he could sit up. He was under only about half a metre of snow but already he could feel it hardening around his legs.

Gerald rolled to his side. He ignored the pain shooting through his ribs. Bit by bit, he dragged himself free of his icy tomb.

He stood groggily and looked around. He'd been carried at least three hundred metres, halfway down the bowl, and jettisoned at the base of a stand of trees. He'd lost his goggles as well as a glove. Above him, up the hill, was a junkyard of broken snow and ice, as if someone had taken a sledgehammer to a wedding cake. Down the hill, all was white destruction. There was carved up powder everywhere.

Gerald saw the sole of a boot poking out from the snow.

It was Sam.

In all the confusion, Gerald had forgotten about his friends.

He strode towards it, ploughing a path behind him.

'Sam!' he called. 'Can you hear me?' He wrapped his hands around the boot, pulled and tumbled onto his backside with the empty boot on his chest. Sam must have lost it in the fall.

'Sam!'

Gerald scanned the area, frantic for any sign of his friend. Then he saw a red-and-green striped foot punched up through the powder. It was only twenty metres away but it seemed an insurmountable task to get there. Gerald lifted his legs and drove himself on.

He dropped to his knees by Sam's foot and scooped away armfuls of snow, desperately aware of the minutes ticking past. He uncovered Sam's other foot, still in its boot, and soon had his legs free. Sam was on his stomach, his head buried deep down, as if someone had fired him into a snow bank from a cannon. Gerald leapt in beside him, digging at his sides.

Sam was not moving.

Gerald didn't look up when Ruby joined him. Felicity was only seconds behind her. Together, they shovelled in a frenzy.

'Is he—?' Ruby couldn't finish the sentence.

'Dig.' It was all Gerald could bring himself to say.

They cleared the snow to Sam's armpits, then Gerald hauled himself to his feet and grabbed one of Sam's legs. 'Get the other one,' he said to Ruby. 'On three, pull.'

Felicity gripped Sam by the jacket and they heaved. Sam slid out like a newborn foal, landing on top of the others in a tangle of legs and arms.

'Sam!' Ruby cried. She scrambled to clear snow from her brother's face. 'Sam!'

He lay in her lap, his face pointing to the sky.

His eyes were closed. His skin was pale.

Ruby shook him. 'Sam!' she cried again. There was no response. Ruby looked to Gerald, desperation in her eyes. Gerald looked back at her, helpless.

Then Sam coughed. A plug of ice shot from his mouth and bounced off Ruby's forehead. He sucked in huge breaths, his chest pumping the mountain air.

Sam opened his eyes. Gerald, Ruby and Felicity stared down at him. He blinked. 'Not sure I want to do that again,' he said.

Ruby wrapped her arms around her brother. 'I thought you were dead,' she whispered. 'You big idiot.'

Gerald looked down the slope. At the very bottom, hundreds of metres away, he could see movement.

'Look,' he said. 'The gunmen are still down there.' The sky was clearing. He shielded his eyes from the glare. 'And they've got Alisha and Ox!'

'They must have surfed the avalanche all the way to the bottom,' Ruby said.

'Thank goodness they're all right,' Felicity said. 'But what do we do now?'

Ruby glanced towards the top of the mountain. 'That snow still looks unstable,' she said. 'We should get over to the trees.'

Gerald helped Sam to his feet and picked up his discarded boot from the slush. They'd taken only a few steps when a rumble rolled down the mountain.

'It's another slide!' Ruby cried. 'Run!'

There was a helter-skelter dash through the ploughed up snow to reach the safety of the tree line. Felicity was the last one to dive behind a trunk when the first rush of tumbling snow whooshed past. They gathered in a tight group and watched as nature's mayhem swept down the slope.

'It's like a river in flood,' Gerald said. 'Amazing.'

'There goes the snowmobile!' Ruby cried, as the machine rolled past, like a toy car thrown into a fairy floss machine.

At the bottom of the slope, the gunmen bundled Alisha and Ox onto the back of their snowmobiles and took off, trying to outrun the approaching snow slide. They disappeared over a rise and were gone.

Gerald, Ruby, Sam and Felicity stood in shocked silence. The river of snow flowed onwards.

Felicity was first to speak.

'Which way do we go?' she asked. 'Up or down?'

'We've got to go get Ox and Alisha, don't we?' Sam said. 'We can't just leave them.'

Ruby shook her head. 'They'll take Ox and Alisha back to the chalet. They'll be warm and safe there.'

'That's where all the adults are,' Felicity said. 'Ox's parents and your—' She looked at Ruby's expression and paused. 'I'm sorry.'

Ruby brushed it aside with a shrug. 'I'm sure they're okay,' she said softly.

Gerald put a hand on Sam's shoulder. 'I think Ruby's right,' he said. 'We've got to stick to the plan. Go get help.' Gerald had no idea whether that was the right decision. But he couldn't see what good it would do to serve themselves up to those gunmen like a sack of Christmas presents.

'Hey,' he said, suddenly remembering. 'It's Christmas Day.'

Sam turned and started up the slope, his eyes following the tree line. 'Terrific,' he said. 'Joy to the world.'

It took two hours of hard slog to reach the top of the bowl. On the way, Felicity described how the avalanche had swept her to one side, and how she pulled Ruby out of a snow bank.

Once they reached the ridgeline they found a trekking hut. There was no radio, but there were snowshoes. The hike to the watchtower took another two hours. They climbed up to the viewing platform and Gerald broke a window to get inside. The first police helicopter arrived an hour after his emergency radio call.

The commander of the SWAT team listened intently as Gerald recounted the events since midnight. Around them, police officers set up a rescue headquarters. 'And this guy you knocked out in the caretaker's cottage,' the commander said, 'was he down for the count or just a bit dazed?'

'He was moaning, so he was still conscious,' Gerald said. 'But he must have been wearing something under his balaclava.'

'Yeah,' Sam said. 'A hockey mask, or something like that.'

'What makes you think that?' the commander said.

'Because his nose didn't go splat when I hit it.'

The commander raised an eyebrow and looked warily at Sam. 'I'm sending in a team of my best people with some locals from the Sierra County Search and Rescue,' he said. 'They know the terrain. We'll get your parents out.'

Gerald, Ruby, Sam and Felicity stood at the watch-tower window, wrapped in blankets and sipping mugs of hot soup, as the SWAT helicopter rose from the snow and disappeared over a rise.

Gerald cradled his mug in his hands, letting the warmth soak into his fingers. 'They'll be fine,' he said.

'What makes you so sure?' Ruby said. Her eyes were fixed on the ridge where the chopper had dropped from view.

'These SWAT guys look like they know what they're doing,' he said. 'And don't forget one important thing.'

'What's that?'

'We've got Ox and his Assertiveness Training on our side.'

Ruby looked at him blankly. 'Do you really think this is the time for jokes.'

'If not now,' Gerald said, 'then when?'

The sun was low in the sky when Sam nudged Gerald, and nodded towards the commander. 'Looks like something's happening.'

The commander stood at a table with a map of the area spread across the top. He held a finger to his ear, listening to a radio call. Then his eyes swivelled to the four people wrapped in blankets.

'The chopper is coming back,' the commander said. 'I need you all to come see something.'

'What is it?' Ruby said. She was trembling. It was not from the cold.

The commander zipped up his jacket and pulled a hat from his pocket. 'It will be easier if you just come and see.'

Ruby gave Gerald a nervous glance, and took Sam's hand. She didn't let it go until the chopper delivered them to the front of the chalet.

A SWAT officer met them at the front door. 'Nothing's been touched,' he told the commander. 'It's just as we found it.'

Gerald's heart raced. A sudden nausea swept his stomach.

The stone chalet stood silent before them. Gerald, Ruby, Felicity and Sam followed the commander into the entry hall.

It was deserted.

Their footsteps echoed as they walked through the house. Gerald stepped on broken glass from a vase that had been knocked from a side table. In the baronial dining room, embers still glowed in the fireplaces. Breakfasts sat half-eaten on plates. But not a soul could be found.

The chalet was empty.

It was as if everyone there had been erased from existence.

Chapter 12

Gerald had been on the phone to the family lawyer for over an hour and he was about to lose control.

'Look Mr Prisk,' Gerald said. 'You can't expect us to just sit around and do nothing. They took everyone. Mum and Dad. Ox and Alisha. Even Mrs Rutherford and Mr Fry. We've got to do something.'

A fog had rolled over San Francisco shortly after lunch. The view from the presidential suite of the Fairmont Hotel was grey, wet and depressing. They had been back in the city for a day, flown there in a police helicopter from Mt Archer. The excitement of their escape had been replaced with a gnawing frustration that threatened to collapse in on itself.

Ruby and Sam sat on a couch opposite Gerald,

staring at him. Felicity stood by a window on the far side of the lounge, her arms hugging her chest. She gazed at the murk outside.

'Really? Good. I'm glad the airport is fogged in.' Gerald had never spoken to Mr Prisk like this before. But he had never been this annoyed. 'There's no point in me going back to London. I may as well be here when the kidnappers call. I'm the one they're looking for anyway.'

Mr Prisk's voice squeaked through the earpiece. Gerald tightened his jaw and listened. 'Yes, I know you're worried about the precious Archer Corporation,' Gerald said. 'I'm worried about my friends. I'll speak to you later.'

He hung up the phone and flopped back onto the couch.

'The jet's grounded till the fog lifts,' Gerald said. 'Mr Prisk wants me back in London straightaway.'

'How can we go?' Ruby said. Her eyes were red from crying. 'I'm not leaving till they find Mum and Dad.' Her voice cracked as she spoke.

Sam put an arm around her shoulder. 'The police will find them,' he said. 'Won't they, detective?'

A man in a blue suit looked up from the dining table where he was writing in his notebook.

He rested his pen on the page and considered the question for a moment. 'We're doing all we can. Crime scene investigators are going through every inch of the place at Mt Archer. If there are any clues, they'll find them.'

'But what if there aren't any clues?' Ruby said. 'What if whoever did this left nothing behind?'

The detective fixed her with a steady stare. 'Nobody is that smart, Miss Valentine.'

Gerald snorted. 'They managed to move about sixty people off a snowbound mountain,' he said. 'I'd say they're smart enough.'

Another detective emerged from the adjoining kitchen, a steaming mug of coffee in each hand. He placed one in front of his partner. 'We've got over a hundred officers working on this case,' he said. 'Not just locals, but statewide. And since the kidnapping involved two minors,' he checked his notes, 'uh, Miss Gupta and Mister Perkins, the FBI has been alerted. They'll be carrying out investigations as well.'

Ruby shrank back into her brother's arm. 'I just want to see Mum and Dad.'

Gerald leaned forward and put a hand on her knee. 'They'll be back. Don't worry.'

'But we haven't heard anything,' Ruby said. She looked across to the detectives. 'Is that usual?'

The two policemen glanced at each other for just long enough to indicate that whatever they were about to say may not be entirely truthful.

'There's nothing about this case that's usual,' the first detective said. 'There has never been a kidnapping on this scale before. Sixty people or more? We're still working to confirm the names of everyone who's missing.'

'But won't there be a ransom demand, or something?' Ruby said.

The second detective gave Ruby a reassuring look. 'Every case is different. Sometimes a ransom demand comes straightaway. Other times, it takes longer.'

'How long?' Sam asked.

The detective took a sip of his coffee. 'Longer,' he said.

Gerald bounced to his feet and paced the floor. 'Then what's keeping them? It's not like I can't afford to pay.'

'It may not be money they're after,' the first detective said. He flicked through his notes. 'You said you heard one of them tell some of the victims to put their jewels and wallets on a table. Right?'

'That doesn't sound like big time thieves, does it,' Sam said. 'A few old watches and some diamond rings.'

'Especially when they flew to the chalet in a helicopter,' Gerald said. 'They can't be too hard up for cash.'

'It sounds like they were looking for something specific,' the first detective said. 'Some particular piece of jewellery.'

A muffled gasp came from over by the windows. Felicity leaned against the wall, her hand clasped to the neck of her black turtleneck jumper.

'Is there something wrong, Flicka?' Ruby asked.

Felicity's eyes darted to the carpet at her feet. 'No,' she said quickly. 'It's just...who would do such a thing?

Go to all that trouble?'

The first detective looked at her intently. 'It depends on what they're looking for. If it was a one-of-a-kind item, a unique piece, a serious collector might be tempted to do almost anything.'

The other detective said, 'Is there something you want to tell us, Miss Upham?'

Felicity's hand tightened at her throat. She shook her head. 'No,' she said, eyes trained on the weave of the carpet. 'It's all just so—'

'Sick-making?' Sam suggested.

Gerald stopped his pacing. 'It has to be Sir Mason Green, doesn't it? All of this happened right after he escaped.'

The first detective flicked back through his notebook. 'Now you mentioned this Green guy before. Who is he? Is he the one that the gang leader called the Falcon?'

Gerald looked up to the ceiling in frustration. 'I told you. Mason Green is the British billionaire arrested for murder after he had my great aunt killed. The story was on the front page of every newspaper in Europe.'

The detective jotted down a note. 'I don't read a lot of European newspapers,' he said, giving his partner a wink. 'And we should contact an Inspector Parakeet, you say?'

'Parrott.' Gerald was about to boil over. 'Inspector Parrott. He knows all about it. I have no idea who this Falcon is. But the man with the deep voice said something about the Falcon coming through with one half of the deal. I'm sure it's important.'

'Talk to Parrott about the Falcon.' The detective made another note in his book. 'I think we've got all that we need for the moment. The phone here has been diverted to a trained police negotiator if the kidnappers call so you don't have to worry about that. There's a uniform at the door to make sure no one gets in and I'll keep in touch with your Mr Prisk. Otherwise, you're free to go back to London once the fog clears, whenever that is. It looks set in.'

The detectives went to leave, but one of them paused near the front door. He turned back to Gerald. 'There's one thing I want to know,' he said.

'Yes?'

'What's it like being a billionaire?'

Gerald thought for a moment. 'There are days when it's the worst thing in the world.'

The detective nodded, and turned to his colleague, 'Still, not a bad position to be in,' he said as they walked out the door.

As the door swung shut, Gerald caught sight of an enormous uniformed officer sitting in the corridor outside their hotel suite.

Sam let out a sigh and rested his head on the back of the couch. 'I'm hungry,' he said.

'Really, Sam?' Ruby said. 'Really? Is that all you can think of?' Then she shook her head. 'I guess you may as well do something.' She tossed Sam the room-service menu.

Sam thumbed through the pages, trying to mask the rumbling from his stomach.

Gerald squatted on the rug in front of Ruby. 'You okay?'

She gave him a tight smile. 'Not even slightly. I can't bear the thought of what might be happening to Mum and Dad. Or Alisha and Ox. Can you imagine what it must be like for them?' She rubbed her eyes.

'Is it too late for blueberry pancakes with a side order of waffles?' Sam asked.

Gerald picked up a phone and passed it to Sam. 'It is never too late for pancakes and waffles,' he said. 'With ice cream.'

Sam dialled room service. 'Ruby, do you want anything? Felicity?'

Ruby shook her head. Felicity hadn't moved from her spot by the window. 'No thank you,' she said. 'I'm really not hungry.'

Gerald looked first to Felicity and then to Ruby. The Christmas hug with Ruby in the chalet seemed an age ago. No one had mentioned it since. It was almost like it had never happened. Felicity had held Gerald's hand in the back of the police helicopter all the way to San Francisco. Ruby had been too upset about her parents for Gerald to talk to her about anything. He looked again at Ruby's red eyes, and at Felicity's vacant stare out the window.

He knew the conversation about that hug had to happen some time.

But not now.

Chapter 13

'I may have over-ordered.'

Sam leaned back in the dining chair, a trail of melted ice cream snaking down his chin.

The table was a mess. Plates of half-eaten pancakes, swimming in maple syrup and whipped butter, were wedged up against soggy waffles soaked in chocolate. A serving trolley, bearing several bowls of melting ice cream, stood against the wall.

Sam rubbed his belly beneath his sweatshirt and groaned again.

Ruby picked up a spoon and twirled it in her fingers. 'Those detectives didn't fill me with confidence,' she said. 'They weren't very interested in hearing about Sir Mason Green.'

'I'm sure he's at the centre of all this,' Gerald said. 'I keep expecting his sneering face to bob up somewhere.' He bit his bottom lip. 'I really don't want to see him again.'

Ruby folded her arms across her chest and shivered. 'I don't like how that man in the cottage said he'd been looking for you, Gerald. If Green is involved, I have the nasty feeling we'll hear from him.'

Then a thought popped into Gerald's head. It landed gentle as a snowflake on a mountaintop, but within seconds it was rolling down the hill in a fully fledged avalanche. 'That dinner jacket of Green's that we got from the dry cleaners.'

Felicity sat at the end of the dining table. The waffle on her plate was untouched. 'What about it?' she asked.

'He left some keys in the pocket. Remember?' Gerald disappeared into a bedroom and reappeared a moment later with a silver key ring. 'These must be for an apartment that Green has here in San Francisco,' he said. He flipped the fob over. 'The Palladium Apartments,' he read. 'Nob Hill.'

Sam let out a giggle. Everyone looked at him. His cheeks reddened. 'Sorry,' he mumbled.

'What are you thinking, Gerald?' Ruby asked, suddenly brightening. 'Do you want to pay a visit?'

'If Green is running this show, I want to know what he's after,' Gerald said. 'There's no way he could sneak back into the US so soon after escaping from jail. So that gives us some time to have a look around his apartment. It probably won't amount to much but who knows—we might find something.'

'You don't want to just call the detectives and tell them?' Sam said.

'No!' Felicity's response was emphatic. Gerald, Sam and Ruby turned to look at her. She blushed. 'They'll be too busy,' she said. 'Looking for everyone.' She dropped her eyes to her uneaten meal. 'And, like Gerald says, there's probably nothing there.'

Gerald pushed himself back from the table. 'It's better than hanging around here,' he said.

Within five minutes they had jackets, gloves and hats, ready to go. They gathered at the door and Gerald was about to pull it open when Ruby grabbed his arm. 'Wait,' she said. 'What about the policeman outside? He's not going to let us just wander out of here.'

Gerald paused. 'You're right. There's got to be a way past him.' Then his eyes fell on the room-service trolley. He reached for the telephone.

It didn't take much to convince the room-service porter.

'A hundred dollars to push you guys down the hall in this trolley?' the man asked, not sure if he'd heard right.

'And there's another hundred when you deliver us back in an hour or so,' Gerald said. 'But our friend outside in the hallway can't know anything about it.'

The porter lifted a corner of the floor-length table-cloth that was draped over the trolley. 'Climb aboard,' he said.

Gerald wasn't sure whose elbow was shoved under his nose, or whose kidneys he'd squashed with his knee, but the cramped journey down the length of the hotel corridor was worth every cent.

A short cab ride later and they bundled out onto the street opposite the Palladium Apartments. The sun had disappeared over the horizon and a dank night had settled on the city.

Gerald jangled the keys in his jacket pocket. Across the street, through a wall of glass at the front of the apartment building, he could see a man sitting behind a reception desk.

'How do we get past him?' Ruby asked, following Gerald's gaze. 'He'll know we don't live here.'

Gerald pondered this for a moment. 'I'll just have to use my Australian charm.'

Ruby snorted. 'Oh, yes. Bend over and let him bask in your sunshine.'

Gerald gave her a dirty look, then scooted across the road and up the front steps. Felicity, Ruby and Sam joined him under the front awning.

Gerald pointed to a panel of door buzzers on the wall. Next to apartment 8 was a neatly typed name: Sir Mason Green.

Through the glass door, the man had his head down, engrossed in a book. Gerald raised his finger to his lips and jerked his head towards the lifts at the rear of the foyer. He eased the door open and slipped inside. The others followed.

They were halfway across the lobby when the man raised his head.

'Can I help you?' he said in much the manner of a cat interrupting a mouse in front of an open pantry door.

Gerald pulled the keys from his pocket and jiggled them in the air. 'No thank you,' he said, smiling pleasantly. 'Just going up to my uncle's apartment.'

'Really?' the man said. 'And who might your uncle be?'

Gerald stopped walking. Felicity almost ran into the back of him.

'Sir Mason Green,' he said, trying to steady the tremor in his voice.

The doorman didn't blink. 'Yeah? Well, he's not home. I haven't seen him for months. So—' the man lifted his hand and wafted it towards the door, as if shooing flies from his soup.

Gerald swallowed tightly. 'I know,' he said. 'But he's coming back next week. He asked if I could, um, check the milk in his refrigerator.'

The man looked Gerald up and down. 'The milk?'

'That's right.'

'And it takes four of you to do that?'

Sam took a half-step forward. 'It's a very big fridge.'

Gerald quickly interjected. 'My uncle's a bit of a neat freak. He likes everything to be just right.'

The man gave Gerald one more look up and down. 'Yes, I know. There were some cleaners here earlier today,' he said. 'Go ahead—I should have recognised the funny accent. Just put the key in next to button 8.'

Gerald uttered a quick thanks and hustled everyone into the lift. He pushed the key in, turned it and pressed button 8. The doors slid shut.

'A very big fridge?' Ruby said to Sam. 'Are you completely insane?'

'It worked, didn't it?' Sam said.

Ruby shook her head, then turned to Gerald. 'What do you think he meant about cleaners being here? Is Green coming back?'

'He's on the run,' Gerald said. 'He's hardly going to tip off the police by calling in the cleaners.' The lift bounced to a stop. The doors slid apart, opening into the foyer of Green's luxury apartment.

Gerald, Sam, Ruby and Felicity stepped into a scene of utter carnage. The place had been ransacked. Completely trashed. Furniture was upturned, cushions were slashed open and the stuffing strewn about. The contents of drawers were flung everywhere. Rugs had been lifted and thrown aside. The apartment looked like an earthquake had struck.

'Oh gosh,' Ruby said, her hands over her mouth. 'What's happened?'

Gerald took a tentative step into the piles of debris. 'If I was Mason Green,' he said, 'I'd be looking for new cleaners.'

The main living room looked through a wall of glass onto the San Francisco night. The order in the grid of streetlights glowing through the fog was in stark contrast to the chaos inside the apartment. They picked their way through the wreckage. Cupboards stood empty, their contents vomited across the carpet in front of them.

Gerald peered into the study. The floor was littered with broken picture frames. Glass was smashed out and documents had been torn from their mountings. It was as if a family of chimpanzees had just moved out. 'I'll say this for the cleaners—they're thorough.'

Ruby leafed through the rubbish at her feet. 'I knew Green liked collecting historical documents, but some of this stuff is amazing,' she said.

Felicity held up a yellowed parchment. 'Is this a copy of the Magna Carta?' she asked.

'What's the Magna Carta?' Gerald said.

'Foundation stone for modern representative government,' Sam said. 'It delivers power to the people through the extension of suffrage to the masses, not just the king.'

Everybody stopped what they were doing and stared at Sam.

'What?' Sam said. 'That stuff is important.'

Ruby shook her head. 'You amaze me.'

'What are we looking for, Gerald?' Felicity asked. She was inspecting a weathered green bottle. The top was sealed with red wax. It was about the only thing in the room that hadn't been broken.

'I'm not sure,' Gerald said. 'But whatever it is, it seems we're not the only ones looking for it.'

Ruby picked up a piece of paper that had been crumpled into a ball. She flattened it out. 'Oh my,' she said. 'This is a letter from Paul McCartney to John Lennon. The Beatles!'

'What's it say?' Gerald asked.

'Um, basically, I don't like your girlfriend.'

Gerald looked at the piles of documents on the floor. 'This lot must be worth a blind fortune,' he said. 'But someone's gone through it and left it all behind.'

'They must be looking for something special,' Ruby said. She gasped. 'You don't think it's the same people who attacked the chalet? Who kidnapped our parents?'

'The detective said they were looking for something specific,' Sam said.

'Then Mason Green can't be responsible for this,' Felicity said, still cradling the bottle in her hands. 'He'd hardly need to turn over his own place.'

Gerald nodded. 'That's a good point.' He thought for a second. 'If it's not Green, then who is it?'

From out in the foyer came a gentle *ding*, and the sound of the lift doors sliding open.

Someone entered the apartment.

Ruby let out a startled gasp and switched off the study light. They froze where they stood—Ruby by the window, Sam and Gerald by the desk. Felicity carefully pushed the study door closed.

Gerald strained to hear. There were footsteps—the sound of someone picking their way through the mess. Then the study door cracked open and swung in slowly. A head, silhouetted against the light outside, popped through the gap.

And Felicity brought down the bottle with a mighty crash, shattering it over the skull as if she was launching a yacht.

Glass shards flew everywhere. A man in a dark suit crumpled to the floor at her feet.

'Do you have to beat up everyone you come across?' Ruby said.

Felicity ignored her. She knelt next to the prone man. A rolled piece of paper, tied with faded ribbon, was lying between his shoulder blades. Felicity picked it up.

'This must have been inside the bottle,' she said.

Gerald snatched it from her. 'Maybe you should ease up on the self-defence. We don't even know if this guy is one of them.' He shoved the paper into his pocket and rolled the man onto his back. He was breathing but his eyes were closed.

Felicity peeled open the man's coat and started going through his pockets.

'Now what are you doing?' Ruby asked.

'We may as well find out who we're dealing with,' Felicity said. She pulled out a black leather wallet and flipped it open.

'Uh oh.'

'What is it?' Sam asked.

Felicity turned the wallet around. It contained a gold shield and a photo ID topped by three large blue letters.

FBI.

Chapter 14

Special Agent de Bruin sat hunched at the kitchen table, with a cup of instant coffee in one hand and his head in the other.

Felicity sat opposite him, biting her bottom lip. 'I am truly sorry,' she said for the tenth time. 'I don't know what came over me. I just got caught up in the excitement.' She grimaced. 'I've never done anything bad before.'

De Bruin ran his fingers over the lump that was forming on the back of his skull. 'For a beginner,' he said, 'you're doing a remarkable job.'

Ruby handed the man an icepack from the freezer. He nodded a thank you, placed it on the back of his head and winced.

Sam had been studying the special agent carefully from across the table. 'Where's your partner?' he asked.

Agent de Bruin raised a tired eye and looked at him. 'Excuse me?'

'You guys always work in pairs,' Sam said. 'I was just wondering where your partner was.'

De Bruin adjusted the icepack to one side. He was a slender man and his lack of width made him appear taller than he really was. His dark hair was cropped short, and he wore his suit like a second skin. 'I work alone,' he said. 'I follow procedures.'

'Do those procedures tell you where our parents are?' Ruby asked. 'Where Ox and Alisha are?'

'Uh, Ox?'

'His name is Oswald,' Gerald said. 'Oswald Perkins. Everyone calls him Ox.'

De Bruin pulled a pad from his coat pocket, folded back the cover and made a note. Then he closed the cover and placed the pad back into his coat.

Ruby looked at him, her brow furrowing. 'Shouldn't you be doing more than just writing stuff down? Like closing airports and rounding up suspects?'

'I am doing everything in order,' de Bruin said. 'I always follow set procedures.'

'So you said. But isn't there a way to speed things up?' Gerald asked.

De Bruin placed the icepack on the table and wiped his hands on a handkerchief, which he then carefully folded and placed in his trouser pocket. 'Routine is my friend. I follow a process. The process is there to get things done in a very specific order.'

'Which order?'

Agent de Bruin fixed Gerald with an intense stare. 'The right order.'

'How about finding my mum and dad?' Ruby said. A tear formed in her eye. 'Is that part of your precious process?'

De Bruin switched his gaze to Ruby. 'The process will be followed.' He offered nothing more.

'Uh, what were you hoping to find here, Agent de Bruin?' Felicity asked, fiddling with the neck of her jumper.

De Bruin turned his head slowly to face Felicity. 'Sir Mason Green may have been in possession of an item that is sought by the kidnappers,' he said. 'I came here to search the premises. Part of the—'

'Process,' Gerald said. 'Yes, we get the idea. What item, exactly? At the chalet they seemed to be looking for a piece of jewellery.'

'Possibly,' de Bruin said. 'Or maybe a document.'

'They're not interested in democracy or the Beatles,' Sam said. 'We know that much.'

Gerald picked up Felicity's jacket from the table and passed it to her. 'We better get back to the hotel,' he said. 'Agent de Bruin, you'll call us if you find anything?'

De Bruin pulled out his notebook and flipped it open. 'Of course. I have one question.'

'Sure.'

'What hat size are you?'

Gerald stared at the agent for a moment. 'I have no idea.'

'I'll put you down as seven and a quarter. That's about average for a boy your age.'

Gerald's mouth popped open. 'Hat size? Is that all part of the—'

'Process,' de Bruin said. 'Oh yes.' He scribbled in the notebook.

Felicity followed Sam, Ruby and Gerald into the lift. She pushed the button for the foyer and the doors slid shut. 'I guess he's just a process kind of guy,' she said.

The presidential suite at the Fairmont Hotel was a sombre place that night. Sam made his usual giant mattress of cushions and pillows on the floor and set himself up in front of the TV. He had the remote in one hand and a cheeseburger in the other. Ruby sat with her feet curled under her in an armchair by the fireplace, trying to read a book. Gerald had dragged a chair up to a window overlooking the city and leaned back with his hands clasped behind his head and his feet up on the sill. Felicity played *Für Elise* on a baby grand.

Ruby tossed her book over her shoulder. It landed on Sam's stomach. 'I've just read the same sentence five times,' she said. 'My mind is mush.'

Gerald stared out at the mist-shrouded city. 'I know what you mean.' He paused for a second. 'I wonder what Ox and Alisha are doing right now.'

'And our parents,' Ruby said.

'Of course,' Gerald said. 'It's horrible for everyone. But I'm really worried about Ox. He still sleeps with a night-light in his bedroom.'

Felicity moved on to the *Moonlight Sonata*, her fingers feather-light across the keys. 'That Agent de Bruin was an odd fellow,' she said, idly. 'Not what I expected an FBI agent to be like at all.'

Gerald looked across from the window. 'That was one of the weirdest things I've ever sat through,' he said. 'What's the business with my hat size?'

Ruby let out a derisive snort. 'Do you even think he is an FBI agent?'

'What do you mean?' Felicity asked.

'We've come across people claiming to be special agents before,' Ruby said. 'Do you remember Leclerc in India?'

Gerald nodded. 'There was this guy in Delhi who pretended to be an agent with Interpol,' he explained to Felicity. 'Then it turned out he was working for Mason Green. Not that it helped him much in the end.' Gerald shivered at the memory of Leclerc sinking into a pit of quicksand.

'Do you think this de Bruin man is working for Sir Mason Green?' Felicity asked.

'At the moment,' Gerald sighed, 'I don't know what to think. But where Green is concerned, I wouldn't rule out anything.'

'Whether he's with the FBI or not, he was very strange,' Ruby said.

'Seriously, Felicity,' Sam said, 'if you hadn't hit him with the bottle at the start I'd have done it by the end. Process this. Procedure that.' He flicked the channel on the TV. 'What a mental case.'

Felicity suddenly stopped playing and sat upright on the piano stool. 'Gerald,' she said. 'I just remembered—the piece of paper that was inside the bottle.'

Gerald shoved his hand into his pocket and pulled out the roll of paper. He held it up between his thumb and forefinger. 'Message in a bottle,' he said.

He knelt by the coffee table and gently eased off the red ribbon, then rolled the paper flat.

'What is it?' Ruby asked, peering over his shoulder.

There was a string of letters, handwritten in faded ink.

Xerxs blu c axtb pxfbi pab cilbnixg hxracib jl snbeebg xis rjiocuibs cp pj pab sbkpao eqp hy rjiorcbirb co cgg xp nbop c xh lclpy hcgbo ib jl rqgkbkkbn cogxis c sj ijp fijv cl c sbobntb nborqb oj c nbgy ji pab dqsubhbip jl pab jib vaj lciso paco hbooxub hxy yjqn ojqg eb nxcobs ji eqppbnlgy vciuo.

At the bottom, in a fine clear hand, was: *Midshipman Jeremy Davey, October 1835. May God have mercy on his humble servant's soul.*

'Well that's complete nonsense,' Sam said.

Gerald turned the paper over. The other side was covered in painted symbols, none of which made any sense.

'It looks like it's been torn from a book,' Gerald said.

'Torn from a book!' Felicity said. 'Who would do such a thing?'

Sam gave Felicity a sidewards glance. 'You're worried about books being vandalised? I take it you're over your guilt for smashing a bottle over an FBI agent's head?'

'That's if he is FBI,' Felicity said. 'Anyway, I can't take it back now. Maybe this paper is what the kidnappers were looking for. Not some piece of jewellery at all. That's a relief.'

Gerald held the paper up to the light, rubbing the fabric-like texture between his fingers. 'Why would that be a relief?' he asked.

Felicity toyed with the neckline of her jumper, and glanced towards the window. The lights of the city seemed to be shining brighter. 'I just mean it will give the police something to work on,' she said. 'That's all.'

'You know who might help us?' Ruby said. 'Professor McElderry. I bet he'd know what these symbols mean.'

'Who's he?' Felicity asked.

'He's from the British Museum,' Ruby said. 'He knew all about the three caskets and the Oracle at Delphi.'

Felicity turned to Gerald, a quizzical look on her face. 'What's she talking about, Gerald? Is there something you haven't told me?'

'It's a long story,' Gerald said. 'I'll tell you later. Much later. But that's a good idea about the professor, Ruby.'

The phone rang.

They all jumped.

It was a discordant, jarring clatter of a ring. The phone ring equivalent of fingernails down the blackboard.

Gerald looked to Ruby and Sam, then picked up the phone.

'Yes?' he said.

Ruby clung to Sam's arm. Her eyes were glued to Gerald's face.

'Is it them?' Ruby asked.

Gerald held up a finger for quiet. After a moment, he gave a simple 'yes', and hung up the phone.

'Well?' Ruby said.

'That was Mr Prisk,' Gerald said. 'The fog has lifted. The jet's ready to go. And if I refuse to go back to London he'll get a court order forcing me to.'

'What are you going to do?' Ruby asked.

'Go back to London, I guess,' he said. 'But I have to seriously think about getting a new lawyer.'

London was grey. Gunmetal grey, and December cold.

Christmas lights were strung along Oxford Street and holly wreaths hung from front doors. But the sparkles and splashes of colour did nothing to distract Gerald from the fact that Ox and Alisha were still missing, along with his parents and everyone else from the chalet.

From the bay window of the main drawing room at the terrace house in Chelsea, the view was grim indeed.

The flight from San Francisco had been a tiring non-event. Gerald had spent an hour of it in the jet's office on the satellite phone to Mr Prisk, listening to updates from the police. A lot of reports, a lot of theories, and one singular thing that baffled them all: no contact from the kidnappers. No demands. No ransom.

'Nothing?' Gerald had said into the phone.

'Nothing,' Mr Prisk responded.

Gerald gave the paper from the bottle to Mr Prisk when they touched down, to pass on to the authorities, but not before he'd made a copy.

And now he was back in his London home, facing a relentless winter and the lonely uncertainty about his family and friends.

'I should be at Bondi,' Gerald grumbled. He turned

his back to the window to face Felicity. She was seated on a rug in front of a crackling fire, doing a crossword from that morning's newspaper.

'Summer at Bondi,' he continued. 'Hot, sandy, sweaty Bondi Beach. Waves rolling in, water cool and refreshing. Swimming till sunset, then fish and chips in the park with a thousand screaming seagulls. That's how you spend December.' He dropped into an armchair and draped his legs over the side.

Felicity didn't look up from her puzzle. 'Mm-hmm,' she said. 'What's a six letter word for tedious? Starts with B.'

'Um...boring?'

'That's it,' Felicity said, filling in the squares. 'Boring.'

'Yeah. And what's with all this rain? All the time. And when it's not raining the sun's gone by, what, three o'clock in the afternoon? That's just ridiculous.'

'Uh-huh,' Felicity said. 'How about a seven letter word starting with W that means constant complaining?'

Gerald thought for a second. 'Whining?'

'Oh, well done. You're good at this,' Felicity said. 'Whining fits perfectly. It connects Dire with Monotonous.'

Gerald gave Felicity a guilty look. 'Have I been going on about the weather a bit?'

'Only to the exclusion of everything else,' Felicity said. She put down her pencil and looked up at Gerald. 'It's okay to talk about your parents, Gerald. It won't make you any less of a man.'

Gerald couldn't maintain the eye contact—he had to look away. 'I prefer to talk to myself,' he mumbled.

Felicity cocked an eyebrow. 'Yes, that's healthy.'

Gerald didn't reply. No one could confront the kidnapping of their parents, or any other major trauma, by bottling everything up. But Gerald had spoken about it with Sam and Ruby—they were in the same situation, after all—and with Mr Prisk, and the San Francisco police, and the assistant housekeeper Mrs Fitzherbert. Frankly, he had nothing left to say.

'By the way, the Colonel is fine with me staying here a while longer,' Felicity said, breaking the silence. 'That is, unless you want me to go back to St Hilda's?'

Gerald tensed. It looked like the Christmas-cuddle conversation was upon him.

'Uh, look,' he said. 'About that thing with Ruby...'

Felicity looked up at him. 'Yes,' she said. 'About that.'

Gerald swallowed and stared at the fire. He had absolutely no idea what he was meant to say. Maybe he should just throw himself into the flames. That would at least be less painful.

'Um...'

'Yes, Gerald?'

Why was there never a signpost pointing to the right thing to say? There were plenty of signs pointing to the M25 or the nearest Tube station. But never one to the nearest escape route.

'It's like this…'

'Yes?'

Then a thought slammed into his head, like a pigeon into a clean window. 'It was Christmas,' he said. 'Ruby's a really good friend and you always give your good friends a Christmas hug. It's traditional.'

He held his breath.

Felicity tilted her head a fraction more. 'That's your tradition, is it?'

'Uh-huh.'

'Cuddling your friends.'

'Yep.'

'And I'm still your girlfriend?'

Gerald saw an escape hatch opening. He dived into it, head first.

'Of course!' he said, a little too forcefully. 'Girlfriend of the Year.' Gerald cringed as the words tumbled out.

'Maybe I should get a T-shirt made up,' Felicity said. She stared at Gerald for a moment then a smile returned to her face. 'Good. That's settled then.'

'It is?'

Felicity nodded and went back to her crossword.

Gerald let out a silent sigh of relief.

That was that sorted.

Felicity understood exactly where everything stood with Ruby.

Gerald wished that he did.

'Are we still meeting Sam and Ruby at the museum

tomorrow to see this professor friend of yours?' Felicity asked. It was as if the previous conversation had never taken place.

'Um, in the morning,' Gerald said, still not quite believing he was off the hook. 'Mr Prisk has something he wants me to do in the afternoon. Want to come along?'

'Sure—what is it?'

'Something to do with me joining some billionaires' club. I think Mr Prisk is trying to keep me busy.'

Felicity chewed on the end of her pencil. 'Sounds a bit—' She paused.

'Six letter word for tedious, starting with B?' said Gerald.

Felicity laughed. Gerald couldn't bring himself to join in.

Chapter 15

Professor McElderry's office at the British Museum was unchanged from the last time Gerald had visited. The same anxious secretary sat in the reception area. Through the open door to the office proper, McElderry's disaster of a desk was visible, with towers of papers and journals all in a state of imminent collapse. Even the professor's pet tortoise was in residence, dormant on the bookshelf. The only thing that was not there was the professor himself.

'He isn't in,' the secretary said, returning her attention to her computer screen.

'Oh, I hadn't counted on that,' Gerald said. Ruby, Sam and Felicity stood behind him, their faces registering disappointment. 'When can we see him?'

The secretary ran a finger down a page on her desk calendar. 'Let's see,' she said, 'How about never? Is that good for you?'

Gerald was taken aback. 'Excuse me?'

The secretary gave him a frail look of defiance, then crumbled. 'I'm sorry,' she said. Her mouth sank and a tear formed at the corner of her eye. 'I have no idea where Knox is.'

'What do you mean?' Ruby asked. 'Is he sick or something?'

'I don't know,' the woman said. She pulled a tissue from the sleeve of her cardigan and dabbed at her eye. 'He took a week off before Christmas and was due back three days ago. He didn't show. There's no answer at his home. The mail hasn't been collected. His phone rings out. I've called his family, his close friends, his academic colleagues. No one has heard a thing.' She blew her nose in a sharp blast. 'I know he's an irascible old bully and a pain in the posterior. But,' she blew her nose again, 'I'm worried about him.'

There was an awkward silence. Then Sam piped up. 'Maybe he had one too many drinks at Christmas, bumped his head and can't remember who he is?'

Everyone turned to look at him.

'I know, I know,' he said. 'I may well be the stupidest boy in the world.'

'Have you called the police?' Felicity asked. 'Missing persons—that sort of thing?'

The woman nodded. 'His brother is handling all that,' she said. 'The worst thing is not knowing. Do you know what I mean?'

Gerald glanced at Ruby and Sam. 'Yes,' he said. 'Yes, we do.'

The secretary crushed the tissue in her hand and took in a calming breath. 'Anyway, what was it you wanted to see the professor about?' she said. 'Perhaps I can help you?'

Gerald pulled a folded page from his pocket—it was the photocopy of the message from the bottle.

The secretary inspected the string of random letters on one side and the hand-painted symbols on the other. 'You need to talk with Dr Efron. Rare and Ancient Documents—third floor. I'll call and let her know you're coming.'

Ruby led the way back to the lifts. 'What was that all about? Professor McElderry going missing?'

Gerald pressed the button for the third floor. 'There seems to be a lot of people disappearing at the moment.'

Dr Efron was not what Gerald had expected. She wore a pair of faded blue jeans, orange Converse sneakers, a slim-fit T-shirt and her hair was a neat tangle of dread-locks. She didn't look more than twenty-five years old.

'You're, um, pretty young to be an expert on old

stuff,' Gerald said.

Dr Efron—'Call me Lucy'—had her feet on a large desk. She rocked back in her chair, studying the paper Gerald had given her.

'And you're pretty young to be a billionaire,' she said with a wink. 'Never underestimate the power of a young mind on a mission.' She ran her eyes over the symbols on the paper. 'And this was in a bottle, you say?'

'That's right,' Felicity said. 'It looked pretty old.'

'Who sends messages in bottles anyway?' Sam asked. 'It's a pretty random way of getting in touch with someone.'

'You'd be surprised,' Dr Efron said. 'Bottles have travelled thousands of miles. Ocean currents can run very fast.' She pulled a thick book from a shelf above her head and flicked through some pages. She stopped and compared the photocopy with a photograph in the book.

'It's a shame you didn't keep the original,' she said.

'Why's that?' Gerald said.

'Because it's probably worth a fortune. This is a page that was torn from the Voynich Manuscript.'

'Torn from the what?'

'The Voynich Manuscript. It's a cypher document from the late sixteenth century.' Dr Efron looked up at four confused faces. 'It's written in a secret code. It supposedly contains the key to turning lead into gold, the recipe to the universal remedy and a bunch of other fantastical stuff.'

'What do you mean "supposedly"?' Ruby asked.

'No one has ever been able to crack the code,' Dr Efron said. 'Even with modern-day supercomputers, the cypher has never been solved.'

She spun the book around for them to see: a double page spread of paintings of mysterious herbs and lines of indecipherable symbols.

'The manuscript was bought by King Rudolph II of Bohemia in the late 1500s for six hundred gold ducats—a small fortune at the time,' Dr Efron said. 'His castle was equipped with the best alchemy laboratories in Europe. Rudolph wanted to own the secrets of science. Alchemy would bring him endless riches and the universal remedy would cure him of any illness. He could rule for the ages.'

'What happened?' Ruby asked.

Dr Efron closed the book. 'He did his dough,' she said. 'The code is either unbreakable, or a complete hoax. I'd vote hoax.'

Ruby studied the note from the bottle. 'If the code is all symbols, what's with the letters on the other side?'

'I'd say those have been added long after Rudolph's time. It's an entirely different type of code. The date at the bottom says 1835—that's about two hundred and twenty years after Rudolph's reign.'

Gerald took the note and held it under a desk lamp. 'If this is a page torn from a manuscript, what happened to the rest of it?'

'Until two weeks ago it was in a library of rare documents at Yale University in the United States,' Dr Efron said. 'But it was stolen. No one knows where it is.'

'You're kidding,' Ruby said. 'Stolen two weeks ago?'

'I wish I was kidding. A man pretending to be from an obscure research institute in the Netherlands made off with it. I'm guessing it was the Falcon.'

'I'm sorry?' Ruby said.

'A professional document thief. He's been raiding the collections of libraries and universities for years. The police can't catch him.'

'The Falcon?' Gerald said. 'Where have I heard that before?'

'He called himself Professor Peregrine,' Dr Efron said.

Gerald looked at her blankly.

'It's a kind of falcon,' she explained. 'His idea of a joke, I suppose. He works for private collectors. They pay big dollars for rare documents like this.'

'How big?' Gerald asked.

'If they want it badly enough? Millions of dollars. Collectors can be kind of obsessive.'

Gerald folded the coded page back into his pocket and got up to leave. 'An obsessive document collector with access to millions of dollars?' he said. 'That narrows the field a bit.'

Gerald warmed his hands around the mug of hot chocolate in the museum coffee shop. 'This has got Mason Green written all over it,' he said. 'An old document worth million of dollars gets stolen. And Green has suddenly escaped from jail. He's got to be connected.'

'Then why was Green's apartment turned upside down in San Francisco?' Sam said.

'Maybe there's more than one person searching for whatever it is they're all looking for,' Felicity said.

Gerald looked at the photocopy. 'If we could unscramble this code we might have some answers.'

'I don't fancy your chances if a supercomputer couldn't manage it,' Sam said.

'That was on the original code,' Gerald said. 'Not this one on the back.' He ran his fingers across the jumble of letters.

'I wouldn't blow a brain stem over it, Gerald,' Ruby said. 'It's not going to get us any closer to finding our parents.'

'Or Ox and Alisha,' Felicity said.

'I guess you're right,' Gerald said. 'We should concentrate on that.' He turned to Sam and Ruby. 'I've got to go to some meeting that Mr Prisk has arranged this afternoon. But do you guys want to come round for dinner tonight? We can order pizza.'

'Sounds great,' Ruby said.

Sam drained his mug and patted his stomach. 'You had me at "dinner",' he said.

Chapter 16

'The Billionaires' Club is one of the world's most exclusive organisations. Membership is reserved for the thirty most wealthy people on Earth,' Gerald read out loud from a letter, printed on heavy linen stationery. The texture of the paper felt like it had been recycled from old banknotes. Or even new ones. Felicity leaned in closer to hear over the drone of the helicopter. They had been in the air for fifteen minutes and still had a way to go.

'Club membership is by invitation only,' Gerald read on, 'and your privacy is assured. After a meeting with the chairman of our admissions committee, Mr Jasper Mantle, both parties will assess whether the membership process should proceed to the next stage.

However, experience has shown that invitees recognise the significant advantages that membership brings. In the club's long history, all offers to join have been accepted. As you would appreciate, vacancies occur rarely, and I would encourage you to view this prospect with favour.' Gerald looked up from the letter. 'It's signed Luis Garcia, Billionaires' Club chairman.'

Felicity looked at Gerald with wide eyes. 'Gosh, Gerald. The thirty richest people in the world! How exciting.'

Gerald scanned the letter again. 'Considering their average age will be about a hundred and six, I don't think it'll be that exciting. Will it, Mr Prisk?'

The Wilkins' family lawyer leaned forward and retrieved the letter from Gerald. He slipped it inside a leather portfolio. 'The Billionaires' Club is not about excitement, Gerald. It is about opportunity.' Mr Prisk eased back into the comfort of his helicopter seat. 'Your great aunt was a longstanding club member until her tragic demise. This offer is about furthering the business of the Archer Corporation and not squandering Geraldine's legacy. In tough business times such as these, making connections with other HNWIs is of paramount importance.'

Felicity wrinkled her brow. 'What's an HNWI?'

'High Net Worth Individual,' Mr Prisk said. 'Someone who is very, very wealthy indeed.'

Gerald's shoulders slouched forward. 'Why can't I

just meet normal people? Isn't it enough that I am filthy rich—do I have to hang around with them as well?'

Mr Prisk inhaled sharply through his nostrils. 'Jasper Mantle is an extremely successful businessman with mining interests in Africa, eastern Europe and South America. As chairman of the admissions committee of the Billionaires' Club, he wields enormous influence. If they want you to join, you should leap at the chance. Those types of connections can only help.'

Gerald nudged Felicity with his elbow. 'Six letter word starting with B,' he said.

Felicity covered her mouth to hold in the giggle.

'The only word beginning with B you should be thinking of is "business",' Mr Prisk said. 'You are responsible for the jobs of many thousands of people. You need to start thinking in those terms.'

'I'm sorry, Mr Prisk,' Gerald said, a little curtly. 'But I've had other things on my mind this week.'

'As have we all, Gerald. And your parents and friends will be located and brought home safely. But business can't grind to a halt while we wait for that. We have to move forward.'

Gerald rolled his eyes at Felicity. 'When was the last time you had a holiday, Mr Prisk?' Gerald asked.

The lawyer looked as if he'd just been accused of stealing from the church collection plate. 'I had a very pleasant Christmas Day at my mother's house, thank you,' he said. 'We ate mince pies while listening to the

Queen's message on the radio.'

Gerald bit his lip. 'You're right, Mr Prisk. That does sound very pleasant.' Gerald gave Felicity another cheeky look. But he was torn. He would give anything to be able to sit and listen to the Queen's boring Christmas message, as long as his mother and father were there with him. And Alisha and Ox. And Mrs Rutherford and Mr Fry. Gerald looked out the helicopter window, and felt a lump form in his throat.

The chopper buzzed onwards. The sun hung low in the afternoon sky, failing to impart any warmth on the day beneath it.

'Is that the place down there?' Felicity pointed to a colossal stone mansion in the distance.

'That's the place, Miss Upham,' Mr Prisk said. 'Blandford Park—Jasper Mantle's country estate.'

Felicity wriggled with excitement. Her hair was pulled back into a ponytail, her designer jeans tucked into a pair of stylish black boots. She wore the dinner jacket from San Francisco, freshly dry-cleaned, with the sleeves rolled to the elbows. The purple silk lining contrasted nicely with the crisp cream top she wore underneath and the cashmere scarf knotted at her neck.

The chopper turned past the mansion and over snow-covered meadows. They left stables and barns behind them. Finally, they settled on a helipad about fifty metres from a huge structure of glass and steel—a hemisphere big enough to cover a sports field.

The helicopter blades wound down to a rhythmic pulse. A voice crackled through the intercom. 'Mr Mantle will meet you in the butterfly house,' the pilot said.

Mr Prisk hopped down first, holding the door for Felicity and Gerald.

'Did he say butterfly house?' Gerald asked. He pulled the collar of his fleece jacket to his ears as they walked along a cleared path towards the enormous glass dome.

'Jasper Mantle has one of Europe's greatest butterfly collections,' Mr Prisk said. 'He's quite the lepidopterist.'

Gerald winked at Felicity. 'His mum must be very proud.'

They reached the front of the butterfly house. 'So we make nice with Mr Mantle and I join the club,' Gerald said. 'Too easy.' He pushed on the revolving glass door.

'Isn't it a bit cold for butterflies here?' Felicity asked as she followed Gerald.

The moment they tumbled out the other side of the revolving door, the question was answered. It was as hot and humid as a tropical rain forest.

Gerald peeled off his jacket. 'Now this is more like the December I know!'

They stood in a spacious foyer before a wall of glass that rose up five storeys above them. The wall held back a jungle, thick and mysterious and threatening to burst free in an explosion of bulging vines and whipping tendrils.

Gerald noticed two men in a shadowy corner. They were deep in conversation, but they broke off and crossed to where Gerald, Felicity and Mr Prisk were standing. The shorter of the two men extended his hand.

'Hello,' he said, a broad smile on his face. The man was in his fifties and barely taller than Gerald. 'Jasper Mantle. So very pleased to meet you.'

The handshake was unremarkable. In fact, not much about the man was remarkable at all. Gerald could have passed him on the street and not noticed he was there.

Gerald introduced Mr Mantle to Felicity and Mr Prisk. He was about to ask about the butterfly house when a sharp cough startled them.

Jasper Mantle jumped a little at the sound. 'Oh yes,' he said. 'My fellow club member. Gerald, may I introduce Tycho Brahe.'

Gerald switched his gaze to the other man. He was far more substantial than Mr Mantle. 'Pleased to meet—'

Gerald stopped mid-sentence. The man loomed over Gerald like a bear rearing up onto its hind legs. He had swimmer's shoulders and a wrestler's chest. A stern gaze and a strong jaw bristling with bushy dark whiskers. And a nose fashioned from a lump of silver.

Tycho Brahe was clearly used to the sight of his face people taking by surprise. He took Gerald's hand and shook it hard, wrenching a gasp from the young billionaire.

'Don't be nervous, Gerald.' The man's voice—deep and resonant—filled the foyer. 'One thing about noses: they don't bite.'

Brahe clamped a sweaty hand on Gerald's shoulder and pushed him towards the entrance to the main butterfly enclosure. 'Come along,' he said. 'Jasper, let's show our guests your bug collection.'

A small voice followed after them. 'Butterflies. Not bugs, Tycho.'

'Whatever you want to call them, Jasper. They're all creepy crawlies to me.'

Automatic doors slid open. It was like walking into a tropical thunderstorm. The humid air poured down Gerald's throat like a stream of warm custard. His lungs struggled to take it in.

The jungle was a nest of moving colours. It took Gerald a moment to realise that the heaving mass of leaves that coated the branches was butterflies. Hundreds of thousands of butterflies, colonies of pulsating wings that seemed to beat and throb in unison, like a giant stained-glass heart.

The sheer scale of life around them, the lushness and fertility, brought a hush over the small group. They stared in silent awe.

Tycho Brahe nudged Gerald with his elbow. 'Watch this,' he said. Then he clapped his enormous hands together as if clashing a pair of cymbals, and let out a booming, 'FLY!'

A million butterflies took to the air. The enclosure was filled with the white noise of wings in flight. The jungle became a storm of insects, swooping and flittering in and out of the light. Butterflies swept around them in a multi-coloured blizzard.

Brahe threw his head back and roared with laughter.

Mantle had a pained look on his face. 'I do wish you wouldn't do that, Tycho. I lose hundreds each time they panic.'

'Panic?' Brahe said. 'You make them sound like children crossing the street. They're bugs. There's millions of them. What's a few hundred in exchange for a good laugh.'

'Oh my gosh,' Felicity said, a squeak of excitement in her voice. 'Look at this.'

She stood with her arms extended. A dozen butterflies had settled on her head and shoulders.

'They like you, Miss Upham,' Mantle said. He smiled. 'Stay very still and others will come.'

Within seconds Felicity was covered from head to foot in a fluttering coat of yellow, orange and black.

'They're very tickly.' Her voice came from deep within a velvet cloak of wings.

'The Monarch—*Danaus plexippus*,' Mantle said. 'They migrate from Canada to Mexico and back every year. Thousands of miles—it's a remarkable journey. Each migration takes three to four generations. So the ones who return are the great-grandchildren of the ones who left. Yet they come back to the same trees in the same valley.'

'How do they know where to go if they weren't even

alive when the migration started?' Gerald said.

'Their parents weren't even alive, Gerald,' Mr Mantle said. 'It is one of nature's great mysteries.'

A tiny voice sounded again from inside the shaggy tower of butterfly wings. 'These are getting kind of heavy,' Felicity said.

Mr Mantle laughed. 'You are butterfly nectar, Miss Upham. Just have a little hop. They'll take off.'

Gerald watched in amazement as Felicity bounced up and down, and the coat of many colours lifted from her, like she was being unveiled at an art gallery. The butterflies swept away into the jungle.

'Oh, Mr Mantle, that was incredible,' Felicity said, her face beaming.

'You must be a very placid person, Miss Upham,' Mr Mantle said. 'Like myself. The butterflies can sense that.'

Gerald snickered. If anyone had asked him to describe Felicity, 'placid' would not be the first word to pop into his head.

Mr Mantle showed them to a round table in a paved area under the jungle canopy. 'This is the largest butterfly collection in the world,' he said, taking a seat. A butler materialised with a tray of cold drinks.

Brahe took a tall glass and swept its frosty exterior across his perspiring forehead. He turned to Gerald. 'You have to understand, Gerald, that Jasper likes his science to be kept under glass. I prefer things on a grander scale.'

'What type of things?' Gerald said.

Brahe swept his arms wide. 'The universe,' he declared. 'All the secrets of the planets and the stars.'

Mr Mantle cleared his throat. 'Tycho fancies himself the astronomer,' he said. 'He keeps an observatory on an island in Sweden.'

'It's a modest affair—a few telescopes and some instruments,' Brahe said. 'Certainly not as grand as this place. The grandeur that interests me is all in the heavens.'

Mantle shone with pride. 'There are specimens here from every continent on earth, apart from Antarctica of course,' he said. He held out a finger and an iridescent blue butterfly settled onto it. He placed it delicately onto the tip of Felicity's nose. She let out a trill of delight.

'Are there any species you don't have?' Gerald asked. He had a score of various kinds on his hair.

'I'm still searching for a Pearl-Bordered Fritillary from Russia. That one has eluded me for years. And of course there's the Xerxes Blue from a remote island in the Galapagos, though, tragically, now thought to be extinct.'

'The Xerxes Blue?' Gerald said. He stared at the tabletop. 'That sounds familiar. Is it a famous butterfly?'

Brahe let out a rough laugh. 'I hope you don't spend your days gazing at beetles, Gerald.'

Mantle turned a light shade of pink. 'Perhaps we should turn to the issue of the club and Gerald's member-ship.' He clasped his hands in front of him and turned to Gerald. 'I think you will find joining our little society extremely beneficial, Gerald. You will meet some of the best business minds in the world. And we do look after our own, if you know what I mean.'

Gerald glanced at Mr Prisk. The lawyer was almost glowing. 'Did you hear that, Gerald?' Mr Prisk said. 'They look after their own!'

'Yes. I'm sitting right here.'

'The opportunity to join does not come up very often,' Mantle said. 'If you do choose to proceed, I think you'll quite enjoy the next stage in the process. It involves a rather fun night out in New York as part of an initiation into the club. But we can talk about all that later on. What do you say, Gerald? Are you onboard?'

A thought suddenly struck Gerald. 'If the club is limited to the thirty richest people in the world, why is there suddenly a vacancy? Did someone die? Or lose their fortune?'

Mantle's eyes flicked across to Brahe. Brahe was leaning back in his chair, running a finger along the length of his silver nose.

'One of our members acted outside the boundaries of behaviour that we regard as acceptable,' Brahe said. 'He is no longer welcome amongst our group.'

'What did he do?' Felicity asked, a butterfly still perched on the tip of her nose. She hadn't taken her eyes off Tycho Brahe's face since sitting down.

'Let's just say that even we billionaires draw the line

at murder,' Brahe said. He directed his gaze straight at Gerald. 'He's British. Perhaps you've heard of him? His name is Sir Mason Green.'

Chapter 17

Gerald had butterflies in his hair and butterflies in his stomach. He was the meat in a butterfly sandwich. Mason Green?

Gerald was being offered Sir Mason Green's membership in one of the world's most exclusive clubs?

He sat silent for a moment, surrounded by the whisper of thousands of gossamer wings. Then he burst out laughing. A raucous hold-nothing-back laugh.

Mr Prisk looked at him with concern. 'Gerald? Are you all right?'

Gerald couldn't hide his glee. 'All right? I'm taking something from Mason Green that he would have treasured. I'm over the moon!' He held out his hand to Jasper Mantle. 'Where do I sign?'

Mantle was taken aback. 'We've had people accept memberships for many reasons but I don't believe we've ever had anyone join the club out of spite.' He accepted Gerald's hand and shook it heartily. 'Congratulations, Mr Wilkins. I think we can happily take you on to the next stage of the process. What do you say, Tycho?'

Everyone at the table turned to look at Brahe. At that moment the butterfly flittered from Felicity's face. It bobbed and weaved and finally lit on the silvery tip of Tycho Brahe's nose.

Felicity gasped.

That nose.

Despite the blue and green wings opening and closing just centimetres from his eyes, Brahe's focus was entirely on Felicity.

'Do you know something, Miss Upham?' he said. 'You're right. These things do tickle.'

Felicity wanted to look away, but her eyes were transfixed on the silver snout in front of her.

'Let me ask you a question, Miss Upham,' Brahe said. The butterfly opened and closed its wings in slow symmetry.

Felicity looked surprised. 'What about?'

'You dress quite spectacularly, my dear,' he said, his eyes fixed on hers. 'That dinner jacket is a bespoke Saville Row if I've ever seen one. Though it looks to have been tailored for someone a little larger than you. Where did you get it?'

Felicity's cheeks flushed. Her hand crossed her chest to cling onto a lapel. 'It was, um, a gift. From a friend.'

'You are lucky,' Brahe said, 'to have such a generous friend. Thank you. Now you may proceed.'

Felicity blinked. 'Proceed?'

'To ask me the question you've been dying to ask since you arrived.'

Jasper Mantle clicked his tongue. 'Must you do this every time, Tycho?'

Brahe ignored him. He didn't shift his gaze from Felicity.

'Go ahead, Miss Upham,' he said. 'They're just words. Believe me—I've heard them all. They can only hurt you if you let them.'

Felicity swallowed, and then stammered out: 'What happened to your nose?'

Brahe slapped his hand on the table, rattling the drinks tray. 'That's more like it!' he roared. The butterfly darted away. 'Hard and to the point—somewhat like my nose. Well done, Miss Upham!'

'Please, Tycho,' Mantle said. He watched the butterfly as it flitted towards the glass ceiling. 'They startle so easily.'

Brahe leaned in close to Felicity. He lowered his voice to an austere whisper. 'I will tell you a tale, Miss Upham. And I promise, it will curl your toenails. Do you like stories of intrigue? Do fables of wonder fascinate you?'

Felicity's eyes widened. Brahe's voice had her in a

snake charmer's trance. 'I do,' she said.

'Excellent,' Brahe said, unblinking. 'I see you wear no rings. No bangles. Are you not fond of jewellery?'

Felicity stared deep into Brahe's gaze. 'Not really,' she said. 'I prefer scarves.'

Brahe regarded her darkly. 'Do you indeed?' He paused, and lowered his voice even further. 'It was at a family wedding,' he said. 'I was in my fiery twenties, and my cousin and I were worse for drink. There was an argument. Over what? Who remembers? There was a fight. He had a knife. And in a few painful seconds, he had half my face as well.'

Felicity raised her hand to her mouth. 'Oh, how sick-making.'

'Not as sick-making as when I get a head cold,' Brahe said, a glint in his eye.

Gerald thought Felicity was going to be ill.

'But why replace it with...' Felicity raised her index finger and pointed at Brahe's face, 'with that?'

'Why shy away from my foolishness?' Brahe said. 'Why shrink from anything at all? Because I look hideous?' He laughed loudly. 'Having half my face hacked away was the best thing that ever happened to me. I felt sorry for myself when it happened. But then I realised: if I can front the world looking like this, I can do anything. I was working in the precious-metals industry at the time, and I had one of the silversmiths fashion me a false nose. Like a badge of honour. Now I have a collection of them. This one—' he tapped a pen against the nugget on his face; it let out a hollow *clonk*—'I wear for important meetings.' He cocked his head to one side, as if posing for a portrait. 'It brings out my regal side, don't you think?'

Brahe slipped a hand into his jacket pocket and pulled out a gnarled lump of copper. He fixed Gerald with a stare. 'This one I use if I'm doing something sporty.'

Brahe wrenched the nose from his face. Gerald gagged at the vision—a slash of scar tissue, a stub of gristle, a gaping hole. A second later, Brahe had his sports nose in place.

Gerald stared in shock. The nose looked as if it had been broken in a bar fight. There was a massive dent right across the bridge.

'What happened to it?' Gerald asked.

'This? A skiing accident,' Brahe said, narrowing his eyes. 'Last weekend.'

Gerald's stomach tightened. The butterflies inside doubled their wing beats. 'Skiing?'

'Yes. Someone hit me across the face with a ski pole. Rotten luck. It's fortunate I have a false nose. It would have made a terrible mess of a real one.'

'You—' Gerald couldn't finish the sentence.

'Jasper,' Brahe said, scraping his chair across the floor as he stood. 'Why don't you go over the next steps of the club membership with Mr Prisk? All that detail. It's just so—' he turned to Felicity and flashed her a humourous smile, 'What's a six letter word for dull, starting with B?'

Felicity's mouth dropped open.

'In the meantime,' Brahe continued, grabbing Gerald hard by the upper arm, 'I want to show young Wilkins one of your very interesting bugs, down by the waterfall.' He hauled Gerald to his feet and they were into the jungle before Gerald could make a sound.

'Butterflies,' Jasper Mantle called after them. 'Not bugs.'

Chapter 18

Tycho Brahe jostled Gerald in front of him, down a rough jungle path. Palm fronds clawed at Gerald's face as he was pushed deeper and deeper into the rain forest. The path twisted and turned. All around were soaring trunks and foliage, thick and impenetrable.

Brahe shoved Gerald hard in the back, sending him sprawling through a curtain of vines and into a clearing. Gerald stumbled and fell onto the mossy ground. A fine mist settled on his face. He looked up through one eye to find a twenty-metre waterfall gushing into a pool at the far edge of the clearing. Butterflies filled the air, adding a swirling vapour of colour to the spray all around them. The roar from the falls was colossal. But Gerald had no problem hearing every word that Tycho Brahe said.

'You have something of mine.' Brahe was furious. He grabbed Gerald by the sleeve and yanked him to his feet.

'Where are my parents?' Gerald demanded. 'Where is Ox and Alisha?' He glared at Brahe and didn't flinch a muscle.

The slap across Gerald's face came as a total surprise.

Once.

Twice.

Three times in quick succession, the back of Brahe's hand found its mark. Brahe grabbed Gerald's ear, and twisted. The pain was excruciating.

'You don't talk,' Brahe said, turning Gerald's head to bark in his other ear. 'If you talk, everyone dies. Do you understand? They will all be dead in one minute from now unless you do as I say.'

Gerald opened his mouth, and Brahe squeezed harder. A cry caught in Gerald's throat.

'No talking,' Brahe said. 'All listening. Understand?'

Gerald nodded.

'Good. You have something I want. A piece of jewellery.' Brahe held up his thumb and forefinger, about seven centimetres apart. 'This big. A brooch, or maybe a pendant. It wasn't at the chalet on Mt Archer when I went looking. Where is it?'

'I don't know anything about it,' Gerald said. His ear hurt so much.

'Ask your pretty friend.' Brahe's dented copper nose pressed into Gerald's cheek. 'It was in the pocket of that dinner jacket you stole. The one belonging to Sir Mason Green.'

Gerald's stomach turned.

Sir Mason Green. That man was a bone-chilling virus that could not be shaken off. Then a thought cut through Gerald's pain. Could Felicity actually have what Brahe was looking for?

'I am a busy man,' Brahe said. 'I have much to achieve and any delay is unacceptable. I will call you at your place in Chelsea. Tomorrow. I'll tell you how to get it to me. Any mistakes—any attempt to contact the police—and everyone suffers. You, Miss Upham and the Valentine twins included.' Brahe whipped off the copper nose and wrenched Gerald's head around to stare into the mutilated face. 'And believe me, I know suffering.'

Gerald screwed his eyes shut with revulsion.

Brahe fixed his flawless silver nose in place and propelled Gerald back up the path.

Felicity had twenty butterflies perched on her head when Gerald and Brahe emerged from the rain forest. She turned to Gerald. Fear was written across her face. The look told him that Felicity had said nothing to Prisk and Mantle about Brahe's skiing accident, or their encounter with him in the caretaker's cottage at Mt Archer.

'Ah, Gerald,' Mr Prisk said, 'Mr Mantle has given me all the details we need. I think you'll quite enjoy what's planned for New York. I'll make arrangements in your schedule. It's a tremendous opportunity to—'

he paused. 'What the devil has happened to your ear?'

Gerald's hand shot up to the right side of his head.

'It's bright red,' Mr Prisk said. 'Are you all right?'

Brahe's whisper landed in Gerald's good ear like an arrow into a bull's-eye. 'Everyone suffers.'

Gerald's throat constricted. 'Must be the change in temperature. It's fine.' He forced a smile. 'Nice to have met you, Mr Mantle, but we probably should be going. We have a dinner to get to.'

They shook hands. And as Gerald followed Felicity and Mr Prisk through the revolving doors and back into the snow, Tycho Brahe's voice went with him: 'I'll be in touch, Gerald. I look forward to seeing you again. Very soon.'

Gerald had no doubt that was true.

The attic in Gerald's swish Chelsea townhouse was not heated. A row of bare bulbs ran the length of the ceiling and cast a harsh light across the hodgepodge of boxes and tea chests on the floor. It was dusty and cramped and uncomfortable. Perfect for Gerald's purpose.

He pushed the door shut at the top of the narrow staircase. Ruby, Sam and Felicity found themselves a place to sit among the jumble of old armchairs and crates.

'Do you really think the house is bugged?' Sam said, at the top of his voice. This sparked off a chorus of shushing. He repeated the question, this time in a whisper.

'Where else would Brahe have heard about that stupid crossword clue?' Gerald said. 'And he knows who you guys are. The place is bugged, or someone's spying on us.'

'You mentioned the crossword in the helicopter on the way to Mr Mantle's place,' Felicity said. 'Maybe the pilot heard us.'

'However he heard it, Brahe was giving us a message,' Gerald said. 'He wanted us to know we're being watched.'

'Who is this Brahe guy?' Sam asked. 'Did I really bust his fake nose?'

'You put a major dent in his nose and in his ego,' Gerald said. 'He's a member of this Billionaires' Club. They want me to join. And guess whose place I'll be taking? Mason Green's.'

Ruby and Sam both jolted upright. 'You're kidding,' Ruby said.

'Nope. They booted him out. Mr Prisk said he wasn't a fit person to be in the club.'

'So Mason Green kidnapped our mum and dad?' Sam said.

'No, Green is involved somehow, but I'm sure Brahe is the kidnapper,' Gerald said. 'He said he would make them suffer unless we did what he said.'

Felicity leaned forward. 'Did he say what he wanted?'

Gerald had chosen not to tell Felicity everything that Brahe had said by the waterfall. Until now.

'A piece of jewellery,' he said. 'A piece of jewellery that Mason Green left in the pocket of his jacket. The one we picked up from the dry cleaners.'

Felicity's hand shot to her throat. She was still wearing the dinner jacket. Sitting in the glare of the bare bulbs, she looked like a guilty suspect in a police line-up.

'What!' Ruby was on her feet.

'Keep your voice down,' Gerald hissed. He could see that Ruby was doing all she could to stay in control. It wasn't likely to last much longer.

'You have it?' Ruby said to Felicity. Her voice teetered on the narrow ledge between disbelief and blind rage.

Felicity's eyes brimmed with tears. 'I didn't know,' she said. Her voice quavered. 'I, I forgot I had it.'

'You forgot!' Ruby clenched her hands into fists and pressed one against her mouth, trying to tamp down a scream. 'Our parents are in danger and you *forgot*.'

Felicity lifted her head, eyes pleading. 'It's not like that,' she said. 'You don't understand.'

'What's not to understand, Felicity?' Gerald said. 'You knew the kidnappers were looking for a piece of jewellery.'

Felicity turned to him, tears trickling down her cheeks. 'It was only after we escaped,' she said. 'Only when we got back to San Francisco that I remembered I even had it—realised it might be what they were looking for. I didn't know what to do. I've never been in trouble before.'

'Why didn't you give it to the police when they were interviewing us at the hotel?' Sam said.

'I don't know,' she said. Then, more forcefully, 'I don't *know*!' She wiped a hand across her face. 'I was paralysed. I've never done anything wrong. I get straight A's. I'm a member of the school honour society. I'm captain of the third form choir.'

'Pity you didn't sing to the police then, isn't it?' Ruby said.

Felicity dropped her head into her hands, sobbing.

Ruby glared at her, then shook her head. 'You could have said something.'

'I'm sorry…I'm so sorry.'

'Let's see it then,' Gerald said.

Felicity pulled at her collar and ran a finger under a fine silver chain and flipped out a triangular prism of crystal. It was about seven centimetres long, with one end set into a silver cap. The crystal was a washed-out blue: milky and dull. Felicity lifted the chain over her head and dropped it into Gerald's hand.

'It was in the jacket pocket,' she said softly. 'It didn't look valuable. I just put it on as a keepsake of our holiday.'

Ruby took the pendant from Gerald and held it up to the light. Her face took on a light blue sheen. 'It's nothing special, is it?' she said. 'With all the fuss those kidnappers were going on about, I expected diamonds at least.'

'Who cares if it's made of petrified dinosaur poo,' Sam said. 'As long as it gets Mum and Dad back.'

'And Ox and Alisha,' Gerald said. 'And Fry and Mrs Rutherford, and all the others.'

'That's a lot of people to kidnap just to get hold of one piece of cut glass,' Ruby said. She looked at Felicity, who had slumped into a ball with her arms wrapped around her knees.

'Don't worry about it, Flicka,' Ruby said. 'I wouldn't think of this as jewellery worth stealing either.'

Felicity raised an eye, and sniffed. 'Are you sure?'

'Yeah,' Gerald said. 'And what if you had given it to the San Francisco police? Brahe wouldn't have been happy that we didn't have it anymore. He wasn't in any mood to listen to reason.' Gerald put his hand to his ear. It still hurt.

'Do you think everyone is still all right?' Ruby said.

Gerald nodded. 'Brahe wants this pendant. He won't do anything to jeopardise getting it.'

Ruby passed the pendant back to Gerald. 'I think we should call the police,' she said. 'This is getting too crazy. What do we know about getting hostages back?'

'No,' Gerald said. 'Brahe was clear. We can't tell anyone. And I'm sure he's got this place bugged. If he finds out we're even thinking of calling the police—'

He was cut off by a sharp banging on the door. They

all jumped. Gerald made his way to the entrance. He shot a glance back to his friends, then turned the doorknob.

The assistant housekeeper, Mrs Fitzherbert, stood in the stairwell. 'So this is where you've been keeping yourselves,' she said. 'I've been looking all over.' She cast a suspicious gaze over the four guilty faces in the attic. 'There's a telephone call for you, Master Gerald. A man. Wouldn't give his name.' She gave them another suspicious look, turned and headed back down the stairs. 'Nearest phone is in the library,' she said over her shoulder.

Chapter 19

'Is it him?'

'Tell him we need to speak to Mum and Dad.'

'What's he saying?'

Gerald clamped his hand over the mouthpiece and let out a loud *shush!*

'Quiet,' he said. 'I can't hear.'

He fumbled with the phone and finally found the button for the speaker.

A calm but authoritative voice sounded out. There was something familiar about it. Gerald couldn't quite place it. But he knew it wasn't Tycho Brahe.

'Gerald Wilkins? I have something important to tell you.'

Gerald dropped into the office chair behind the desk.

'Who is this?' he asked.

'My name is Ursus.'

Gerald looked to the others. Blank responses. They'd never heard of him either.

'Yes?'

'I have news of your parents. And the others.'

Ruby took in a sharp breath and grabbed Sam's arm.

'They are safe. I am informed they will be released when the time is right.'

'What does that mean?' Gerald said. 'When the time is right? How do you know all this?'

'You have been contacted by Tycho Brahe?' the man asked.

Gerald touched his cheek. It still burned from the slap that afternoon. 'Yeah, we've had words,' he said.

'Then you know he is not to be trifled with,' the man said. 'He is seeking the crystal pendant. Do you have it?'

Gerald looked sideways at Felicity. 'It turns out we do,' he said. Felicity lowered her eyes to the carpet.

'I suggest you give it to him,' the man said.

'We're going to—we want to—but we haven't heard from him.'

'He will be in touch very soon, I am sure. He will ask you to meet him in Prague, in the Czech Republic, away from the hands of the British Police.'

'How do you know this?' Gerald said. 'Who are you?'

'I am the only hope you have of ever seeing your

parents again. I advise you to do everything that Mr Brahe instructs. Do not doubt his tenacity; do nothing to impede him. And under no circumstances mention that we have spoken. That would be disastrous. For everyone.'

There was a click, and the line went dead.

'What do you make of that?' Ruby said.

'I guess I pack a bag and wait for Brahe to call,' Gerald said.

'You're not seriously thinking of going to Prague?' Felicity said. 'If Brahe is as dangerous as you say, that's insane.'

Gerald leaned back in the chair. 'Do we have a choice? First Brahe and now this Ursus guy. Every man and his dog seems to know what's going on except us.'

'Bear,' Sam said.

'What?'

'Everyman and his bear,' Sam said. 'Ursus. It's Latin—it means bear.'

Gerald narrowed his eyes at Sam. 'How do you know all this stuff?'

'I have no idea,' Sam said. 'I guess if teachers throw enough at you some of it's bound to stick.'

'If you're going, Gerald, Sam and I are coming too,' Ruby said.

'What happened to going to the police?' Gerald said.

Ruby shrugged. 'I guess we don't have a choice but to do what Brahe tells us to do.'

'I'm coming too,' Felicity said. 'It's my fault we're in this mess.'

Gerald looked at each of his friends in turn. He didn't feel confident. But at least he didn't feel alone.

'That's settled, then,' he said. 'Now we just wait for the call.'

It came the next morning, soon after breakfast.

Brahe's instructions were to the point. And Mr Ursus had been right.

'You will travel to Prague. Bring the crystal with you. You will be under the Astronomical Clock in the Old Town Square at 3 p.m. on Wednesday. You will not be late.'

Gerald scribbled the details on a sheet of paper. 'What about Ox and Alisha, and—'

'Your friends will be released once I have the crystal.' Then, in a voice so low a mole would struggle to hear it, 'Tell no one.'

It took Gerald over an hour to convince Mr Prisk to allow him to use the Archer corporate jet. It was the comment 'I could always hire another lawyer' that proved the clincher.

'But why Prague?' Mr Prisk asked as he lifted the telephone to make the arrangements. 'It's even colder there than it is here.'

'I've always wanted a white New Year's Eve,' Gerald said, not sounding particularly convincing.

Mr Prisk eyed him archly. 'In the absence of Mr Fry,

I will send Mr Pimbury from Avonleigh as chaperone,' he said. 'There needs to be some adult supervision.'

'Fine,' Gerald said. 'As long as he knows who's the boss.'

It took Captain Baulch three attempts to land the jet at Prague international airport. The snow was driving across the runway in thick flurries. Visibility was close to zero. Five minutes after she taxied to the terminal building, the airport was closed due to the blizzard conditions.

The sky over Prague was gutted—every trace of life and joy had ebbed away. Clouds of ice draped over the city like a sodden blanket.

Gerald had never felt so cold. It was like the marrow in his bones had formed glaciers, tiny frozen rivers immobile in his frostbitten interior.

'This is ridiculous,' Ruby said as she banged her gloved hands together. 'How are we supposed to get anywhere in this snow?'

They stood in the airport concourse while Mr Pimbury tried to explain to a limo driver where they needed to go.

Felicity dropped a daypack at Gerald's feet and pulled his arm around her shoulders. 'I hope there's a fire at the hotel,' she said. 'I love an open fire.' She snuggled tighter into Gerald's chest.

Ruby stared at them for a second. Gerald gave her an apologetic shrug. She turned and marched towards the exit. 'I think Mr Pimbury has the driver sorted,' she said, without looking back.

The automatic doors slid open. An arctic blast took their breath away.

The limousine ride into Prague took them through streets barely wider than the car. They weaved in and out of a maze of buildings straight from a fairy-tale village. Tall, narrow windows looked down upon them as they crawled through the city. There were no people. No cars. The flawless carpet of snow only added to the feeling they were in a town that had been recently vacated—packed up, vacuumed clean, waiting for the next tenants to move in.

'This is so weird,' Sam said, his breath fogging the car window. 'Anyone else got the feeling we've stepped out of a time machine?'

'Didn't anyone own a ruler when they were building this place?' Gerald said. 'None of these streets are even vaguely straight. And these buildings don't look like they've changed in the past five hundred years.'

When they arrived at the hotel there was a dash for the door. They paused in the foyer, glad to be out of the piercing cold.

'Oh, there is a fire,' Felicity said, poking her head into an adjoining lounge. 'Come on, let's defrost.' She disappeared around the corner with Sam close behind.

Gerald hesitated next to Ruby. 'I'm sorry about the whole Felicity thing,' he said.

Ruby cut him off. 'Don't start, Gerald. It seems to bother you way more than it bothers me. Like I said before, getting Mum and Dad back safely is all I'm thinking about at the moment. I thought Christmas Eve might have meant something to you, but clearly not. Felicity tells me you two are solid. Fine. You can play footsies together as much as you like.' She brushed past Gerald and walked towards the lounge area. She turned the corner at a trot.

Gerald's shoulders slumped. He was too young for all this.

He looked to Mr Pimbury, who was at the reception desk, checking in. A grandfather clock in the corner chimed twice. It was only an hour until Gerald was due to make the handover with Brahe.

'Mr Pimbury?' Gerald said. 'Everything all right?'

'As good as can be expected,' Mr Pimbury said. 'No one speaks English and I can't make myself understood, no matter how loudly I speak.'

'Yep,' Gerald said, looking at his watch. 'Life's a puzzle. Look, we're all talking about going for a look around. Just to let you know.'

'A look around?' Mr Pimbury said. 'In this weather? Are you barking mad? You'll catch your death.'

'I think the snow's easing up,' Gerald said. He looked through the hotel's front doors. The blizzard had doubled in intensity. He looked back to Mr Pimbury. 'It's not like we're going to get into any trouble. And you can sit by the fire with a pot of tea and put your feet up. That'll be nice.'

Mr Pimbury signed the last of the check-in paper-work. 'Assuming they have any tea here,' he muttered. 'Very well. I'll be waiting by the fire. Don't be long.'

Gerald collected a duffle bag from their pile of luggage and headed into the lounge. Felicity and Sam were drinking hot chocolate by the fireplace. Ruby sat on a couch, studying a tourist map of the city. Gerald dumped the bag at her feet. 'There are some jackets and gear in here,' he said. 'What have you found?' He sat next to her. Ruby shuffled a few centimetres away.

'The old town square is just a few blocks from here,' she said, pointing to the map. 'The astronomical clock is at the south end, here.'

'What exactly is an astronomical clock?' Sam said. 'Tells you the time and the winning lottery numbers?'

'Astronomy,' Ruby said. 'Not astrology, you clot. The movement of the planets and the universe. Not whether you'll fall in love with a tall, handsome stranger.'

Felicity looped her arm through Gerald's and squeezed. 'He's not that strange,' she said, gazing at Gerald with a sweet smile.

Ruby closed her eyes for a moment. 'It's a clock that has figurines out the front,' she said. 'Puppets and moons and stuff like that. They move around on the hour.'

'Sounds fascinating,' Sam said.

Ruby opened the zip on the bag and tossed a down jacket to her brother. 'Put this on,' she said. She threw another at Felicity, hitting her in the chest. 'It's frosty outside.'

Gerald pulled out a red jacket for himself. 'Frosty in here, too,' he mumbled to himself.

Just then a hotel porter approached them. 'Excuse me, Mr Wilkins?'

Gerald paused in pulling on his jacket. 'Yes?'

'There's a phone call for you, sir.'

Gerald gave the others a curious look and followed the porter to a telephone on an antique table.

'Hello?'

'Gerald?'

Gerald's fingers tightened on the hand piece. He would recognise that voice anywhere.

'Gerald,' the voice continued, 'this is Mason Green...'

Chapter 20

Gerald could feel the blood washing through his eardrums like tiny timpani rolling in his brain. He felt like he was going to be sick on the floor.

'Can you hear me, Gerald? You've gone awfully quiet.'

Gerald closed his eyes. 'I can hear you.'

'I understand you're meeting my old friend Tycho very soon,' Green said. 'Do you have my crystal pendant?'

'Yes.'

'Excellent. Don't lose it, will you. There's a good chap. It may not look much, but it bought me a ticket out of prison.'

'Why are you calling me? Can't you just leave me alone?'

'Gerald, I'm calling you to warn you.'

'You! Warn me! About what?'

'You must do everything that Tycho tells you to do. He is a good man but he is prone to sudden tempers. I wouldn't want anything to happen to your pals Alisha and Oswald. Or to you, Gerald, old friend.'

Gerald couldn't believe what he was hearing. This from the man who had tried to kill him on half a dozen different occasions. 'What a load of rubbish,' Gerald said. 'The only thing you care about is yourself.'

'You sell me short, Gerald. I am working very hard at the moment to keep you and your friends alive.'

'What do you mean?'

'That crystal pendant you stole from me. It turns out it is a rather important collector's piece. I picked it up years ago among some interesting bits and pieces that my friend Alphonse was selling. I used to wear it as a good luck charm, you know. I must have left it in my dinner jacket when it was sent off to the cleaners. Tycho has always admired it. So it was an easy choice when he contacted me in that filthy Athens prison and offered to get me out.'

'He helped you escape in exchange for the pendant?'

'The pendant, and another item that I asked my friend Alphonse to acquire. Imagine Tycho's anger when he found out the crystal had been stolen. By you.'

Gerald's mind folded back to the scene in the chalet when Brahe and his thugs were demanding everyone hand over their jewellery. He shivered. 'So it was Brahe who ransacked your apartment in San Francisco looking for the pendant,' Gerald said.

There was a pause on the other end of the phone. 'I hadn't heard about that,' Green said. He did not sound impressed. 'But you are missing the point, Gerald. Tycho is determined. I hold genuine fears for the safety of Alisha and Oswald. On my word as an Englishman, your parents and the others will be fine—I will see to that. But Alisha and Oswald...'

Gerald's chest tightened. 'What?'

'Don't give Tycho any cause to be upset. Deliver the crystal on time. No police. No heroics. It must be done, or Alisha and Oswald will most likely die. And if that happens, I will be coming to find you, Gerald.' Green paused to let his words soak in. 'I'm sure that's not something you desire.'

Gerald took a deep breath and let it flow out through his nostrils. 'No,' he said.

'Excellent,' Green said. 'It is almost time. Do not be late.'

Gerald replaced the receiver. Then he ran to the men's room and was violently ill in the toilet.

The Old Town Square in Prague could have been designed by Grimm Brothers Architects. A dour-faced statue stood in its centre, surrounded on four sides by build-ings topped with spires and cupolas. The twin towers of the Tyn Church were to the east, the old town hall to the south. It looked like nothing had changed there for hundreds of years.

Gerald pushed his way through a thick blanket of snow. His feet felt like ice blocks in socks. He shoved his hands deep into his pockets. His head, clad in a beanie, bowed to the pianissimo patter of flake upon flake landing on the top of his skull.

'It must be twenty below,' Sam said, his breath a plume of fog before him. 'Who'd come out in this?'

The answer was all around them.

No one.

The square was deserted. Gerald, Sam, Ruby and Felicity walked through the snow to the clock tower. Christmas lights flickered outside the deserted restaurants, failing to entice the tourists out of their cosy hotels.

'Brahe's supposed to be here at three,' Gerald said. They stopped at the foot of the stone tower and gazed up at the ornate clock face. A collection of gothic figurines stared back at them. It was still a few minutes before three.

The snow tumbled down.

Ruby looked up at Gerald and put her hand on his arm. 'Are you okay?'

Gerald gave a slow nod. 'Hearing from Green like

that really threw me. Just when I had got him out of my head he's stuffed himself back in there.'

'He's out of prison,' Sam said. 'What does he care if Brahe gets his pendant or not.'

'Maybe he believes in paying his debts,' Ruby said.

Gerald grunted. 'Mason Green and honesty don't exactly go together. He's brewing something. And I really don't like what he said about Alisha and Ox.'

A gust of wind blew across the square, kicking up a flurry of snowflakes. 'Do you think Brahe will bring your parents?' Felicity asked.

'I doubt it,' Gerald said. 'He'll probably phone someone and have them released from wherever he's holding them. They could be anywhere.'

'You've got the crystal?' Ruby asked.

Gerald's gloved hand closed tighter around the pendant in his pocket. 'For the fourth time, yes.'

They stared up at the clock. The minute hand crawled towards the twelve. As the hour began to strike, a skeleton perched on one side of the clock face sprang to action, swinging a silver bell. Two wooden doors slid open and a parade of puppet figures revolved past the openings.

'What's with the skeleton?' Sam asked.

'Death,' Ruby said. 'Every toll of the bell is a mark closer to when you get to meet him.'

'And you get reminded of that every hour?' Sam said. 'Cheery.'

As the last of the tolls rang through the still afternoon air, a trumpeter in a uniform trimmed in red and yellow appeared high on the tower ramparts. He sounded a clarion call. As the notes floated away, he banged his gloved hands against his sides, then disappeared back into the warmth of the guard house.

Gerald looked around. Nothing stirred. He sucked frozen air into his lungs. 'I don't like the look of this,' he said.

Then a low rumble sounded from across the square. Two motorcycles appeared from a narrow laneway.

Sam nudged Gerald. 'I think your man's arrived.'

Twin figures dressed in black leathers rode towards them, their spiked winter tyres biting into the snow. Gerald, Sam, Felicity and Ruby edged closer together, shoulders pressed against shoulders.

The bikes spun around on the slippery surface and pulled up beside them.

Neither rider wore a helmet. The smaller man had a face like the last dog left in the pound—round, pressed flat and eyes that looked like they could roll out of their sockets at any moment. The larger man wore a black balaclava. He pulled it from his head, and Sam and Ruby suppressed a gasp. Tycho Brahe's silver nose seemed to glow blue in the dusk light.

'A little cooler than our last meeting, Gerald,' Brahe said, snowflakes settling in the tangle of his beard. He coughed into his gloved hand. Despite the cold, a sheen of perspiration glistened across his brow.

Sam stood opened-mouthed. He couldn't take his eyes from Brahe's face.

The man glared down at him. 'Didn't your mother teach you it's rude to stare?'

Sam bridled at the mention of his mother. He opened his mouth to say something but Ruby grabbed him by the arm and flashed her eyes. Now was not the time to argue.

Brahe laughed. 'What's the matter, Mr Valentine? Cat got your tongue?'

Sam couldn't help himself. 'No. Jack Frost been nipping at your nose?'

The man's face went dark. He spun around to Gerald. 'You have the prism?'

Gerald nodded. 'Of course,' he said. 'But not here.'

Brahe bristled—and he was not the only one. Ruby took Gerald by the elbow and hissed in his ear. 'What are you doing?'

Gerald shrugged her off, not taking his eyes from Brahe. 'Where are our parents? Where are Ox and Alisha?' he asked. 'I'm not handing over anything until I know they're free.'

Brahe tilted his head. A thought crackled across his eyes, like lightning in a bottle. Then the edge of his mouth curled up a fraction.

'They're not here,' he said. 'But they're not far away.' Snow continued to pile onto Brahe's head and shoulders. He ignored it. 'Do not think for a second that you are in a position to negotiate,' he said. He chucked his chin towards his companion, who had remained silent, straddling his motorbike. 'A word to my colleague here and you will be rejoicing in your new status as an orphan.'

The smaller man leaned into Brahe. 'We must hurry,' he said. 'There's still the castle. We need to find Vaclav. And Jan and Sigmund.'

Brahe waved him off. He glared at Gerald. 'Give me the prism.'

Ruby grabbed Gerald's arm again and swung him around. 'Give it to him, Gerald! What's the matter with you?'

Gerald shook himself free. 'We don't know where they are,' he said, glaring at Ruby, 'or even if they're okay.'

Ruby tore the glove from her hand and shoved it into Gerald's jacket pocket, reefing him from side to side as she searched for the pendant.

She pulled her hand free and shoved Gerald away, sending him tumbling into the snow. 'Here,' Ruby said to Brahe. 'Take it. Take the stupid thing.' Her voice caught in her throat. The pendant swung from its silver chain, looped around Ruby's finger.

Brahe reached for the prism.

Gerald struggled to get up.

Then the world caved in on them.

A chorus of shrill whistles cut the air. From his position on his back in the snow, Gerald looked up to see three coils of rope launch over the parapet of the clock tower. Moments later, three figures clad in black military fatigues were rappelling face first down the side of the ancient building. Shouts broke out across the square. Sharp, urgent calls. Gerald couldn't make out the words, but he could tell they meant business. He rolled onto his knees. From laneways and shopfronts, men brandishing handguns and assault rifles emptied into the square. A single shot echoed like a thunderclap.

Brahe moved quickly. He snatched the chain from Ruby's hand and threw his leg over his idling motorbike. His hand flew to the throttle and he opened it wide. The machine roared and smoke shot from the exhaust.

Gerald knew he had to act.

He threw out his hand a second before the bike kicked into gear. He wrapped his fingers around the sissy bar at the back of Brahe's seat just as the machine surged forward. Gerald's arm snapped taut, his shoulder was almost yanked from its socket. The rear of the bike spun around, flipping Gerald onto his backside. The snow tyres buzzed bare centimetres from his ear as the spikes struggled to grip the powder. Gerald could feel his fingers slipping. Brahe slammed the machine sidewards. The impact twisted Gerald into the air. He landed on his feet, square behind the bike. Without thinking, he latched his free hand onto the other side of the sissy bar. The rear wheel bit into the snow and the bike took off across the square, towing Gerald behind it like a water skier.

Gerald could still make out shouts coming from behind him, but the roar of the engine drowned out almost everything. His eyes dropped to the spiked snow tyre that was now spinning uncomfortably close to the crotch of his jeans. A sudden bump and that would be the end of the Wilkins family line.

Gerald clenched his teeth and looked up. Brahe was heading towards the far corner of the square, gunning the engine for all it was worth. Gerald clung on, his boots buffeting across the snow. They were following Brahe's partner, who made a sudden turn towards the church on the eastern perimeter. Gerald shot a look over his shoulder. Ruby, Sam and Felicity were surrounded by armed men—and three police motorcycles were surging after him.

Gerald spun his head forwards again—and spotted the crystal pendant. It was strung around Brahe's right wrist, the prism flailing in the wind.

It was the only bargaining chip Gerald had. If he ever wanted to see his parents again, he had to get it back.

At that point, Brahe noticed he had a passenger.

His head swivelled and Gerald stared straight into his eyes. Brahe threw a hand back, swiping at him. Gerald ducked, then had the unnerving sensation of the fork of his pants being shredded. He looked down to see the snow tyre had sliced clean through the main seam of his jeans. His purple boxer shorts were flapping in the very cold wind.

'Eep!' Gerald cried.

He looked up just in time to duck another swinging fist from Brahe. Instinctively, Gerald shot out a hand to scrabble at Brahe's face. His fingers closed around something cold and hard.

Brahe lost control of the bike for a second. It wobbled and the shake reverberated though the machine like an earthquake. Gerald was flung clear. He sailed through the air and smacked hard into a snow bank. He struggled upright to find his pants full of snow and a silver nose in the palm of his right hand.

Brahe leapt from the still-moving bike and disappeared through a doorway at the base of the Tyn Church.

Gerald scrambled after him, diving through the door and up a covered lane. He skidded through an archway and found himself inside the ancient church. The ceiling soared high above. The air carried a trace of incense. The cold was accentuated by the bare stone floor and the kilogram of snow that was still packed into Gerald's underpants. He looked around.

Candles.

Stained glass.

The fug of wood polish.

And a trail of snow leading up the right aisle.

Gerald scarpered past rows of pews, following the trail towards the front of the church. Rounding the corner near the altar, his feet flew out from beneath him. He crashed onto his chest, knocking the wind from his lungs. Momentum carried him across the floor, and he came to a stop at the edge of an open grave. A large slab of black granite lay next to the pit.

Gerald peered down.

The grave was empty.

Police arrived behind him, guns drawn, calling into radios. But Gerald was oblivious to the commotion. All he could see were the two words chiselled into the gravestone, weathered and chipped with age.

The name of the grave's one-time occupant.

Tycho Brahe.

Chapter 21

Mr Pimbury stood before them, his arms crossed and his face set to maximum fury.

Gerald, Sam, Felicity and Ruby had just endured two hours with the Prague police, answering questions and making excuses. Gerald was in no mood to sit through a repeat session in their hotel suite with his stand-in butler.

'Look, Mr Pimbury,' he said, 'we've said we're sorry and there's really nothing else to say. We told the police everything we know. And that's that.' He tossed Brahe's silver nose from hand to hand. 'We're no closer to finding our parents, or Ox and Alisha. So unless you want to start the girls crying again, I suggest you leave it.'

Gerald gave Ruby and Felicity a meaningful look. They both started sniffling.

Mr Pimbury raised his eyes to the crystal chandelier hanging from the ceiling. 'I've spoken with Mr Prisk in London,' he said. 'He has instructed that you are not to leave this suite until the snow clears and we can fly home. You can drown in your tears for all I care. Now, I am going down to the lounge, and I shan't be drinking tea.'

Mr Pimbury closed the double doors behind him with a bang.

Gerald flopped onto an ottoman opposite the others who were seated on a long couch.

Felicity, Ruby and Sam recoiled. '*Whoa!*'

Gerald looked at them, surprised. 'What's the matter?'

Sam covered his face with a hand and pointed to Gerald's pants. 'You might want to do something about that,' he said.

Gerald looked down to the gaping hole in his jeans.

'Whoops,' he said, jumping to his feet. He dived into the main bedroom and rummaged around for a change of clothes.

Ruby's voice floated in from the lounge. 'What's the story with the open grave in the church, Gerald?'

Gerald found a fresh pair of jeans and pulled them on. 'Brahe's name was on the gravestone,' Gerald called back. 'It looked really old. Like hundreds of years old.'

'What are you saying?' Felicity called out. 'That we're chasing after a ghost?'

Gerald wandered back into the lounge, pulling his shirt free from his waistband.

'Thank you for doing that,' Sam said. 'It was quite off-putting.'

Gerald settled back onto the ottoman. 'You're welcome,' he said with a polite nod, and turned to Felicity. 'Now, as for ghosts—'

Ruby interrupted him. 'Don't even start talking that nonsense, Gerald. Ghosts do not exist. Let's not waste any time going down that path.'

Gerald held up a hand. 'Don't be so hasty,' he said. 'Let's look at the facts. There's an empty grave in that church with Brahe's name on it.'

'Maybe it's a common name around here,' Ruby said.

'A common name?' Gerald said. 'Oh yes, you can't go ten steps down the street without bumping into a dozen Tycho Brahes. Every year the maternity wards are pumping out tiny Tychos by the truckload. Call out "Tycho Brahe" in any schoolyard and you'll be deafened by the cries of "*Yes?*" I've heard that—'

'All right,' Ruby said. 'You've made your point.'

'My point is that we can't discount anything,' Gerald said.

'Even ghosts?' Felicity said.

Gerald grabbed his jacket from the floor. 'When the police were taking me out of the church, I passed a table with a bunch of postcards for sale. This was one of them.' He pulled a card from the pocket and flicked it to Ruby.

It was a photograph of a marble bas-relief sculpture. On the top was a life-size image of a man dressed in ancient armour. One hand gripped the hilt of a sword while the other rested on a globe of the world. The man's nose had a large gash carved into it.

'What's this say?' Ruby asked. She pointed to lettering that ran around the border of the tombstone.

'It's Latin, I think,' Gerald said. 'But there's Tycho Brahe's name and if I've got my Roman numbers right it says he died in 1601.'

Ruby studied the card, shaking her head. 'How can that be?' she said. 'That looks exactly like—' She couldn't finish the sentence.

'Like Tycho Brahe,' Gerald said. 'The same man we just saw walking and talking down in the square.'

They sat in silence. Felicity tapped Gerald on the arm. 'I'm totally lost. How does this empty grave fit in with the crystal pendant?'

Gerald rubbed his eyes with the heels of his hands. 'I don't know,' he said. 'Let's go back to the beginning. Mason Green took his dinner jacket to the cleaners, and he left the pendant in his pocket.'

'Brahe's gone to a lot of trouble to get it,' Felicity said. 'It must be really valuable.'

'So valuable that Green leaves it in his jacket?' Ruby said. 'That doesn't seem likely.'

'Green said he just wore it as a lucky charm,' Gerald said.

'Odd for a billionaire not to know the value of something,' Sam said. 'Especially since he likes collecting old stuff.'

'But mostly old documents,' Gerald said. 'Not stuff like jewellery.'

'There was that old bottle,' Ruby said. 'Not that there's much of that left, thanks to Felicity.'

Felicity's cheeks went pink. 'I hope Special Agent de Bruin is all right.'

'Agent de Useless, more like,' Gerald said. 'There's no way he's with the FBI. The Czech police told me they were waiting for Brahe in the square after they were tipped off by the UK authorities who had been monitoring my phone in case the kidnappers made contact.'

Sam leaned across and took the silver nose from Gerald. He rolled it around in his hand. 'Whether he's a ghost or not, that Brahe's face is something else.'

'How about his little friend?' Felicity said, giggling. 'He was pug ugly.'

'And what's with Brahe perspiring all the time?' Gerald said. 'Have you noticed? It doesn't matter if it's hot or cold, he sweats like a fat man in a sauna.'

Sam laughed. 'Sweaty and Pugly. Quite the team.' He buffed the silver nose against his shirt and held it up to the shimmering chandelier.

Gerald held out his hand. 'Here, toss that over.'

Sam gave him a sly grin. 'Make me.'

There was a gunslinger's silence.

Gerald glanced at Sam.

Ruby's eyes flicked towards Felicity.

Felicity slowly reached out a hand and wrapped her fingers around the corner of a cushion...

The first shot hit Sam square in the jaw. Felicity's cushion had enough force behind it to send him jolting into the back of the couch. It was followed by three more in quick succession as Gerald and Ruby whipped cushions at Sam's head, before diving for cover behind a chaise lounge.

'You'll pay for that!' Sam called. He rolled over the back of the couch to the floor and scrambled to collect ammunition.

The battle of Prague was on.

Sam flung a bolster over the couch like a grenade. It smacked into an end table and knocked a stack of magazines across the floor. He poked his head above the parapet and was instantly claimed by a whirling pillow that struck like a padded Ninja star.

Felicity yelled a victory cry. 'Gotcha!'

Gerald was on his feet, gathering up things to hurl. 'This is why they call them throw cushions!' He skidded around the side of the couch where Sam was sheltering and let loose a barrage.

Ruby had raced into the bedrooms and returned with

pillows stacked under both arms. She tossed a couple to Felicity. 'It's girls versus boys, Flicka! Let's get 'em!'

Gerald looked to Sam under a pile of cushions and jumped down beside him. 'Shove over,' he said. 'Looks like I'm switching teams.'

Sam emerged from beneath his padded pile. 'Good to have you onboard,' he said.

They both grabbed a cushion in each hand and stood up. They hadn't counted on the girls kneeling on the couch, pillows cocked and ready to go. Ruby and Felicity hit as one. The impact split the covers and an explosion of goose feathers billowed into the air.

'Eat hot feathers, turkeys!' Felicity was really getting into the spirit of things.

Feathers snowed down as the squealing, whirling, cascading pillow fight rolled around the hotel suite. Lamps toppled, chairs tumbled, vases were deflowered.

Sam and Gerald sought refuge under the dining table. 'We're down to one cushion,' Sam said, breathless.

Gerald punched him on the shoulder. 'Make it count.'

Sam gave a tight nod, and rolled out into no man's land. He was immediately hit by a bolster across his ribs. Ruby was pulling back for another swing when Sam wound up with his last throw. But just as he released the cushion his hand was hit by a hard flying pillow from Felicity. Sam's shot aired high…straight into the crystal chandelier.

There was a colossal crash as cushion met glass. The

projectile sailed out the other side, shaking loose a dozen prisms. They rained down like shrapnel onto the carpet.

Everyone stopped.

The chandelier swung on its mount. The last of the goose feathers settled. Gerald emerged from under the table to survey the damage.

'Oops,' Sam said.

Ruby grinned wide. 'You idiot,' she said, and gave her brother a hug.

Felicity scooped up some cushions and tossed them back onto the sofa, and laughed. 'I think I needed that.'

Gerald smiled. There was nothing like a pillow fight to vent steam. He knelt down to clear away the crystals. A large one had landed on an open magazine. His hand paused just as he was about to pick it up.

'Oh, wow,' he said.

Ruby looked his way. 'What is it?'

'Come and see this.'

They crowded over Gerald's shoulder and looked at the crystal where it lay on the magazine. Through the glass prism, the words on the page bent and twisted like alphabet pretzels.

'Very pretty,' Sam said.

'Don't you see?' Gerald said. 'Look at how the glass bends the letters?' He moved the crystal back and forth, stretching and morphing the images in the magazine. 'The pendant that Brahe was after, the one that we just gave him. It's just a chunk of quartz on a cheap silver chain. It can't be worth more than a couple of dollars. Its value is in what it does.'

'What does it do?' Sam said.

'It's a key,' Gerald said.

'To what?' Sam said. 'A chest of gold or something?'

'No,' Gerald said. 'To a code.'

'You're thinking about the manuscript that was stolen from that university a few weeks ago,' Felicity said.

'Exactly,' Gerald said. 'What did Dr Efron from the museum call it?'

'Wasn't it something like Boy Itch?' Sam said.

'That's Voynich, you numpty,' Ruby said.

'Do you remember back in the chalet, when we were hiding in that blacked-out passageway?' Gerald said. 'The voice we heard through the wall was Brahe. I'm sure of it. And he said something about the Falcon coming through with one half of the deal. That must be the manuscript that was stolen from Yale University. Mason Green's crystal pendant was the other half of the deal.'

'So Brahe is trying to solve the code in the manuscript,' Felicity said.

'That's why it has never been deciphered,' Gerald said. 'Without the crystal prism it's impossible, no matter how many supercomputers you have.'

Ruby looked at Gerald, impressed. 'Gerald, you might be onto something.'

'I'm sure of it,' he said.

'What's in this manuscript that's worth all this trouble?' Sam said.

'Dr Efron said it was rumoured to hold the secret to alchemy—to turning lead into gold,' Gerald said. 'If Brahe could do that—'

'He'd have slightly more money than he already does,' Ruby said, shaking her head. 'He's a billionaire, Gerald. A member of your new club. He's not short of cash. I think your idea might need some more work.'

The wind fell out of Gerald's sails. 'There must be more to it than the money.'

'Well, Brahe has got the pendant now,' Ruby said. 'There's nothing we can do about that. He will release everyone, won't he?'

Gerald looked blank. 'Mason Green promised our parents would be released. But he said Ox and Alisha were in danger.'

'I don't understand,' Ruby said. 'What's different about Ox and Alisha?'

'I don't know,' Gerald said. 'But what more can we do? Brahe doesn't need anything else from us.'

Felicity straightened in her seat. 'But he does need something more,' she said. 'Do you remember down in the square. Pugly said something about going to a castle, and looking for three people. Jan, Sigmund and someone else.'

'Rudolph?' Sam suggested.

'No, that was the name of the old emperor, wasn't

it?' Felicity said. 'The one who bought the manuscript in the first place.'

There was a rattle at the door. A hotel waiter appeared with a large trolley, bearing plates topped with silver cloches. He glanced at the mayhem in the room and shook his head.

Gerald looked at the clock on the wall. He was surprised to see it was after eight in the evening. And he was famished.

The waiter set bowls of steaming dumplings and beef stew across the dining table.

'Excuse me,' Felicity said.

'Yes, ma'am,' the waiter replied.

'Is there a castle near here?'

The waiter looked at her dumbly for a second, then picked up a remote control from the sideboard and pointed it towards the windows. He pressed a button and the curtains tracked open, revealing an astounding night vista. On a steep hill overlooking the city stood the most extraordinary stone castle.

'There is that one,' the waiter said.

Chapter 22

Snow continued to fall under grim skies in the dull light of morning. The castle was no less intimidating. It stood over the city like a bully's fist.

Breakfast was laid out across the dining table. Gerald turned to Ruby and said, 'Can you read that again?' His brain couldn't process what he had just heard.

Ruby pushed her bowl of cereal to one side and folded back the page of the *International Herald Tribune*. 'Some of Britain's leading historians have gone missing, sparking a major police investigation,' Ruby read. Even Sam put his fork down to listen. 'A police spokesman said at least five senior academics have disappeared in the past week—all of whom worked at the British Museum.' Ruby ran her finger down the page. 'It lists their names. Professor McElderry is there. And so is that Dr Efron. It goes on to say that—oh my, listen to this—police have not ruled out a link to the theft of the Voynich Manuscript from Yale University.'

'We only saw Dr Efron a couple of days ago,' Felicity said. 'How awful.'

'Both McElderry and Efron,' Ruby said. 'That can't be a coincidence.'

Gerald gazed out the window. Too many people had gone missing. A memory of Ox came to him, of them playing together for the school rugby team back in Sydney. Ox was always the last man to the ruck, always lumbering behind the play. But he was always there. Trying. Having a go. Gerald blinked. Then he could see Alisha. She was smiling as she haggled with a street vendor in a Delhi market. Her face was so vibrant, so full of life.

Gerald blinked again.

'We need to get up to that castle,' he said. He fished in his pocket and pulled out Brahe's silver nose, rolling it between his fingers. 'I want to know what Brahe is looking for.'

'But we haven't heard if our parents have been released,' Ruby said. 'We need to wait here for the police to call.'

'I don't like coincidences,' Gerald said. He grabbed up his jacket. 'And I don't like waiting.'

As it turned out, neither did Ruby, Sam or Felicity.

And just as it can in San Francisco, in Prague a hundred-dollar tip can buy you a ride in a hotel dining trolley.

They plodded across the Charles Bridge, huddled together in a vain attempt to ward off the cold. Only the occasional tourist crossed their path as they slogged through the snowdrifts and up the hill towards the castle.

'You'd never forget who the boss was, would you?' Gerald said, peering through the tumbling curtain of white towards the sheer stone walls high above.

Felicity nudged him with a shoulder. 'What do you mean?'

'If you were a peasant back then. You'd wake up every morning to see that thing staring down at you. You wouldn't be game to do anything wrong. It'd be straight out to the fields for work or you'd have a platoon of soldiers on your case.' He thought for a second. 'It'd be like living next door to the school principal.'

Felicity laughed. 'A lot like boarding school, then.'

They climbed a winding stairway cut into the hillside. At the top it opened out to a large square. At one end stood a tall set of iron gates capped by two enormous statues: a pair of giants engaged in ferocious battle. One was armed with a dagger and the other was wielding a club. Gerald, Felicity, Sam and Ruby stared up at them.

'Yep,' Gerald said, gazing into a giant face that was contorted with unspeakable rage, 'just like boarding school.'

There was a slender sentry box at the base of each statue. Inside each one was a guard, wrapped in an overcoat and standing to attention with a rifle slung over his shoulder. The guards looked only slightly less ferocious than the giant statues that stood above them.

Ruby elbowed Gerald in the ribs and pointed to a sign on the gate. It read: 'Closed for Christmas–New Year.' Ruby looked up to the spired turrets of the castle beyond. 'That puts a stop to all that, then.'

Gerald considered the guards in the sentry boxes, and their rifles.

'We can get around those two,' he said.

'How, exactly?' Ruby said.

'It'll come to me.'

The answer arrived a moment later, in the form of more guards. Muffled boot steps from behind caught Gerald's attention. He turned to see four sentries marching their way across the square. He checked his watch. Right on nine o'clock.

'The changing of the guard,' Ruby said. 'Just like at Buckingham Palace.'

They watched as the two soldiers in the sentry boxes emerged and marched out to meet their replacements.

There was a convoluted exchange of orders and salutes, and Gerald saw their chance.

'Quick,' he hissed. 'While they're busy.'

He slipped behind one of the sentry boxes, and through the gates. He didn't look back as he scurried across the courtyard, but he could hear footsteps following him. He hoped they didn't belong to the guards.

Gerald ducked inside an arched carriageway and pressed his back against the cold stone wall. Felicity scooted in beside him, followed by Ruby and Sam.

'Did they see us?' Felicity said, craning her neck to peek back towards the gates.

'Since we haven't been shot, I think we're okay,' Sam said.

They crept to the far end of the carriageway, where it opened into a snow-filled courtyard. 'What do we do now?' Sam asked.

'We try to find those guys that Brahe was talking about,' Gerald said. 'Jan and whatsisface.'

Ruby looked at Gerald and sucked on her teeth. 'You haven't given this a lot of thought, have you?'

'What do you mean?'

'We've just broken into a castle. We can hardly front up to complete strangers and ask if they know someone called Jan. And what if they do? Where does that get us?'

Gerald kept staring across the courtyard at the building opposite. 'It gets us closer to solving this mystery,' he said flatly.

'Have you ever considered that some mysteries are best left unsolved?'

Gerald thought for a second. 'Nope,' he said, and started off across the courtyard.

Ruby scurried after him. 'You can be so stubborn,' she said, catching up to him. 'Why can't you just ease up for once?'

Gerald stopped at a large doorway and turned to face Ruby.

'Look,' he said, staring hard into her eyes. 'I may be entirely clueless when it comes to girls—'

'Yes,' Ruby said. 'Entirely.'

'But I am certain about two things. Our parents are fine and they'll be free soon. And Brahe is not going to get away with this.' Gerald didn't say it, but after Mason Green's warning, he still had a gnawing doubt about Ox and Alisha's safety.

Ruby's cheeks turned pink. She and Gerald looked at each other in silence until Sam and Felicity caught up.

Sam pushed open the door and stepped inside. 'Let's go you two,' he called back to Gerald and Ruby. 'What's keeping you?'

Ruby opened her mouth to speak but was lost for words.

'Come on,' Gerald said to her. 'Don't stand in the way of a stubborn man.'

They climbed a broad set of stairs and found themselves inside a cavernous hall.

Sam let out a low whistle. 'You could play a football match in here,' he said.

Banks of windows ran the length of the hall and the grey daylight seeped inside. Chandeliers were suspended in a line along the centre of the stone-vaulted ceiling, their unlit bulbs casting no cheer in the chilly chamber.

Felicity called over from the far wall, where she was reading an information card. 'It says here that there used to be jousting in this place.'

'People in suits of armour on horses and all that?' Sam said. He snorted to himself. 'Mum loses it if I come inside with my football boots on.'

'Sounds like this King Rudolph knew how to have fun,' Gerald said.

Ruby wandered over to a window. 'It's good to be the king,' she said, and gazed down at the courtyard outside. 'This place is enormous. We could look for days and not find anything.'

Gerald joined her at the window. 'It'd be good to get some height,' he said. 'To get an idea of how big this place is.' He pointed to a tower across the courtyard. 'That looks like the tallest part of the castle. Want to climb up and check the view?'

'If I said no, would that stop you?'

'Probably not.'

Gerald led the way across the courtyard and up some stairs to a door at the base of the tower. They peered inside a musty entrance hall. Apart from a stand of postcards against one wall, the room looked much as it would have done six hundred years before. At the back of the hall, a tight spiral staircase wound up into the shadows.

Gerald put his foot onto the bottom step and squinted up the barrel of the staircase. 'I can't see a thing,' he said. Then he started to climb.

He flattened his left hand against the wall, feeling his way in the dark. The cold stonework was worn smooth by centuries of others making the same dim journey up the narrow winding stairs. On and on they went. Every few turns they would pass an arched window set into the thick wall, giving a spectacular view of the castle surrounds and the city of Prague beyond.

'I'm beginning to see why Rapunzel got her visitors to take a shortcut,' Ruby said, plodding higher and higher. 'This is killer on the thighs.'

After a few more turns up the corkscrew, the stairs opened out to a landing and an enormous bell suspended inside a large wire cage.

'Check that out,' Sam said. The bell hung a metre or so above the floor. Ropes attached to its top trailed down through holes in the floorboards. It appeared to be extremely old.

Gerald tugged at Sam's elbow. 'Let's keep going.'

The stairs wound on up into the tower. Gerald strained to see, but the darkness was complete. All he could sense was the soft shuffle of their boots on the worn steps and the rub of stone wall against the skin of his hand.

Again, after a few turns of the narrow stairway, they came to a landing, and another bell suspended in a cage.

Snow swirled past the narrow window. The silence was absolute.

Gerald indicated the stairs with a nod and he set off again into the shadows. The stairway seemed to become narrower the higher they wound. Gerald arrived on a third landing to find the same arrangement as before: a huge bell suspended inside a room with iron bars for walls, like a prison cell. This bell was by far the largest. And the door to the room was ajar.

Gerald slipped through the gap. Ruby, Sam and Felicity followed. He wrinkled his nose at the stale mustiness in the air. The room was bare, apart from a wooden table against the far wall. It was covered in sheets of old paper. Sam lifted a large lump of coal from the pile and picked up a yellowed magazine.

'It's from 1984,' he said, holding the cover up to the spare light filtering in from an arched window.

There was a sudden fluttering sound above their heads. Felicity gasped, grabbing Ruby's arm. They looked up to see a pigeon flapping its wings before settling back in its nest.

'I don't think anyone has been here for a very long time,' Gerald said.

But just as he spoke there was a loud *bang*.

They all jumped at the sound.

The door to the caged room had slammed shut. The bolt shot home. Gerald swung around to see someone disappear down the stairwell, heavy boots pounding into the darkness.

'Hey!' he yelled, rattling the door. '*Hey*!'

'Was it Brahe?' Felicity asked. She squeezed an arm between the bars but couldn't reach the bolt.

'Or Pugly, maybe,' Ruby said. She joined Gerald shaking the door against its hinges. It wouldn't budge.

'Now what do we do?' Felicity said.

The pigeon above them fluttered in its nest again, sending down a shower of feathers and dried droppings.

Then there was a creaking. And a noise Gerald hadn't heard since he'd last played tug of war at school: a long stretching noise, a rope under strain.

The bell started to move. Slowly at first, back and forth. But it soon built into a full-blooded swing.

'Look out, Sam!' Ruby yelled.

Sam was still standing by the window and seventeen tonnes of bronze bell was about to swing straight at him. He ducked just as the rim shot over his head. The massive clapper missed him by inches before it struck the side of the bell and emitted a colossal tone.

Sam threw himself to the floor. He rolled across the boards just as the bell started on its return path. The front rim caught him under the ribs and lifted him into the air. There was another resounding toll as Sam flew into Gerald and Felicity, knocking them to the ground like bowling pins.

The sound of the bell was deafening.

And, locked in the cage, they had no escape.

Gerald scrambled to his knees. He pressed his hands to his ears trying to smother the noise.

But it made no difference.

The bell assailed the tower with a fusillade of sound.

Every strike was like a blow to the head, the reverberations echoing inside the skull. Gerald screwed his eyes tight and rolled back and forward with each pounding blow, mimicking the movement of the enormous instrument of torture. Ruby, Sam and Felicity had their hands over their ears. They curled into balls on the floor.

Gerald knew he had to do something. Much more of this and his eardrums were likely to rupture.

Again and again the percussion pounded his head. The vibrations juddered his teeth and his bones.

He sat there, hands clamped over his ears, wishing the noise away.

Chapter 23

It was too much.

Gerald toppled onto his side.

A pain shot into his left thigh—sharp enough to cut through the incessant ringing. He had rolled onto Brahe's silver nose that he had stuffed in his pocket.

Then Gerald's eyes flashed open.

The nose.

Still with his hands clamped over his ears, he turned onto his back and looked up at the bell.

It hung on a crossbar on a wooden frame, suspended from iron scaffolding. Gerald tried to focus, tried to block out the noise. Then his eyes lit on a chance. He just had to get up there.

He pulled a tissue from his pocket and tore it in two.

He wadded each bit up and drove them into his ears with his thumbs. The bell's toll still pounded into his brain but it would have to do.

The giant clapper was the size of a tree trunk. It extended beyond the lip of the bell and swung with enormous force. At its lowest point it cleared the floorboards by bare centimetres. To climb up the scaffolding, Gerald had to get to the far side of the room. That meant getting past the bell and the clapper.

He crouched to his haunches, like he was about to start a sprint. His eyes traced the bell's path as it rose and fell.

Easy now.

Get the timing right.

Go!

Gerald shot out of the blocks. He dived under the swinging edge of the bell, sliding across the floor on his belly. But he mistimed the swing of the clapper. It clipped him on the ankle as he was almost clear, and sent him spinning across the boards like a fallen ice skater. He slammed into the table on the far wall, splintering its legs and sending sheets of paper flying in the air. The lump of coal that had been serving as a paperweight bounced off his head.

Gerald gathered himself and studied the scaffolding looming above him. He took hold of the lowest bar. The iron was slippery with the cold and it shook with each swing of the bell. He clambered up, hand over hand, struggling to hold on as the bell's shockwaves rode through him. The sound seemed to reach an entirely new level the closer he got to the top. Gerald could feel his eyeballs vibrating in their sockets.

To and fro, to and fro, the bell swept past him. His hands cramped in the cold, but finally Gerald reached the top of the scaffold. He folded an arm around the upper beam and clung on. His eyes darted about the wooden frame that supported the bell, searching for an opening, a point of weakness. Then he spotted it. Where the frame reached its upper point on the backswing. A notch in the woodwork. If he could wedge Brahe's silver nose in there, it could jam the mechanism. Maybe still the bell.

Gerald screwed his eyes shut and opened them again. His vision was blurring. The noise was just so intense. He fumbled in his pocket and pulled out the lump of silver. He had one shot at this. The timing had to be perfect. If he got it wrong, the bell would crush his fingers to mush.

He reached out his right arm.

His hand shook. He fought to control it.

The bell tolled.

Again.

And again.

This time.

No. *This* time.

Gerald extended his arm.

And he dropped the silver nose.

His mouth shot open in a silent cry of despair. He watched, horrified, as the lump of metal tumbled from his grasp. It bounced among the limbs of iron like a pinball bound for the drain. It pinged off the lowest arm of scaffolding and bounced into the air.

Then, to Gerald's amazement, the nose landed right into the notch that he'd been aiming for! Jammed in tight, as if driven by a hammer. It was a one in a million chance—all the planets must have been in alignment. He watched with wide eyes as the wooden frame supporting the bell swung back. The mechanism hit the metal lump. And squashed it flat.

The bell didn't miss a beat. Seventeen tonnes of bronze swung on, clanging out the last ounce of Gerald's will to live.

Gerald slumped against the top of the scaffold. He was spent. He strained to open his eyes and looked down to the floor below. He wondered whether it would really hurt that much if he jumped. At least the ringing would stop.

Then Gerald noticed something. He shook his head to clear the clamour in his brain.

The ringing *had* stopped.

He looked across to the bell and saw with astonishment that it was slowing; the clapper was no longer striking the rim. The mechanism was winding down.

Stunned, Gerald again looked down to the floor, to

see Felicity smiling back at him, a pocketknife in one hand, and a cut bell rope in the other.

Gerald clambered down the scaffold to be met by Felicity's embrace.

She pulled back, holding him by the shoulders, and started talking. But Gerald couldn't make out anything she was saying. He realised he still had tissue stuffed in his ears. He plucked out the wads of paper.

'—you all right?'

Gerald stuck his little finger in his ear and wiggled. 'A bit deaf,' he said, through a lingering peal of bells. 'But in better shape than Brahe's nose.'

He picked up the bell rope and inspected the severed end. 'I guess that was a better idea than mine.'

Felicity grinned. 'The Colonel's pretty big on the whole "be prepared" thing actually,' she said. She held up the pocketknife. 'This was a birthday present. Nifty.'

There was a call from near the door. Ruby had gathered herself from the floor and was studying a placard on the wall. 'Look at this,' she said. Sam picked himself up and staggered over, still rubbing his ears.

'What is it?'

Ruby pointed to the words on the placard, in Czech and translated into English.

'The bells of St Vitus Cathedral date from the mid-sixteenth century,' she read out loud. 'This is the largest of them. Weighing 17 tonnes and 2.6 metres in diameter, Zikmund was struck in 1549.'

'Zikmund?' Gerald said. 'The bell is Zikmund?'

'Yes,' Ruby said, her eyes lighting with realisation. 'All large bells have nicknames. Like Big Ben in London.'

'I thought that was the name of the building,' Gerald said.

'No. Big Ben is the bell inside the clock tower at the Houses of Parliament. Maybe the Zikmund that Brahe was looking for wasn't a person. It was this bell.'

Gerald looked back to the massive bronze instrument. It hung straight down, its enormous clapper stilled and silent.

'So the other two people Brahe and Pugly were talking about—Vaclav and Jan, was it?—what's the bet they're the two bells we passed on the way up,' he said.

'What would Brahe want with some four-hundred-and-sixty-year-old bells?' Ruby said. 'It's not like he's going to steal them and melt them down for spare change.'

Sam wandered across to the long clapper. He dropped to his knees and gave it a shove. It swung up and kissed the rim. Even the lightest touch set off a humming ring.

'Please don't,' Ruby said. 'You might find this hard to believe, but I have a headache.'

Sam stood up. 'Hey,' his voice chimed out from inside. 'There are some engravings and stuff in here.'

Gerald and Ruby looked at each other, then made a dive for the bell. Felicity shuffled in with them.

Sam pointed to an array of swirling lines, and a

jumble of letters spread across the pattern like alphabet soup: P R H A H R B R.

'What's that supposed to mean?' Sam asked.

Felicity ran her fingertips across the engraving. She pursed her lips. 'This reminds me of something.'

A faint breeze blew through the arched window, fluttering the sheets of paper that were now spread across the floor. A sheet wafted in under the bell and brushed against Felicity's leg. She bent down to scoop it up.

'Gerald, wasn't there a piece of charcoal or something on top of that pile of paper?'

Gerald nodded, rubbing his head where the black lump had hit him.

'Could you fetch it for me?' Felicity asked. Gerald ducked out from under the bell to search for the lump of coal.

'How did you manage to train him so well?' Ruby asked.

Felicity gave a shy grin. 'Boys are like puppies,' she said. 'Tickle them under the chin and you've got a friend for life.'

'Hey!' said Sam. 'I'm a boy.'

'And a very good boy at that,' Felicity said, flicking him under the jaw with her finger. He blushed.

Ruby looked on in awe. 'It's that simple?'

'Oh, yes,' Felicity said. 'It's that simple.'

Gerald crawled back in with them and handed Felicity the charcoal. 'Here you go.'

'Thank you, Gerald,' she said, smiling sweetly. 'Now, hold the paper up against the side of the bell just there.'

Gerald laid the sheet flat across the tangle of lines and letters.

'What are you doing, Felicity?' Ruby asked.

'Brass rubbing,' Felicity said. 'The Colonel used to take me to old churchyards in the Lake District. We'd spend the day doing rubbings of brass plaques. It's fun. See?'

Felicity scraped the charcoal across the paper and an impression of part of the engraving appeared. 'I won't go too hard,' Felicity said, concentrating on the task, lines and letters transferring to the sheet with each stroke. 'I'm guessing that the other two bells have similar markings on them. If we use the same piece of paper I bet we can build up an answer to this riddle.'

'Like a 3-D jigsaw puzzle,' Ruby said.

'That's genius,' Sam said.

Felicity smiled. 'Why, thank you.'

Sam blushed again.

They crawled back into the bell room and Felicity held out the paper for everyone to see.

'It's still just a jumble,' Sam said.

Felicity carefully rolled up the sheet. 'Let's see how it looks once we've spoken to Jan and Vaclav,' she said.

Gerald rattled the cage door. He reached through the bars but couldn't get to the bolt. 'Can I have your pocketknife, Felicity?'

Felicity held it out but snatched it back just as Gerald was about to take it. 'What's the magic word?'

Gerald arched an eyebrow. 'Please?'

Felicity put the knife into Gerald's palm. 'There's a good boy.' She gave Ruby a wink. Ruby just shook her head.

Gerald pulled out a short blade and dropped to his knees. He pressed the edge of the blade against the door hinge and jemmied out the pin. A minute later he repeated the trick on the top hinge and they were able to wrench the door open.

Gerald led the scamper down the worn stone steps.

The door to the cage around the second bell stood open. Ruby pointed to a placard on the wall.

'This one's called Jan,' she said, excitement bubbling in her voice.

Sam kept watch as Felicity and Gerald disappeared inside the bell. They crawled out a minute later.

'What's it look like?' Sam asked.

Felicity showed him the paper. More twisting lines intersected across the page, joining up with those from Zikmund. And there were more letters: A D A N B I T A H.

'What do you think?' Ruby asked.

'I don't know,' Gerald said, studying the image. 'It could be part of someone's face maybe.'

Sam looked over Gerald's shoulder. 'World's ugliest human if it is.'

Felicity rolled up the paper again. 'Come on. Only Vaclav to go.'

They emerged from the shadows of the stairwell to find the final bell cage open, the door hanging askew from its top hinge. Gerald stopped at the entry, and Sam, Felicity and Ruby piled into the back of him.

'What's the problem?' Sam said.

Gerald spun around to face them. He took a deep breath. 'What are we doing?' he said. 'Brahe just tried to kill us. He's probably still nearby. Maybe we should take the hint and ease off a bit.'

'What are you saying, Gerald?' Ruby asked. 'That we should go home and wait quietly by the phone to see whether our parents are all right?'

Gerald lowered his eyes to his boots and frowned.

Ruby's jaw dropped open. 'What happened to all your bluster about not being patient? Not waiting for the police or the FBI to get their game together?' She shoved Gerald's shoulder. 'I don't believe you. You drag us out here, put us through the seven rings of hell and now you bottle it?' She shoved Gerald again, this time knocking him clear of the doorway. 'Well if you want to go home and cry into your pillow, go right ahead. But I've had it with waiting. Come on, Flicka. Let's see what Vaclav has to say.'

Ruby stormed into the cage, leaving Gerald blinking after her. She and Felicity crawled in under the bell.

'What was that all about?' Felicity asked, rubbing

the charcoal against the sheet of paper.

'You train him your way,' Ruby said. 'I'll train him mine.'

Ruby helped Felicity out from under the bell. 'Let's see what we've got,' Felicity said. She laid the sheet of paper flat on the floorboards.

'Oh my,' Ruby said. 'Is that a map?'

The three layers of lines, swirls and letters had married together to form a rough chart.

'Look,' Gerald said, elbowing Ruby in the ribs. 'The letters have formed some words.'

Ruby eyed Gerald closely. 'Back in the game, are we?'

Gerald allowed himself a half-smile. 'The coach gave me a rev up at half-time,' he said. He ran his finger under a word at the top left of the map. '*Praha*. Where have I seen that before?'

'On signposts all over town, dopey,' Ruby said. '*Praha* is Czech for Prague.'

'There's a picture of this belltower,' Sam said. 'So where does this line go?'

He traced his index finger along a winding route towards the north-east. It came to rest on an engraving of a small cluster of buildings, and the word *Hadanka*.

'Maybe that's the name of a town,' Ruby said.

'What do you suppose this is?' Felicity asked, pointing to a small collection of crosses just outside the township with the word *Hrbitov* next to it.

'What's a cross usually represent on a map?' Sam said. 'A hospital?'

'Seeing as this was probably engraved a few hundred years ago, I don't imagine the health system was that sophisticated,' Ruby said. 'A church, maybe?'

'Or,' said Gerald, 'a graveyard.'

A silence settled over them. The snow continued to tumble past the arched window above their heads. Gerald suddenly remembered how cold he was.

After what seemed an age, Felicity spoke. 'Can anyone make out this word next to the cross at the bottom?' she said.

Ruby moved her head in close to the paper. 'I'm not sure,' she said. 'Is that a D?'

A rough voice sounded from behind them. 'It's a B.'

Gerald spun around. A man in a black overcoat blocked the doorway.

'B, as in Brahe,' said Tycho Brahe. A fresh silver nose covered the gash in his face.

Chapter 24

They walked along a windowless corridor, deep in the bowels of the castle. Gerald scuffed his boots and stumbled to the stone floor. Felicity stopped to help him, leaving Ruby to trudge on ahead. Sam was last, the point of Brahe's knife at his back.

'How much further?' Gerald said, his voice low, defeated.

'You'll know when you get there,' Brahe growled.

The miserable caravan trekked onwards. The corridor turned and ended at a heavy oak door. Ruby looked over her shoulder and Brahe told her to open it. She needed Felicity's help to push the door in.

They passed through the doorway. The walls were at least two metres thick. There was no use in shouting.

Nothing was going to penetrate. Then Sam slammed into Gerald. They both fell to the floor.

'This was once a torture chamber,' Brahe said. He sheathed his knife. 'Let's not revisit those times.'

Ruby helped Sam to his feet and shot Brahe a defiant look. 'Where are our parents?' she said.

'Again with the question of your parents,' he said. 'You attach some importance to them?'

'Of course we do,' Ruby said. 'Who wouldn't?'

Brahe shrugged. 'I haven't seen mine for so long, I no longer care.'

'That's because you're old,' Sam said.

A glint shone in Brahe's eye, a speck of gold in a seam of granite. 'Older than you can possibly imagine, Mr Valentine.' Brahe pulled a handkerchief from his pocket.

Sam's eyes fell upon it. 'What's the matter?' he said. 'Got a runny nose?'

Brahe dabbed the handkerchief across his sweat-drenched forehead. 'You truly are an annoying child. I don't expect you to understand what is at stake here. That's the problem with the young. You have all the time in the world and do absolutely nothing with it. One day you'll wake up and wonder where it all went.'

Gerald was still on the floor, glowering up at the figure in the doorway. 'Why was there an open grave with your name on it in that church?' he asked. 'And a gravestone with your face carved on top?' Gerald tried to contain his anger, but it bubbled over. 'What is it you want? Money? I can pay.'

'Ah! The gravestone.' Brahe ran a finger along the scar that divided his face. 'A good likeness, yes?' He waved Gerald off with an irritated flick of his hand. 'What I seek, Gerald, can't be bought. It has to be earned. Earned and learned. And that takes time.'

Brahe gathered his overcoat around him like a bat's wings and turned to leave. 'And I have wasted enough time dealing with you. The castle opens for tourists again in a few days. You'll be found then. There is water here—you may go hungry but you will survive. I regret the inconvenience, but I can't afford any further delays.'

Then he paused. 'Miss Valentine?' he said.

Ruby looked at him through red-rimmed eyes. 'What?'

'I have no idea where your parents are.'

Ruby's mouth fell open. 'But you kidnapped them!'

Brahe wrapped his hands around a metal ring on the door and pulled. 'I only took what I needed from Mt Archer. If your mother and father were kidnapped,' he said through the shrinking gap in the doorway, 'it was not by me.'

The door closed with a dull thud. Sam rushed and heaved on the handle. It wouldn't budge.

Ruby stood forlorn, her expression frozen in place. 'He doesn't know where they are?' It was barely a whisper.

Gerald gave Sam a concerned look, then he laid

an arm across Ruby's shoulders. 'They'll be okay,' he said.

Ruby's head fell forward.

'Ruby?' Gerald said.

She didn't respond. Gerald said her name again and jostled her shoulders.

Nothing.

Then a tear rolled down her cheek. 'I don't think I can do this anymore,' she said.

Gerald put his hand under Ruby's chin and tilted her head back. It was like looking at a department store mannequin. The spark was gone from her eyes. The brightness and the joy, the warmth and the vitality—all the ingredients for a proper Ruby—had disappeared.

'We'll find them,' Gerald said to her. 'I promise.'

Ruby closed her eyes.

Gerald was left holding a shell. He was glad when Felicity took her away to sit by the wall.

'We've got to find a way out of here,' Gerald said to Sam, joining him by a large wooden cabinet further inside the room. 'Ruby's not doing so well.'

The old torture chamber was becoming lost in shadows. The early winter evening had begun its descent. The only light came from a barred window high in an outer wall and it was half-covered by a snowdrift. Gerald tightened the scarf around his neck.

He was astonished when Sam handed him a torch. 'Where did you find this?'

Sam pointed to a door in the cabinet. 'I think this must be part of a museum now,' he said, flicking on his own flashlight. He swung the beam into the shadows. It played across display cases housing dusty suits of armour. There were racks of weapons—swords, flintlock rifles, a small cannon—a pyramid of cannonballs and rows of flasks and mixing bowls.

'Shame we didn't know this lot was here before,' Gerald said. He picked up a heavy sword. 'We could have jumped Brahe.'

Sam was inspecting an information board attached to a cabinet of glass bottles. 'Speaking of Brahe,' he said. 'Maybe we are chasing a ghost.'

'What do you mean?' Gerald said.

'It says here that King Rudolph II appointed a Royal Astronomer in 1599. A guy with a silver nose by the name of Tycho Brahe.'

Gerald beamed his torch onto a line drawing of a man who looked exactly like the one who had just locked them up in a dungeon. 'This is getting more bizarre by the minute,' he said.

Sam kept reading. 'Brahe became one of the king's most trusted advisers. When he died, the entire kingdom went into mourning. He was given the highest honour: a grave in the historic Tyn Church in the heart of Prague.'

'That's where I was yesterday,' Gerald said. 'And the grave was empty.'

'So what are we talking about?' Sam asked. 'Zombies?'

'Don't talk rubbish,' Felicity said, with a sharp edge to her voice.

Sam winked at Gerald, and shuffled over towards the girls. 'Now that I think of it,' he said, cupping a hand over Felicity's head. 'I am a bit hungry.'

'Sam!'

'Braaiinnzzz…'

'SAM!'

Gerald trained his light on the flasks and beakers and scales in the display. 'It says that Brahe was at the very heart of Rudolph's court and a keeper of the secrets in his alchemy laboratory. He was rumoured to hold the recipe to the universal remedy.'

'The universal remedy?' Felicity said. 'Dr Efron mentioned that at the museum.'

Gerald's eyes grew wide. 'Anyone who possessed the secret of the remedy,' he read, 'could live for hundreds of years.'

'Surely you don't think it's the same person,' Felicity said.

'But it's all connected,' Gerald said. 'This drawing of Brahe, right down to the fake nose. The missing manuscript with the recipe for the universal remedy. And Brahe's desperation to get the crystal pendant so he can break the code. It all adds up.'

Felicity was at a loss. Then a thought hit her. 'How do you explain the grave in the church, then?' she said.

'If he'd been alive all this time, why is there a grave there at all?'

'Zombies have to die before they come back,' Sam said.

'Sam.'

'Braaiinnzzz...'

'*SAM!*'

'Wait,' Gerald said. 'It says that Brahe died in 1601 from—' He paused, then burst out laughing.

'What?' said Felicity.

Gerald tried to compose himself. 'It says he died because he held on too long when he needed to pee.'

'You're joking,' Felicity said.

'Nope. He was at a royal banquet and everyone was drinking heavily. It was rude to leave the table if the king was still there. So Brahe couldn't get to the toilet.'

'Even though he was busting?' Sam said.

'Apparently. He held on, something got kinked and he was dead a week later.'

There was a pained silence.

Sam crossed his legs. 'It must have really hurt.'

'Dire,' said Felicity. 'That would make your eyes water.'

'Or your nose fall off,' said Sam.

'That's if it's true,' Gerald said.

'What do you mean?' Felicity asked.

'What if Brahe faked his death? What if he cracked the code on the manuscript and brewed up a batch of this miracle juice that cured any illness he ever had?'

'But surely that's not possible,' Felicity said. 'A cure to everything?'

'No more hospitals,' Sam said. 'No need for doctors. Just a sip of Professor Brahe's magic cure-all potion and you're on your way.'

'To be able to live for centuries,' Gerald said. 'How amazing would that be?'

'You might create a population problem,' Ruby said.

Everybody looked to where Ruby was sitting by the wall, her eyes fixed on the floor between her feet.

'What do you mean?' Sam asked.

'If everybody's getting cured and living forever, then no one's dying,' Ruby said. 'Babies are still being born. It'll be hard to feed all those extra people.'

'Trust you to put a downer on things,' Sam said.

Ruby rounded on her brother. 'What's there to be happy about? Mum and Dad are still missing. So are Ox and Alisha. And Gerald's parents. Who cares if Brahe's a zombie or a ghost or a mental case? And believe me, I'm betting on the last option. We're still stuck in here and I want to find Mum.'

Sam's face fell. 'Sorry,' he mumbled.

'How do we get out?' Felicity asked.

Sam kicked a desultory boot at the flagstones. 'It's probably a dumb idea...'

'What's that?' Gerald said.

'Those cannon balls back there.'

'What about them?'

'It said on the poster that they've still got gunpowder in them.'

Gerald, Felicity and Ruby all stared at Sam.

'What?' Gerald said.

'Yeah—still stuffed with gunpowder from when they were made a couple of hundred years ago. Maybe we could blow our way out.'

'Sam, I wouldn't trust you to blow your nose,' Ruby said.

'You don't have to be snotty,' Sam said.

'Do you think we could stop with the nose jokes,' Ruby said, 'just for a minute?'

'No need to be so picky either,' Sam said.

'Enough!'

'You could blow that door open?' Gerald asked.

'Oh, sure. It's simple chemistry and a bit of physics. Nothing to it.'

'Since when are you an expert in chemistry and physics?' Felicity said.

'Actually,' Ruby said, 'he's pretty good at that stuff.'

Sam gave Felicity a smug grin.

The four of them manoeuvred the small cannon out of the display and wheeled it across to the doorway. Sam took a cannonball from the top of the pile and lifted it over his head. It took three throws onto the stone floor to bust it open. A pile of black powder spilled out.

'I guess we pour it in here,' Sam said. He scooped

the powder down the barrel of the cannon. Gerald broke open two more balls and they tamped the contents down tight with a wooden plunger.

Sam rolled a cannonball down the barrel and funnelled the last of the gunpowder into a hole on the top of the cannon, near the end.

'Right,' he said. 'I light this batch of gunpowder here and that should explode the powder inside the cannon and send the ball straight into the door. Simple.'

'Don't you think a wick would be a good idea?' Ruby said. "So you don't have to stand so close when it goes off.'

Sam thought for a second. 'Good idea,' he said. He hunted about and found a cotton rope holding a flag in place. With Felicity's pocketknife he cut a five-centimetre length and frayed the end.

'How are you going to light it?' Gerald said.

Felicity took the pocketknife back from Sam and slid out a strip of metal the size of a match from the side. 'This has a flint in it,' she said. 'The Colonel likes his campfires.'

Felicity struck the metal strip down the side of the knife, sending a shower of sparks onto the wick. Sam coaxed the embers along with light breaths, then carefully placed the burning cord into the pile of gunpowder on top of the cannon. He joined the others a few metres back.

They watched as the wick fizzled and burned.

'Think we put enough in there?' Gerald asked.

'Enough what?' Sam said.

'Gunpowder.'

'Oh, yes. Heaps and heaps.'

The wick burned on.

'Probably enough to blow the whole cannon up,' Sam laughed.

'What?'

Sam looked at the fizzling cord.

'Maybe we should stand back a bit further,' he said.

'Good idea,' Gerald said. 'How far?'

The wick smoked and crackled.

'Maybe a really long way back.'

Gerald looked at Sam. Felicity looked at Ruby. They all bolted towards the far end of the room and dived behind an old wooden cabinet. A colossal BOOM rocked the rafters.

Gerald opened his eyes to find Sam lying on top of him. A cloud of black smoke wafted around them. 'Well, the chemistry bit worked,' Sam said, cheerfully. 'Let's see how the physics went.'

They untangled themselves and looked out from behind what was left of the cabinet.

The cannon had disintegrated. There was a scorched circle on the floor where it had been standing. Sam looked up to the wooden door. It was untouched.

'You great clot,' Ruby said. 'Only you could miss a door.'

'Maybe we used too much powder,' Sam said.

Gerald clapped him on the shoulder. 'Never mind about that,' he said. 'Look.' Sam followed the direction of Gerald's pointed finger to the window set high in the wall. The glass had shattered and the iron bars were swinging from a single corner bolt.

'The explosion must have jolted the bars free,' Gerald said. He went to the back of the room and returned with a siege ladder tucked under his arm.

It was only after Sam helped Gerald lean the ladder up to the window that they noticed the telephone on the wall.

Ruby took one look at it, and turned to her brother. 'You idiot,' she said.

Chapter 25

The ticket queue had stalled. The woman three places in front of Gerald in the line was having a long and loud discussion with the ticket seller. All progress had stopped.

Gerald shifted from one foot to the other, trying to keep his blood moving. There was heating in the bus station but it seemed to be avoiding anywhere that Gerald was standing.

'How long will it take to get to Hadanka?'

Gerald was so lost in his thoughts that Ruby had to repeat the question, and finally flick him on the ear, before he heard her.

'Huh? What?' he said. 'I don't know. How would I know—I haven't even spoken with the ticket lady yet.'

'All right—no need to get shirty,' Ruby said. 'I was just asking.'

'Yeah? Well don't ask stupid questions that I can't possibly know the answers to.'

Ruby stared at Gerald for a moment. 'Feeling a bit tired and grumpy, are we?'

Gerald screwed up his face. 'Sorry. I'm still annoyed at how the police reacted when I called them.'

'You can't really blame them, can you?' Ruby said. 'I'm not surprised they didn't believe you.'

'I guess I shouldn't have said we were locked up by a four-hundred-year-old astronomer.'

'That may have been a fundamental error.'

'I was thinking about Ox and Alisha as well,' Gerald said. 'And about something Brahe mentioned down in the dungeon.'

'What's that?'

'When he said he had no idea where our parents are. He said he'd only taken what he needed from Mt Archer.'

'So?'

'Well, the only people we actually saw being picked up by Brahe's goons were Ox and Alisha. Maybe he really doesn't have everyone else.'

It was Ruby's turn to screw up her face. 'Where could they be, then? And what would Brahe want with Ox and Alisha beyond using them as hostages to get the crystal pendant?'

Gerald shrugged. 'At least those are good questions,' he said.

Felicity ran up to them, her face beaming. She grabbed Gerald and Ruby by the arm and dragged them out of the ticket queue. 'Come quick! You've got to see this!'

'What is it, Felicity?' Ruby asked. 'What's the matter?'

'It's your parents. And yours too, Gerald.' Felicity was babbling as she hauled them into the bus station waiting room.

'What about them?' Gerald said.

'They're on TV!'

'They're what?'

'They've been released, and they're on TV!'

There was a television on the wall showing a cable news channel. Sam was standing in front if it with his mouth open.

Ruby rushed up to her brother.

'They're free,' he said. 'I can't understand what the announcer is saying but there's Mum and Dad, and Gerald's parents too.'

A group of adults were milling around in a large room. Reporters and cameramen were jostling to get close to Vi Wilkins. Then Vi began to speak, and Czech subtitles appeared on the screen.

'Ladies and gentlemen of the press,' she said, assuming her natural position at the centre of attention, 'I am pleased to say that our entire party has come through this frightful experience unscathed. Our spirits are high. We are healthy. And above all else, we are British!'

Ruby grabbed Gerald's arm and squeezed. 'They're okay! They're all okay.' A tear ran down her cheek. 'I can't believe it.'

'Your mum sounds like she's taken charge,' Sam said.

Gerald shook his head. 'Those kidnappers never stood a chance.'

Vi beamed out at the cameras. 'And I want to let my brave little soldier Gerald know that Mummy and Daddy miss him and we'll be home very soon to squeeze his little cheeks.'

Gerald's ears turned a bright crimson. Sam opened his mouth, but before he could make a sound Gerald prodded a finger into his chest. 'Don't. Say. A. Word. All right?'

Sam grinned. 'Not a word. My little soldier.'

The vision on the television cut to two photographs, clearly taken from passport files.

Ox and Alisha.

The announcer continued in Czech.

'What do you think she's saying?' Felicity looked up at the two young faces staring out of the screen, like photos on a wanted poster.

'The police are still searching for the children.' A man in an overcoat, who had been watching the news program, leaned over them and spoke in an accent. He chucked his chin at the screen. 'The adults were released in Miami in the United States. But there is no sign of the two children.'

Gerald looked at Ruby. 'Mum said that everyone she was with was all right,' he said. 'Ox and Alisha can't have been with them.'

'So Brahe wasn't lying,' Ruby said. 'He only took Ox and Alisha.'

Gerald nodded, then turned to leave.

'What are you doing?' Ruby said.

'Getting bus tickets to Hadanka.'

'You're still going?'

'Of course,' Gerald said. 'Brahe has Ox and Alisha. I can't abandon them just because the local police don't believe me.'

'But what about our parents?'

'My mum and dad looked fine on the TV. I know you'll want to see your parents, so you should head back to the hotel and get Mr Pimbury to arrange a flight to London. But I'm going to find Ox and Alisha.'

Ruby glanced back at the television, to a grainy image of her parents among the crowd of released hostages. Then she looked back to Gerald.

'Why do you always do this to me?' she said.

'Do what?'

'Put me in these impossible situations.' She pressed her lips together. 'I can't do it, Gerald. I have to see Mum and Dad.'

Gerald nodded again. Felicity took him by the hand. 'I'll come,' she said. 'It's not like I've got anyone to go home to at the moment.'

Gerald squeezed her hand. He said an awkward goodbye to Sam and Ruby, then went to join the ticket queue.

He and Felicity had just climbed inside the bus, with the doors hissing shut, when Ruby thrust a shoulder into the gap and pushed herself onboard. She held the doors open long enough for Sam to squeeze through too.

Gerald couldn't hide his smile. 'I thought you were going home,' he said.

Ruby brushed a stray strand of hair behind her ear as they shuffled down the aisle. 'Lucky for you that I enjoy your company then, isn't it?'

Since inheriting his enormous fortune, Gerald had criss-crossed the globe in a private jet, skimmed the English Channel in a helicopter and skied down his own private mountain. He could now add to the list: crossing more of the Czech Republic than he would care to in the back of a donkey cart.

Gerald, Sam, Ruby and Felicity had tumbled off the bus from Prague in a small village in the grey light of early afternoon. The bus stop consisted of a pole in the ground and a park bench half-buried under a mound of snow. It was the closest they could get to Hadanka using public transport. From there they would have to make their own way. It was Felicity's polite inquiry of a passing farmer that had hitched them the lift in the back of the donkey cart.

Gerald shifted uncomfortably on his cushion of hessian sacks. He reached under his backside and, with a grunt of effort, extracted a gnarled turnip. 'Oh, that's better,' he said, tossing the vegetable into the back of the cart. 'That was right in the wrong spot.'

He pulled a horse blanket up to his chin and snuggled in closer to Felicity. The four of them were packed in tight, like pink-cheeked urchins off to market.

'How much further is it, do you think?' Sam asked. The cart lurched over a pothole in the road, jostling them about.

'He doesn't speak much English,' Felicity said, indicating the farmer with a nod. The man sat on an old crate at the front of the cart, reins held slack in one hand, giving the occasional word of encouragement to the donkey. 'But I gather it's a fair way.'

Gerald shifted on his bottom again. 'Any distance on this thing would be a fair way. My bum feels like it's about to drop off.' He glanced across to Ruby. She was staring out at the snow-draped countryside. She hadn't spoken since getting off the bus.

'I'm curious,' she said.

'That you are,' Sam said.

Ruby gave him an annoyed glare. 'If Brahe didn't kidnap the adults, then who did? And how did they end up in Miami?'

Gerald tugged at the blanket, trying to keep warm. 'I get the feeling that Mason Green might have something to do with it,' he said. He wrestled another turnip out from underneath his bottom. 'I'm sure we'll hear all about it from my mother. Many times.'

The donkey cart rolled onwards, bumping its way along rough country roads. All around were snow-covered fields separated by windbreaks of fir trees.

'Have you noticed something?' Felicity asked, swaying in time to the rhythm of the cart.

'What's that?' Sam asked.

'There's no one around.'

Sam shrugged. 'We're in the country. What were you expecting? Mardi Gras?'

Felicity shook her head. 'There were people around when we got off the bus. But for the last few hours we haven't seen another living soul. Not even any birds. Don't you find that kind of creepy?'

Sam let out a sharp laugh. 'Nah.' But he did pull the rug up tight under his chin, and shifted in closer to the others.

The cart arrived in Hadanka just as the sun dipped behind the white-crested hills that surrounded the village. The temperature plummeted.

The farmer declined Gerald's offer to pay for the

ride. He glanced at the setting sun and urged the donkey onwards. The cart set off at a clip and disappeared around a bend.

'What a kind man,' Felicity said, waving after him. 'It's nice when people take the time to help.'

'He was certainly in a hurry to get on,' Ruby said. 'But it was good of him to give us a lift.'

'Yeah, yeah,' Sam said, clapping his arms across his chest to ward off the cold. 'Renews your faith in the world. So, where to now?'

Gerald looked around them. They were in a small village square. A fountain stood in the centre—its metal centrepiece wrapped in canvas. Lights shone from shopfronts that had stared across the square at each other for centuries. Shutters on upper floors were closed. Window boxes were barren, longing for spring. The square was deserted.

One shopfront in particular caught Gerald's eye. 'Over there,' he said, pointing. 'That could be a hotel.'

'Hopefully with a kitchen,' Sam said. 'I'm starving.'

Gerald climbed the three steps to the front door and pushed his way in. He was greeted by a wave of warm air. A fire blazed in a grate in a cosy lounge area on the left, with comfy armchairs arranged on a rug before it. On the right a bearded man sat at a table, lit by a desk lamp. He held a tiny screwdriver in an enormous hand. His head was bent low as he tended to a model of a sailing ship. Metal springs and cogs littered the tabletop.

It looked as if someone had gutted an alarm clock.

The man did not look up. He said something in Czech.

Gerald glanced at the others. 'Excuse me,' he said. 'Is this a hotel?'

The man stopped his work and raised his head. A jeweller's glass was wedged into one eye socket and a smouldering pipe jutted from his bearded mouth. Fingers of smoke crawled out of the bowl, filling the room with a pungent mixture of burning hay and rum.

The man looked at Gerald with surprise. 'You are English?' he said in a voice leathered by age and smoke.

'I'm Australian,' Gerald said. 'But these guys are English.'

The man removed the jeweller's glass from his eye and studied the four travellers. The burning tobacco glowed and crackled and popped as he drew on his pipe. He expelled a ball of smoke from a cheek as tanned as a saddlebag.

'Well, Australian and English, welcome to my hotel.' The man set down his screwdriver and pushed himself up from the table.

Ruby muttered a cautious thanks as the man hobbled towards them.

'Come,' he said. 'Take a seat. I don't get to practise my English very often.'

Gerald, Felicity, Sam and Ruby settled into armchairs. Gerald propped his feet near the fire and savoured

264

being warm for the first time that day.

'Thank you,' Gerald said. 'We've been on the go for ages. Do you have any rooms available?'

The man prodded at the fire with a blackened poker. He dropped another log on top, sending a fountain of sparks up the chimney. 'At this time of year, you can take your choice of room. And tonight—' he paused to prod the embers again, '—well, tonight you will be the only travellers for miles around.'

Felicity rubbed her hands by the flames. 'Oh really?' she said. 'Don't you get many tourists here?'

The man slowly turned his head towards Felicity and was about to reply when the front door banged open. A woman wrapped in a shawl and dusted with snow bowled into the room, muttering and grizzling. She carried a large wicker basket laden with vegetables. She dumped the basket on the floor and, from among the potatoes and the onions, she pulled out a long string of white bulbs, each the size of a baby's fist. With a practised kick, she hooked a wooden stool with her foot and climbed up to latch the door, straining to push the heavy iron bolt. Once the lock was in place, she strung the white vegetables from a notch on the back of the door. She stepped down and turned to face the man. The moment she saw the strangers in the room, she froze.

Her eyes darted from one face to the next.

The man took a step towards her. 'It's okay,' he said. 'They are in for the night.' He gave her a reassuring nod.

265

The woman ran her tongue across her teeth and gave Gerald and his friends another wary look. 'I will make dinner,' she said. She picked up the basket and disappeared through a curtain behind the table.

'Is everything all right?' Ruby asked.

The man tapped out his pipe on the hearthstone and pulled a beaten leather pouch from his pocket. 'Do not worry. Everything is fine,' he said. He tamped a plug of tobacco into the bowl of the pipe and worked it with his thumb. Then he shot a glance towards the bolted front door. 'Just fine.'

Gerald followed the man's gaze. Through the front windows he could see the square was dark. The night had closed in.

'That's garlic, isn't it?' Felicity said, nodding to the string of bulbs hanging from the door.

The man struck a match and put it to his pipe. His cheeks worked like a pair of bellows. 'Yes,' he said, his eyes never leaving the flame as it bucked and dived with each puff. 'It gives the room a lovely smell.'

Felicity started to respond when the man lurched back to the table. 'But now I must check you in.' He cleared a space on the table, sweeping aside a scattering of screws, springs and widgets, and pulled a battered book from a drawer.

'Well, Mr Gerald Wilkins and friends,' the man said, peering over Gerald's shoulder as he wrote his name in the register, 'it is good to meet you. My name is Novak, my wife is Stephanie. I will call you down when dinner is ready.'

'That's quite a boat you have there,' Sam said, studying the model ship on the end of the table. 'Did you make it?'

The man turned his gaze to the galleon and smiled at it as if it was a favourite child. It was just over half a metre long and the main mast stood about the same again high. 'I wish I had the skill to create such a beautiful thing,' the man said. 'I am merely trying to repair it.'

Sam poked his nose in close to the metal cladding around the hull. 'There's so much detail,' he said. 'Is this real gold?'

Novak grinned behind his beard. 'That is what they tell me. Watch.'

He turned the ship around. From his pocket he pulled a golden key. Sam watched entranced as the man inserted the key into a hole in the stern and wound it three times.

From deep inside the bilges came a whirring. Then, to Sam's delight, the ship lurched forward. It set off along the table on unseen wheels, swaying to and fro as if buffeted by the roaring forties. A sailor in the crow's nest raised and lowered a spyglass, searching for new lands. Four tiny portholes opened on each side, and out of each one popped a tiny cannon. Sam's eyes flew wide as the cannons shot out puffs of smoke. A jaunty nautical tune played from the hull as the ship ran down. Novak took hold of the galleon in loving hands as it reached the end of the table.

Sam looked at him, gobsmacked. 'That is awesome!'

Novak returned the smile. 'See here?' he said to Sam, chuffed at finding another enthusiast. 'The little people in the wheel house? This one is King Rudolph II, emperor of Bohemia.'

Sam peered in close to four tiny figurines standing on the high deck. 'Oh yeah,' he said. 'The one with the crown. We've heard all about Rudolph.'

Novak placed the galleon gingerly into a cradle and made a slight adjustment with the screwdriver. 'This was once part of his collection,' he said. 'He loved the wind-up toys. The more elaborate, the better.'

'How did you get it?' Sam asked. 'If that's not a rude question.'

Novak placed a giant hand on Sam's shoulder, and spared a glance to the curtain through which his wife had disappeared.

'We should have time before dinner is ready,' he said. He guided Sam back towards the lounge. 'Come. I have a story to tell you.'

Chapter 26

The fire cast shapes across the hearthrug in a puppet show of dancing shadows. Two lamps did little to fill the darkness that had descended with the night.

Novak stood by the grate, an elbow on the mantle and his pipe belching as much smoke as the chimney. 'Rudolph was not a good leader,' he said, his voice low and deliberate. 'He never wanted to be king. But when his father died, he had no choice. Overnight he became the most powerful man in the western world. His kingdom was large and he was the head of the Catholic church. He had the say of life and death over millions of people.' Novak blew a stream of smoke into the air. Apart from the crackle of the firewood in the grate, there was no other sound.

'He had castles. He had armies. But he did not have the passion to be a leader, to be a conqueror of lands.'

'What did he do all day?' Sam asked.

'He collected,' Novak said. 'He collected everything.'

He drew heavily on his pipe, infusing the room with its pungent odour. 'Rudolph turned the castle in Prague into his personal ark. Every kind of animal he could find would go into the private zoo. There were elephants, lions, giraffes. It was said that he even had a dodo.

'His passion was acquiring objects and he had the money to do it. It went beyond animals. He had three thousand oil paintings, display cases of minerals from around the world. There were birds and butterflies. He had two special collections: his Cabinet of Curiosities and his Cabinet of Wonders. Rudolph would show them off to visiting ambassadors, like a proud parent.'

'What was in them?' Ruby asked.

'Everything you could imagine,' Novak said. 'A unicorn horn, phoenix feathers, nails from Noah's ark. There were magic books and manuscripts—volumes that promised the secrets of the natural world, and the unnatural world for that matter.'

'Unicorn horns and phoenix feathers?' Ruby said with a snort. 'Sounds like he had every con man in Europe coming to visit.'

'Like the men who sold him the Voynich Manuscript,' Gerald said.

Novak pulled the pipe from his mouth and stared at

Gerald. 'You know of the manuscript?'

Gerald mumbled a 'yes'. The sudden change in the man's expression threw him.

Novak narrowed his eyes. 'There are some who believe the manuscript was not a hoax,' he said. 'That it contains real secrets to limitless wealth. And more. Rudolph's collection of animals and artefacts was impressive, but what really stood out was his collection of people.'

'People?' Sam said. 'How do you collect people?'

'The same way you collect dodos,' Novak said. 'With money. Rudolph surrounded himself with the best minds of the day. He had two hundred alchemists and their assistants working in his laboratories in the castle in Prague, all of them trying to locate the secret that would turn base metals into gold.'

'What about the universal remedy?' Ruby said. 'Were they trying to find that as well?'

Again, Novak narrowed his eyes. 'You know much on this topic.'

Ruby's cheeks flushed. 'I read travel guides,' she said.

Novak grunted. Gerald could see that Ruby had touched a sore point and he tried to change the subject. 'And your ship?' he said. 'How did it end up here?'

Novak cast a glance towards the golden galleon on the table. 'Rudolph was fond of anything mechanical. He was obsessed with controlling nature. Part of his collection of people was a man named Cornelius Drebbel.

It is said that he invented a perpetual motion machine.'

'What's that?' Felicity asked.

'A machine that once started would run forever. Rudolph had hundreds of clocks and automata—wind-up models and figurines. My galleon once graced the king's dining table. Rudolph would let it set sail to entertain his guests. Those must have been amazing gatherings in the castle. But nothing lasts forever. At the end of Rudolph's life there was a war with Sweden. His collection was looted by the invading troops. This hotel fed and housed some Swedish officers on their homeward journey. They paid their bill with the boat. My father found it packed in the attic years ago. After he passed on, I took over the job of restoring it.'

'You've done a brilliant job,' Sam said. 'It's amazing.'

Novak bowed his head. 'You are very kind.' The man stared into the flames that danced in the grate; the light played across his wrinkled face. He seemed lost in thought. Then he spoke again. 'Not all of Rudolph's collection survived,' he said. 'There was a girl. A girl not much older than you two.' He gave Ruby and Felicity a grave look. 'She was a singer, said to have the finest voice in Europe. Rudolph heard stories of her performances in Vienna and insisted she come to his court in Prague. But her father did not want his daughter to go.'

'What happened?' Sam said.

'You do not defy an emperor,' Novak said. 'The girl came to Prague. Her father was forced to bring her. When they arrived at the castle gates, the girl was admitted but the guards refused to let the father in. He was distraught, screaming to be allowed to go with his beloved daughter. She was dragged away. Some legends say the guards threw the father into the castle bear pit. Others say he stayed by the gates until he starved to death.'

'How horrible,' Felicity said.

'The girl was so upset by her father's death that she never sang again. Rudolph lost interest in her and she spent the rest of her life begging for scraps in the alleys of the castle.' The fire flickered as a draught swirled down the chimney, sending the shadows into a frenzy.

Novak looked deep into the flames. 'On the first full moon of each new year, the spirit of the father is said to rise from his grave to search once more for his daughter. He can take the form of a man or of a bear. When he can't find her, he steals the soul of the first female he sees.'

Ruby turned her head to the window.

'Is the full moon tonight?' she asked.

The man nodded.

'And that's what the garlic is for?' Ruby said. 'To keep the spirit away?'

Novak dropped his eyes. 'It is a silly superstition,' he said.

'*It is no such thing.*'

The man's wife stood in the kitchen doorway, a tray of food in her hands. She bustled into the room and set the platter onto the table. 'I don't see you putting the talisman aside,' she said to Novak. 'Look to the window. The moon is rising. Do you dare to take the garlic down?'

The man muttered into his beard.

The woman set out plates of stew and dumplings. 'Come,' she said, calling them all to the table. 'Eat. And be thankful that we are safe indoors on the night that Ursus roams.'

Ruby was pulling out a chair to sit at the table when she stopped. 'I'm sorry,' she said to the woman. 'What did you say the father's name was?'

The woman knocked three times on the wooden tabletop. 'His name was Ursus—the bear,' she said. 'His grave is in the *hrbitov*, the cemetery, beyond the hill.'

Chapter 27

Gerald checked the lock on the door and joined Ruby, Sam and Felicity on the rug in front of the fireplace. The evening meal had been consumed in near silence. Sam even waved away an inviting-looking apple strudel for dessert so they could retreat to their room as quickly as possible.

'They're not going to get the tourists flooding in here with stories like that,' Sam said. 'Ghost bears rising from the grave to abduct girls—happy new year.'

Felicity rolled out the brass rubbing she had made from the belltower at the castle. She ran a finger along the route they'd taken to get to Hadanka.

'Here's the graveyard, just like Stephanie said.' Felicity rubbed her hands along the goosebumps on her arms. 'I love a good ghost story.'

Gerald studied the map. 'I say we go there tonight,' he said.

Sam gave Gerald an incredulous stare. 'Are you insane? You heard what Novak said. There's a bear out there.'

'Sam,' Ruby said, 'surely you don't believe that silly story about a father searching for his lost daughter.'

'I don't know,' he said. 'Is it any more silly than a daughter searching for her lost father?'

'Our situation has nothing to do with some stupid old superstition.'

'A lot of those old superstitions are based on fact,' Sam said.

'Even the stupid ones?' Ruby asked.

'There's a lot of stupid facts out there,' Sam said. 'Like Tycho Brahe being dead for more than four hundred years. That's a good stupid fact. And now the guy who warned us about Brahe? Ursus. Well, it turns out he has been dead for four hundred years as well. I say we let the bear have his big night out and we check the graveyard in the morning.'

Gerald shook his head. 'I don't buy it,' he said. 'I don't believe in ghosts and I don't believe in bears stealing souls. What I do believe is that tonight is the perfect opportunity for Brahe to do whatever he wants without having to worry about anyone seeing him. If the whole of Hadanka is tucked up behind locked doors and strings of garlic, he's free to do whatever he wants away from prying eyes.'

'So you think Brahe's in town?' Felicity asked.

'I think we're about three steps behind him on whatever bizarre journey he's on. But Brahe holds the key to finding Alisha and Ox.'

'What about Ursus?' Sam asked.

Gerald pulled on his jacket and fished his gloves from the pockets. 'If you're lucky you can ask him yourself, tonight.'

The snow had finally stopped falling.

Light remnants of cloud dotted the heavens as Gerald, Felicity, Sam and Ruby trekked out of the village. As they left the last of the houses behind, a huge full moon poked above the line of hills ahead and an ethereal glow coloured the sky.

They wandered in silence. Past tennis courts closed for the season. Beyond a snowbound aero club, the runway a long strip of white. Past a junkyard, where a howl from the resident guard dog startled them.

'Are you sure this is the way?' Felicity asked Gerald as she re-wrapped her scarf around her neck.

Gerald trudged on, following the country lane. 'The sign back there said *Hrbitov*. I don't think we'd miss it.'

'Did you notice all the houses back in the village?'

Ruby said. 'There was a string of garlic hanging in every front window.'

'Superstitions can be stubborn,' Gerald said. He wrinkled his brow. 'What's that smell?' He turned a suspicious eye to Sam, then grabbed him by the front of the jacket.

'Hey!' Sam protested. 'What are you doing?'

Gerald managed to unzip Sam's fleece. He pulled open the jacket to reveal a large string of garlic around Sam's neck.

Ruby's glare would have cut glass. 'You must be joking,' she said.

Sam zipped up his jacket, his cheeks burning red. 'There was a spare one in Stephanie's shopping basket as we snuck out,' he said. 'It's not doing anyone any harm.'

'Unless they're downwind of you,' Gerald said, screwing up his nose.

Sam was unrepentant. 'Well, that's one thing we don't have to worry about with Brahe,' Sam said, as they trudged up the hillside.

'What's that?' Felicity said.

'He won't be able to smell us coming.'

They broached the top of the hill and stopped. The moon hung above the horizon, an enormous yellow disk in the sky. The lightly wooded hillside was carpeted with snow. At the bottom of the hill in the bowl of a valley, lit like a film-set beneath the full moon, nestled the grave-yard.

Ruby pointed, but she didn't need to. Everyone had already seen it. A path cut across the hill and led straight to the cemetery gates.

Gerald's stomach tightened. The words of Mason Green echoed in his ears: *I hold genuine fears for the safety of Alisha and Oswald.* Gerald had to find his friends. He couldn't shake the gnawing feeling it was his fault that they were in danger.

He raised a finger to his lips. Sound would travel for miles on a night like this. He gave a quick thumbs up and started the downhill journey through the snow.

The four friends cut a swathe across the hillside until they reached the path to the cemetery. Gerald knew that anyone in the graveyard would be able to see the trail they had left. It stood out like a scar. He hoped that whoever was in the cemetery was too busy to be looking their way—or too dead.

The gates stood ajar, as if unsure whether their task was to keep intruders out, or occupants in. Gerald shivered as he walked beneath the gothic arch that spanned the entrance. Ruby, Felicity and Sam were close behind.

Good.

Gerald needed friends on a night like this.

Inside the gate the path forked, encircling a forest of gravestones. To the right, the snow was a pristine carpet; to the left, the path was clearly marked with two sets of bootprints.

Gerald's breath caught in his throat. Who were they about to find?

Brahe or Ursus?

Man or ghost?

Gerald knew they couldn't follow the path—they'd be too exposed. He turned to his friends and pointed straight ahead. They'd have to sneak through the labyrinth of gravestones. At any other time, the look on Sam's face would have had Gerald in fits of laughter. But not this night.

Gerald stepped from the path and between two gravestones.

A layer of mist hung low over the ground. It parted like a curtain and welcomed the four souls as they stepped inside.

The ground was pitched and rutted in corrugations where graves had collapsed under the combined weight of time, earth and sorrow. Headstones lay toppled and tiered like rows of giant teeth. Snow had settled along the tops of the blocks of granite that remained upright, like icing on Death's birthday cake.

Gerald moved gingerly between the stones, desperate to make no noise to alert the living, or disturb the dead. He soon lost sight of the paths. The mist closed in. A frozen forest of shadow and death surrounded them.

Chink-chink-chink.

The sound was like a metronome—a steady pulse in a place where pulses were not meant to be. Gerald held up his hand. He ducked a glance over his shoulder. Ruby, Felicity and Sam stood like marble memorials. Gerald pointed to a line of gravestones a few metres ahead. He crouched and crept to them, crawling into the shroud of mist. When Ruby, Felicity and Sam had joined him Gerald dared to ease an eye around the corner...

Two men stood in the moonlight.

One, wearing a large black coat, was perched on the side of an open grave. The other had shed his jacket, and stood in his shirtsleeves waist-deep in the ground, hacking at the frozen earth with a shovel.

Chink-chink-chink.

Gerald stared open-mouthed. The man in the coat turned his head a fraction—just enough for the moonlight to glint off his silver nose.

'This is hopeless,' the man with the shovel said. It was Pugly. His words came in pants of exhaustion. 'This ground isn't giving up any secrets.'

Brahe glared down at him. 'Dig,' he commanded.

Then Brahe swivelled his head towards Gerald, as if he had heard something.

Gerald froze, half his head still poking out from behind the gravestone. A collar of mist gathered at his neck.

'What was—' Brahe began.

Then the shovel blade hit wood.

It was a clear, hollow sound. Like a knock on a door. A door that was never meant to be opened.

'This is it!' Pugly doubled his efforts with the shovel, clearing the soil from what must have been an ancient coffin.

Brahe peered down from the edge of the hole. When the last of the dirt was removed he extended a hand and hauled Pugly out. The smaller man landed on his backside in a pile of freshly dug soil.

'Wait there,' Brahe said.

Then he jumped into the grave.

His heavy boots crashed through the coffin lid, splintering it into shards. The impact catapulted a skeleton upright, as if it had been shaken awake by the shock arrival. The skull bobbled on the top of the spine, silently protesting the intrusion.

Pugly smothered a cry. His right hand clutched at the cross that hung around his neck.

Brahe ignored his companion and batted the skull to one side. It landed at the smaller man's feet, its sightless eyes staring at him accusingly.

Brahe plunged both fists into the coffin and fished around among the ribs and vertebrae. Then his hand closed on an object. He pulled it up to his face and nodded before shoving it deep inside his overcoat.

'Here, give me a hand up.'

Pugly struggled to help him out of the hole. Brahe dusted himself down and tossed the shovel to his companion. 'Fill it in,' he said.

As the smaller man set to work, Brahe dug into his

pocket and retrieved the item he'd taken from the grave. He held it to the moonlight. Gerald caught a glint of metal.

Then, from behind him, a pile of snow tumbled from a branch and hit the ground.

Whether it was the movement or the sound, Brahe looked up. His face was as dark as murder. He pushed the stolen item into the folds of his coat, and in the same movement pulled out a handgun.

Gerald whipped his head back and pressed himself into the gravestone. He shot a warning look to Ruby, and mimed a gun with his hand. Ruby's eyes popped.

Then there were boots scuffling through snow and the heavy breathing of a man on edge.

Gerald tilted his head to look to the black sky. The business end of the barrel of a gun appeared over the edge of the gravestone just centimetres away, moving like a ship into port.

Brahe was right above them.

Gerald held his breath, biting the inside of his cheek.

Then the bulbous end of a large metal nose hovered above. Gerald stared up into two carefully moulded silver nostrils. To his astonishment, he saw that the silversmith had etched in individual nose hairs. The whiskers on Brahe's chin bristled. If Brahe should glance down, it would all be over.

Then Gerald understood. The silver nose was blocking Brahe's sight. The reflection from the moonlight was shining up into his eyes, obscuring his downward vision. All Gerald had to do was keep perfectly still, and wait...

After a long moment, Brahe retreated. Gerald allowed himself a slow, silent intake of air. He glanced across to Ruby. Her eyes were still wide.

'It's done.' The sound of a spade patting down earth floated to them. Brahe's voice cut the night air. 'Come. We have work to do.'

Gerald tensed. If the two men came back their way, there was nowhere to hide. But the sound of boots crunching through snow receded as Brahe and Pugly made their way out to the path. Within a minute, the graveyard had returned to silence.

Gerald placed a finger to his lips and indicated for Ruby, Sam and Felicity to stay put. He poked his head around the side of the gravestone. Then he stole out into the night.

It took Ruby just five seconds to break cover and follow him. Sam and Felicity were only a second behind.

Snow had started falling again, already covering Pugly's handiwork. Gerald stood before the dirt mounded on top of the freshly covered grave.

'Will you look at that,' Sam said. He pointed to the headstone on the neighbouring grave. Carved into a slab of ancient granite was *Ursus*.

'I guess he didn't go looking for his daughter this year,' Felicity said.

Sam unzipped his jacket and gave the string of garlic

a jiggle, releasing a fog of fumes. 'Maybe he's still hiber-
nating,' he said.

The headstone on the desecrated gravesite tilted
sharply backwards. Gerald leaned across the pile of earth
and wiped away a layer of snow. What he revealed made
them all shudder.

A single name, carved centuries before.
BRAHE.

Chapter 28

'How many graves does one man need?' Sam said. 'And still be walking around? I mean, how dead do you have to be to need two graves?'

'Not dead enough to stop you digging them up, apparently,' Ruby said. She aimed a kick at the mound of dirt.

Gerald cleared more snow from the bottom of the headstone. 'Look, it's got a date on it,' he said. '1627. But didn't Brahe die before that?'

'I think the information at the castle said around 1601,' Felicity said. 'So this is a different Brahe?'

'Whoever it is, or was, our Brahe stole something from his grave,' Gerald said. 'Something small and made of metal.'

'Spare nose?' Sam said.

Ruby clipped her brother over the ear. 'Enough with the nose jokes,' she said.

Sam rubbed the side of his head. 'Well if we're going to find out what it was, we better get after Brahe and his buddy before we lose them.'

They headed straight to the path, and saw fresh footprints leading back towards the gates.

'Hey Gerald?' Sam said, boots crunching on ice.

'Yeah?'

'Won't Brahe see the trail we left in the snow getting down here.'

The path curved. The arched entry was just ahead.

Gerald considered the question for a second. 'If he looked that way, I guess he would,' Gerald said.

'Well, don't you think that's a bit risky?' Sam said.

'What do you mean?'

'He's not stupid. He's sure to notice a trail that wasn't there when he came over the hill.'

Gerald walked on. 'He was in a hurry to get going. Brahe and his precious time. I don't think he'll see it.' They reached the gates and Gerald looked up the rise. 'See?' he said, turning to Sam, 'The snow is already covering—'

Gerald stopped at the sight of Brahe holding a gun to Sam's left temple.

The four-wheel drive sped along a country lane. In the locked rear compartment, Gerald bounced into the air and landed on top of Sam, jolting an elbow into his ribs.

'Ow!' Sam cried.

Gerald wrestled himself upright. Brahe was driving like a man running late for his wedding. There were no seat belts and the four of them were being tumbled about like socks in a drier.

The countryside zipped past the window in a blur. There were no buildings, no signs of life. Just open fields and snow. When they pulled up next to a decrepit wooden barn, Gerald feared the worst.

The rear door of the four-wheel drive opened and Pugly grabbed Felicity and Ruby and dragged them out. Gerald threw himself outside. 'Let go!' he shouted, diving towards the little man. But Brahe was too fast. He took Gerald by the arm and swung him around. Then slapped him hard across the face.

Gerald held a hand to his cheek and lowered his head like a whipped dog.

'Enough of the heroics,' Brahe said in a rumbling growl. 'Inside.'

A hurricane lamp cast the interior of the barn in a yellow haze.

Brahe shoved Gerald hard in the back, sending him sprawling into a stack of hay bales. Gerald rolled to his side and spat a ball of blood-streaked saliva onto the floor. Felicity rushed to his side and helped him onto a bale of hay. Ruby and Sam joined them: a row of disconsolate figures, heads bowed.

Brahe crossed to a makeshift table—a plank of wood resting between two fuel drums. Pugly stood to his side, training a handgun on Gerald. Brahe motioned for the short man to join him. 'Hold this down,' he said, indicating a sheet of paper.

Pugly kept the gun on Gerald. 'There's a forecast for shut-out conditions around Landskrona,' he said to Brahe. 'The island may be cut off.'

Brahe grunted, absorbed in his work. 'I need to check the translation.'

After a moment, Brahe stood back, rubbing his eyes. 'This is taking too long,' he said.

As Brahe stepped clear, Gerald could see what he had been working on. A large bundle of paper was spread across the tabletop. Mason Green's crystal pendant lay on the top sheet. Gerald squinted. The paper looked familiar.

'Is that the Voynich Manuscript?' Gerald said.

The effect of the question on Brahe was instantaneous and monumental. The man swung around and advanced on Gerald. He took him by the collar and hauled him to his feet. 'What did you say?'

Gerald jutted out his chin. 'You're looking for the universal remedy, aren't you?'

Brahe glowered at him. But said nothing.

'And you're using the crystal to decipher the Voynich

Manuscript to find out how to make it.'

Again, no response.

'You've got everything you need,' Gerald said. 'Why are you keeping Ox and Alisha?'

Brahe threw Gerald back to the hay bale. 'I don't need to explain myself to you,' Brahe said. 'You could never understand the science.'

'Science!' Ruby said. 'You call digging up graves and robbing the dead, science?'

Brahe tilted his head towards her. 'What do you think archeologists do for a living? Half the economy of the undeveloped world is based on organised grave robbery.'

'But mummies in pyramids have been dead for thousands of years,' Ruby said.

'And that makes them more dead than other corpses, does it? It's okay to dig up Tutankhamun but not all right to dig up your Aunt Tammy. Or even Tycho Brahe?'

Sam gasped, his eyes widening. 'So that was your grave. You...you are a...'

Brahe managed a self-satisfied smile. 'What's the matter, Mr Valentine? You look like you've seen a ghost.'

Sam's mouth hung open.

'I took what was rightfully mine,' Brahe said. He fished a small metal container from his coat pocket. 'The last piece in my jigsaw.'

'What is it?' Ruby asked, curious despite herself.

Brahe eyed her with interest. 'It's a key, Miss

Valentine. A key to a code that has not been broken for half a millennium.' He lunged forward and grabbed Ruby by the sleeve. 'Come. You seem a clever girl. You can help me.'

'Hey!' Ruby protested.

Sam jumped to his feet and unzipped his jacket. He tore the string of garlic from his neck and flung it to his sister.

'Ruby!' he called. 'Use this!'

Ruby caught the garlic in one hand and brandished it before her.

Brahe's face blanched at the sight of the pungent talisman—then he snatched the string of bulbs from Ruby and hung it from the tip of his silver nose.

'What do you think?' he said to Ruby as the garlic jiggled about in front of him. 'As a fashion statement, I mean. A little over the top?'

Brahe laughed like it was the funniest thing he had ever seen. 'Your brother isn't the sharpest tool in the box, is he? I hope you are more enlightened.'

He tossed the garlic aside and marched Ruby to the table and handed her a pen and notepad. 'Write this down as I read it out.'

Brahe placed the crystal pendant on a page from the manuscript. Seen through the prism, the symbols morphed into entirely different shapes. He consulted a separate sheet of paper, creased a dozen times.

'Is that from the grave you dug up?' Ruby asked.

'It was buried a long time ago,' Brahe said. 'For safekeeping.'

'And you're matching the symbol from the crystal with the letters on that paper.'

Brahe glanced at Ruby from the corner of his eye. 'You are quite the cryptographer, aren't you Miss Valentine.'

He dictated a string of letters for Ruby to write down. Pugly looked on anxiously. 'Hurry,' he said. 'The weather.'

Brahe did not look up. 'We will make it to Ven,' he snapped. 'Don't interrupt.'

Brahe ran the crystal across the manuscript, deciphering the ancient script as he went. 'c...o...r... a...p...u...e...l...l...a.' Ruby wrote down the last of the letters.

Felicity straightened next to Gerald. '*Cor a puella*?' she said.

'What is it?' Gerald asked. He didn't like the look of horror that appeared on Felicity's face.

Brahe took the notepad and scanned it quickly. 'I was right,' he said. 'This confirms it.' He cast a considered glance at Ruby. 'Thank you for your help, Miss Valentine. I think there may be one more contribution you can make to my work.'

He went to take Ruby by the arm, but she ducked clear. In an instant she had grabbed the hurricane lamp. A mighty kick from her boot sent the makeshift table flying. Pages of parchment scattered into the air.

'No,' Brahe cried. 'The manuscript!' He dived at the flying pages, trying to gather them in.

Ruby lashed out again with her boot, this time smashing one of the drums onto its side. Fuel gushed onto a stack of hay bales.

Gerald, Felicity and Sam were on their feet. Pugly aimed his gun from one person to the next, unsure what to do.

Ruby held the hurricane lamp high above her head. Brahe made a move towards her, but she brandished the lamp like a weapon. 'Stop!' she cried. 'Or I'll light this place up.'

Brahe froze, clutching manuscript pages to his chest. He slowly extended a hand. 'Give me the lamp, Miss Valentine,' he said. His eyes were focused on the yellow flame that danced inside the glass cage. 'You know you can't escape.'

Ruby squared her jaw and swallowed tightly. 'Maybe not,' she said, her voice cracking. 'But they can.' She turned her head towards Gerald, her eyes saying what words could not.

Then she smashed the lamp into the fuel-soaked hay. And the barn exploded in flames.

Chapter 29

A sheet of fire split the barn in two: Gerald, Sam and Felicity on one side; Ruby, Brahe and Pugly on the other.

Intense heat.

A pall of blinding smoke.

Total confusion.

Gerald felt himself stumbling across the ground. Felicity had him by the hand, dragging him through a door into the cold night and flinging him into a snow bank. 'Don't move,' she ordered. Without waiting for a response, she turned and ran back into the inferno.

Gerald raised himself onto his elbows and was about to go after her when she reappeared. She had an arm around Sam's shoulders and was helping him stagger out of the barn.

Smoke rolled out of the upper windows. Flames licked at the rafters.

Sam coughed, and spat into the snow. 'We've got to go back for Ruby,' he said. His voice was a rasp. He was barely able to breathe. He lunged forward.

Felicity still had her arm around him, holding him back. 'No!' she cried. 'The flames are too high.'

Sam dropped to his knees. He gazed up at the burning building. His face glowed in the light from the fire. 'No,' he whispered, stricken.

'They would have got out,' Felicity said. Her voice trailed off. 'I'm sure of it.'

Gerald lay propped in the snow. He stared at the flames. A lump lodged in his throat, about the same size as the hole that had just been ripped out of his heart.

Ruby.

Ruby.

What have you done?

Gerald struggled to his feet, and took Felicity's hand. 'The other side,' he said.

She looked at him in alarm. 'What?'

'The other side of the barn,' he said. 'If they got out, that's where they'll be.'

Gerald stumbled through the snow, his mind fixed on the sole prospect of finding Ruby alive on the far side of the building.

They reached the corner of the barn and Gerald heard something above the roar of the fire. He skidded to a stop and pulled Felicity back just as a four-wheel drive vehicle burst from behind the building, missing them by centimetres.

Gerald stared after the speeding tail lights.

'Was that them?' he said. 'Did you see her?'

Sam slid into Gerald's back. 'There were two people in the front. I think there was someone in the back seat. It must be Ruby.' Sam sounded like he had been reborn.

'Are you sure?' Gerald said.

'No,' Sam said. 'But who else could it be?'

Of course it had to be them. And it had to be Ruby. It *had* to be.

The tail lights disappeared around a bend in the distance. Gerald looked down at the tyre tracks in the snow, fresh and sharp. He looked at Sam and Felicity, then started jogging down the path. Sam and Felicity fell in behind.

The going was hard. The cold air cut at Gerald's throat and razored at his lungs. But they kept on. After about a kilometre, Gerald realised they were heading back towards Hadanka. He started recognising landmarks. As they neared the junkyard on the outskirts of the village, he had a sudden thought.

The aero club.

Brahe was going to fly out of there.

The tyre tracks turned off the road. Up ahead, Gerald

could see the aero club hangar. The four-wheel drive was parked next to it. Gerald breathed deep and urged his legs on. He had no grand plan, no masterful scheme to mount a rescue.

He just wanted to see if Ruby was there.

If Ruby was alive.

Gerald ran straight up to the four-wheel drive. He grabbed a door handle and pulled it open.

The vehicle was empty.

There was no sign whether Ruby had been there or not.

Sam and Felicity ran up to him, breathing hard. Gerald cast a despairing look to them. Before he could speak the night air was rent by the sound of an engine—an engine far more powerful than that in a four-wheel drive.

An aeroplane emerged from the front of the hangar, twin propellers spinning fast, skis sliding towards the airstrip.

Gerald ran after it, slogging through the snow. He could see Brahe in the pilot's seat on the left, and Pugly sitting beside him.

In the back, with her face pressed to the window and staring right at him, was Ruby.

Gerald trundled to a stop. He stared after the plane as it neared the end of the runway and turned.

Brahe fired the engines. The propellers roared. The plane rolled forward and sped along the airstrip. As it drew level with Gerald it left the ground and soared into the night sky. When Felicity and Sam reached Gerald, he was looking into the heavens as if searching for shooting stars.

'She's alive,' he said, still gazing skywards. 'Ruby's alive.'

Gerald had the strange sensation that he was about to drown on dry land. It was like he'd forgotten how to breathe. Then his chest filled with air, like an over-inflated balloon.

Ruby was alive.

Then he started to cry.

The more he tried to stop, the more his lungs filled with air, the more his shoulders heaved, the more tears ran down his face.

Ruby was alive.

Gerald felt Sam's arm across his shoulders and Felicity's hand taking his. His vision blurred, the tears were a curtain.

'I'm okay,' he said, sounding anything but.

'It's all right,' Felicity said into his ear. 'It's all right to cry.'

Gerald took a deep breath, trying to staunch the sobs. Why was he doing this? Ruby was alive. It was all okay. But it could easily have been so very different.

Gerald's eyes slowly cleared. But the hole in his heart stood gaping. He would do anything to see his friend again.

'Gerald,' Felicity said. Her voice was soft, comforting. 'We have to call someone. The police.'

Gerald sniffed. Blinked his eyes. Wiped his tears. 'Of course,' he said. 'Of course we have to call the police.'

'There's more to it, Gerald,' Sam said. 'Tell him, Felicity.'

Felicity cupped Gerald's chin in her gloved hand. 'When Brahe was decoding the manuscript back in the barn, and Ruby was writing it down—'

'Yeah,' Gerald said. 'What about it?'

'I think he was reading out the ingredients for the universal remedy.'

'But it was just a bunch of random letters,' Gerald said. 'None of it made sense.'

'I'm fairly sure it was Latin,' Felicity said, shooting a concerned look at Sam. 'They make us study Latin at St Hilda's—I think I recognised some of it.'

'So?' Gerald said. 'What's the big deal about ingredients?'

'One of them was *cor a puella*. I think that means—' Felicity took a deep breath. 'It means, the heart of a girl.'

Gerald looked at Felicity as if she was insane.

'The heart of a girl,' Felicity said. 'And then Brahe said something about Ruby making a contribution to his work. Gerald, I think Brahe's going to use Ruby as part of his potion.'

Chapter 30

Gerald led the dash to the aero club hangar.

'There must be a phone in here,' he said, skidding through the open door. He looked around in a panic. The inside was lost in shadow.

'No sign of anything over here,' Felicity called from the far side of the building.

Sam raced up to Gerald and grabbed him by the shoulder. 'What about that?' He pointed to a single-engine aeroplane at the rear of the hangar. 'Would it have a radio or something?'

Gerald stared at the little Cessna. Compared with the majesty of the Archer corporate jet, it looked like a toy—a wind-up toy, with a rubber band for power.

But to Gerald, it was a lifeline.

He ran to the plane. 'Come on,' he shouted back to Sam and Felicity. He ducked past the propeller and under the wing. He pulled open the door, clambered up into the pilot's seat and started flicking switches.

Sam appeared in the doorway. 'You know how to work the radio on this?'

Gerald pulled a set of headphones over his ears and adjusted the microphone in front of his mouth. 'This isn't like the chopper back in California,' he said. 'Not only can I work the radio,' he broke into a manic grin, 'but I reckon I can fly it too.'

Sam gaped at him. 'You what?'

Gerald pressed a button on the steering control. 'This is Oscar Kilo Echo India November, from Hadanka aero club. I need to report a kidnapping. A twin-engine aircraft has just left Hadanka airstrip with two men on board, destination unknown. They have kidnapped a girl: Ruby Valentine. Thirteen years old. Blonde. Please alert the Czech police immediately.'

Gerald released the button and waited. Sam went to speak but Gerald held up a hand as he listened to a voice over the headphones. 'Affirmative,' Gerald replied into the microphone. Then a pause. 'Uh, who am I?' He gave Sam and Felicity a panicked look. 'An interested bystander. Out.'

Gerald tore off the headphones and climbed out of the plane, pushing past Sam and Felicity. 'They're calling the police,' he said.

'Who is?' Felicity asked.

'I think it was the control tower at Prague Airport.' Gerald pulled a chock from a wheel under the left wing and ducked across to the other side.

'They spoke English?' Sam said.

'International language of flying,' Gerald said. 'They could see Brahe on the radar. He's heading north.' He tugged on the other chock and sent it skating across the floor. 'Take a side.' Gerald grabbed a strut under one wing; Sam and Felicity did the same on the opposite side. They pushed the plane towards the hangar doors.

'How did you know all that radio stuff?' Sam asked. 'You sounded like the real deal.'

Gerald nodded to the side of the plane, on which was painted in large black letters, OK-EIN. 'That's the plane's call sign. Its tail number. You spell it out with the phonetic alphabet.'

The Cessna juddered out of the hangar and onto the apron, and rolled to a stop.

'This is a Cessna 185. It's a classic tail dragger,' Gerald said. 'This is exactly what we've been learning to fly in aero club at school.'

Sam stared at him in wonder. 'I keep forgetting you go to Gazillionaire Grammar. You can really fly this?'

Gerald shifted the pilot's seat forward so Sam could get in the back. Sam hesitated.

Gerald gave him a reassuring pat on the shoulder. 'I'm certain I can.'

Sam narrowed his eyes, then climbed into the back of the plane. Felicity hopped into the co-pilot's seat. Gerald settled in the pilot's seat and studied the array of switches and dials and gauges and indicators. 'Almost certain of it.'

He toggled a knob.

The windshield wipers turned on.

Sam watched as the blades tracked back and forth. 'Almost certain, huh?'

Gerald bit his lip and switched off the wipers. 'Good,' he said. 'Windscreen's clean. Now, we can get underway. Where's the checklist?'

Felicity handed him a clipboard from a pocket in her door. 'Is this it?'

'Thanks,' Gerald said, and started checking off items from the list. 'We've got plenty of fuel. Batteries are charged. It's all good.'

'Yeah, great,' Sam said, without enthusiasm. 'Where exactly are we going?'

'After Brahe,' Gerald said. 'We can't just rely on the police tracking him on radar.'

'But we don't know where he's going, apart from north.'

'Do you remember Pugly, back in the barn?' Gerald said. 'How he was saying something about the weather closing in?'

'That's right,' Felicity said. 'At some odd-sounding place. Scandinavian, maybe. What was it? Lansdrone?'

Gerald tapped at a small screen in the centre panel. 'Landskrona,' he said. 'In southern Sweden.'

'How do you know that?' Sam asked.

'Global Positioning System,' Gerald said. 'Satellite navigation will get us there.' A tiny map of central Europe glowed on the screen. He entered the destination into its menu. 'Are we ready?'

Sam closed his eyes. 'Do we have an option?'

Gerald pulled his seat belt over his shoulders and fastened the clasp. 'Not really.'

He turned the key and the engine sputtered into life. The propeller sliced the air. The little plane shunted forward on its skis and turned towards the airstrip. Gerald radioed the control tower to tell them Brahe could be heading to Sweden. He manoeuvred the Cessna to head straight down the runway.

'Gerald?' Sam said from the back seat.

Gerald made final adjustments to the instruments. 'Yep?'

'How many times have you flown without an instructor in the plane?'

Gerald gripped the control column and took a deep breath. 'Let's see. Including this flight,' he said, gunning the engine, 'once.'

Sam's head flopped back. 'I was afraid you were going to say that.'

They headed off, sliding across the hard-packed snow. The plane accelerated in a juddering howl.

The tail lifted.

Gerald pulled back on the control column.

The nose lifted.

The rattling stopped.

They were airborne.

Gerald tried to ignore Sam's heavy breathing to set his coordinates for Landskrona. They climbed steadily and after a few minutes Gerald flicked a button. He turned to face Sam, resting his arms on the back of his seat.

'Hands!' Sam yelled, his eyes popping. 'On the steering wheel!'

Gerald grinned. 'Autopilot,' he said. 'I shouldn't have to do much till we get closer to Sweden, in about seven hundred miles.'

Sam gripped his armrest with white-knuckled intensity. 'I think I prefer the Archer jet.'

The engine droned as the little plane sliced its way through the night. The full moon had reached its peak and the landscape below was painted ghost white. Soon, the thrill of the chase subsided and the ache returned to Gerald's chest.

Ruby had sacrificed her safety to let them escape. She must have known that the fire in the barn would trap her with Brahe. And if Felicity was right—if she had translated the Latin correctly—Ruby was in real danger.

The heart of a girl? What sort of witch's brew was Brahe planning?

Gerald turned to look at Felicity. She was asleep, her head slumped forward onto her chest. Felicity obviously liked him—a lot. And Gerald liked her. But a gnawing doubt chewed in his gut. Gerald had never felt the sensations he'd experienced when he thought Ruby had perished in the fire. A total sense of loss. An emptiness that felt like he could never be made whole again.

Gerald suddenly felt so tired. He rubbed the heels of his hands into his eyes, setting off sparks that spun and coalesced into the shape of Ruby's face. He kept his eyelids closed, trying to preserve the image forever.

Gerald must have dozed off. He was jolted awake by Sam's voice cutting through the drone of the engine.

'What does "Terrain Ahead" mean?'

Gerald sat upright, disorientated. 'Huh? What did you say?'

'On the GPS screen there,' Sam said, pointing. 'The words "Terrain Ahead" are flashing.'

Gerald spun his head around to stare at the screen, his eyes bulging. 'How long has that been there?'

'A couple of minutes,' Sam said. 'I would have told you sooner but you looked so peaceful, I didn't want to disturb you.'

Gerald grabbed hold of the control column and flicked some buttons on the panel.

'Hold on everybody!' he called.

Felicity stirred and looked up, droopy-eyed. 'What is it?'

Gerald worked the trim wheel by his right leg, furiously turning it. 'I think we're about to fly into a hill.'

Sam's grip tore two chunks of foam clean off the armrests.

Chapter 31

The words were flashing on the screen. *Terrain Ahead. Terrain Ahead.*

Gerald hauled back on the control column.

'What are you doing?' Sam asked from the back seat. His eyes were fixed on the window and the night outside.

'Trying not to crash,' Gerald said through gritted teeth.

'Anything I can do to help?'

'Shutting up would be good.'

'Right you are.'

An alarm sounded, beeping in time to the flashing message. Lights blinked red on the navigation display. Through the windscreen Gerald could see the brow of a hill, fast rising in front of them. They were flying straight towards the trees along the top of the ridge.

'Oh, crud,' Gerald muttered.

He pushed the throttle to its limit and hauled back as hard as he could on the control column. The engine strained. The nose pulled up.

Gerald's hand reached for the radio button. He was ready to call in a mayday. The plane jostled in the turbulent air crossing the ridge, tossing the three occupants about in their seats. A sudden whooshing noise came from the tail.

Then the alarm fell silent. The flashing message disappeared from the screen. The cockpit returned to normal. And Gerald started breathing again.

There was a long pause. 'Are we okay?' Sam asked.

Gerald swallowed. 'Yeah. But we might need to clean some pinecones from the tailskid. I think we almost landed in a tree.'

Sam leaned back into his seat. Pieces of yellow foam littered his lap. His armrests were stripped bare.

Felicity gave Gerald a nervous glance. 'Good work, Gerald,' she said. 'I think.'

Gerald tapped on the GPS screen and looked at his watch. 'Not far to go. We should be able to see something soon.'

'Why is it suddenly so dark down there?' Felicity said. 'Where have all the lights gone?'

'We're flying over the Baltic Sea,' Gerald said. 'Copenhagen will be coming up on the left, see?' He pointed to the little digital map. 'And Landskrona is on the other side of this body of water.' His finger paused over a tiny dot in the middle of the Oresund Sound.

'What is it?' Felicity said.

'This island,' Gerald said. His eyes strained to make out the tiny lettering next to it. 'Can you read that?'

Felicity leaned across to get a better view. 'Is it... Ven?'

'Ven?' Sam said. 'Why does that sound familiar?'

'Isn't that the other place that Brahe mentioned back in the barn?' Felicity said. 'Something about not being able to land there because of the weather.'

'You're right,' Gerald said. 'That must be where they're heading. Jasper Mantle said something about Brahe having an observatory on an island in Sweden.' He adjusted some dials. 'That's our new destination.'

Sam leaned over Gerald's shoulder to look at the map, then out the window into the darkness beneath them. 'It looks very small,' he said. 'What if we can't find it?'

Gerald chewed on the inside of his cheek. 'Then we'll get as close as we can.'

Sam collapsed back into his seat and closed his eyes.

Ahead, the inky blanket beneath them gave way to a ribbon of lights as the Swedish coastline came into view. Gerald teased the plane a little to the left. He was desperate to know if the local police had been able to track Brahe on radar. But he didn't want to use the radio again in case Brahe was listening.

Wind buffeted the plane, tossing the little craft around in the sky. Gerald tried to concentrate but Sam's moaning was distracting.

Then, after another sudden gust, Gerald saw a tiny speck in the expanse of water.

The island of Ven.

He could just make out a few pinpricks of light in the darkness. The island was about four kilometres long and two kilometres wide—far smaller than Gerald's country estate near Glastonbury.

Gerald put the Cessna into a long arcing turn. 'Now comes the fun part,' he said.

'What's that?' Felicity asked.

'Landing,' Gerald said. 'And Sam, can you stop moaning? It's very off-putting.'

A meek 'sorry' floated across from the back seat.

'We'll only get one go at this,' Gerald said. 'There's a fog bank rolling in from the north and I don't fancy putting this thing down in the dark and in a fog.'

The island grew larger. They could make out scattered farmhouses, boats moored in a small harbour and the outline of paddocks framed by windbreaks of tall trees. What they could not see was an airstrip.

'Gerald?' Sam said.

'Yes, Sam.'

'Where are we going to land?'

'On the ground.'

'Okay.'

Gerald banked the aircraft, giving them a grandstand view of the island.

'How about there?' Felicity said, pointing. 'That paddock looks pretty long and flat.'

Gerald sized up the strip of land and gave a curt nod. Whatever usually grew there in the spring seemed to be buried under a lot of snow. 'It'll do,' Gerald said. 'And just as well.'

Sam raised his head from the back seat. 'Why just as well?'

'We're almost out of fuel.'

Sam slithered back into his hole. 'I've got to stop asking questions.'

Wind buffeted the little Cessna as it made its approach. Gerald tightened his seatbelt and worked the wheel by his leg, trying to keep the plane in trim. Lower and lower it came. Its skis barely cleared the windbreak at one end of the paddock.

Five metres above ground.

Three metres.

The plane smacked down with a bump. Gerald cut the throttle and hauled the control column back to his stomach. He held on as they skidded to the left. A ski dug into a snow bank, throwing the tail violently around.

Inside the plane it was like the world had flown off its axis. The view through the window was a cartwheel of white, then black, then white and black again. There was a sharp wrenching of metal. Sam looked over his shoulder to see the tail section sheer away just behind his seat. The paddock wheeled around in an eye-popping panorama as what was left of the Cessna came to a stop. Gerald ripped his seat belt off and did the same for Felicity. He tried his door but it was jammed.

Sam crawled over the back of his seat and fell straight onto the snow. 'Out this way!' he yelled. Felicity clambered into the back, with Gerald close behind. They got clear just as the first flame appeared from the engine cowl. A second later, the plane erupted in a fireball.

They watched the flames light the sky, their faces washed in orange and yellow. Gerald let out a loud breath. 'Well, that was a good landing,' he said.

Sam dropped his mouth open. 'How is that?' he asked.

Gerald put a hand on his friend's shoulder and started towards the end of the paddock, leaving the burning wreckage behind them. 'We're walking, aren't we?'

They reached a line of trees and climbed a stile into the next paddock. Gerald stopped short. 'Will you look at that,' he said.

On the far side of the field, shielded beneath the lower branches of a cluster of pine trees, was a squat building. Two large sliding doors stood apart. Just visible through the opening was the nose of a twin-engined aeroplane.

'Is that Brahe's plane?' Felicity asked.

'What else could it be?' Sam said.

'It has to be,' Gerald said. 'These paddocks are the only place on the island that you could land a plane. I bet under all this snow there's an airstrip.'

'What do we do now?' Felicity asked.

It was seventy metres of open terrain between them and the hangar. Gerald weighed up the options. 'Let's keep to the tree line and go the long way around,' he said.

'You don't think a fiery crash landing in the neighbouring paddock might have tipped Brahe that he's got company?' Sam said.

Gerald set off, grim-faced. 'My guess is he's concentrating on other things.'

Chapter 32

The hangar stood dark as a tomb and twice as quiet, as Gerald, Felicity and Sam approached from the cover of a line of pine trees.

Gerald scuttled low across to the near wall, dropping to his haunches in the snow. Sam and Felicity followed. The moon cast a glow across the night as they edged silently towards the hangar doors. Gerald paused for a moment, held a breath, and inched his eye around the opening.

The twin-engined plane that had taken Ruby from him in Hadanka stood inside. There was a workbench and a large toolbox against one wall. Mismatched office chairs and a desk stood opposite. There was nobody about.

They crept inside. Felicity scooped something up from the floor near the plane. 'Ruby's scarf,' she said, holding it up to Gerald. 'We're on the right path.' She folded it into her jacket pocket.

'Well, Brahe and Pugly aren't here now,' Gerald said. 'They must have taken her somewhere else.'

'There are tyre tracks in the snow out here,' Sam said from the doorway. 'They should be easy to follow. Brahe can't be far away on an island this size.'

Gerald crossed to the toolbox and opened the metal cover. He pulled out three large wrenches and handed one each to Sam and Felicity. 'We may as well have some weapons,' he said.

Felicity tested the weight of the wrench in the palm of her hand. 'Do you really think Brahe would use a human heart?' She shivered. 'It just seems so desperate.'

Gerald zipped his jacket to his chin. 'In the last few months, one thing I've learned is that desperate people do desperate things.'

The tyre tracks led onto a narrow road. Gerald, Felicity and Sam followed them, the setting moon lighting their way.

They passed endless fields and the occasional farmhouse. Apart from the whinny of some horses in a lone stable, all was silent. The island of Ven was tucked up for the long winter's night.

After about a kilometre, the tyre tracks turned up a rough lane. On the right, well back from the laneway, was a farmhouse.

Gerald pulled Felicity and Sam into the shelter of a tall hedge that ran the length of the lane. 'Did you see that?' he said. 'There's smoke coming from the chimney. Someone's awake.'

'Brahe?' Felicity said.

'There's only one way to find out.'

Gerald went to push through the hedge but came up against a chain wire fence hidden amongst the foliage.

'I'm going to have to climb over,' he said. He wedged his feet into the links in the fence and struggled through a tangle of branches. Twigs scratched at his face and stabbed into his ears as Gerald forced his way up. He reached out to grab at another link then whipped his hand back in sudden pain. A surgical cut ran the length of his forefinger. Gerald stared as a ribbon of blood appeared through the wound.

He thrust the finger into his mouth and half-climbed, half-fell back to the ground.

'Razor wire,' he said with disgust. He held his finger out for Sam and Felicity to see. 'There's no way over the top of this. We'll have to follow the lane and see if there's another way in.'

Sam took Felicity's pocketknife and cut a strip of cloth from the bottom of his T-shirt. Gerald wrapped his finger as best he could. They crept along in the shadow of the hedge. After a moment Sam stopped. He grabbed Gerald and Felicity by the arms and pulled them to the ground. Gerald looked to Sam, but before he could say anything, Sam pointed ahead. The farm gate was about thirty metres away.

Gerald strained to see in the dim light. The gate appeared to be flanked by two tall trees, growing in the hedge line. Then Gerald saw it. A glowing red ember, about a metre and a half above the ground. It flared bright, then faded.

A cigarette.

There was someone by the gate.

Sam motioned with a nod of his head and they retreated back to the main road, well out of earshot.

'What do you think?' he whispered. 'Someone on guard duty?'

'It has to be,' Gerald whispered back. 'You hardly need razor wire in a hedge. Someone's hiding something here.'

'How do we get past them?' Felicity said. 'That gate looks like the only way in.'

From his jacket, Gerald pulled the wrench that he'd taken from the hangar. 'We could rush them,' he said. 'Take them by surprise.'

Sam and Felicity looked at him doubtfully. 'That's not exactly a plan, is it?' Felicity said. 'Pretty hopeless, actually.'

Gerald dropped his shoulders. 'So what do we do?'

Sam peered back up the laneway. 'Tell you what. I'll sneak back there to get a closer look. At least see how many guards we're dealing with. Okay?'

It was Gerald's turn to look dubious. 'Just be quiet,' he said.

Sam gave him a broad grin. 'Have you ever known me to be anything else?'

He ducked across the lane and climbed into the paddock opposite the farm gate. Once he was behind the hedge, he was hidden.

Felicity let out a weary sigh. 'I'm exhausted,' she said.

'We all are,' Gerald said. 'I can't imagine how Ruby is going.'

Felicity turned to face him. 'And Alisha,' she said.

Gerald looked at her blankly for a second. 'Yeah, of course,' he said. 'Alisha too.'

Felicity held his gaze for a moment, then Gerald looked away.

Sam returned moments later, ducking through the hedge and scampering over the lane.

'There's just one,' he said, puffing. 'But he's a big unit. Dressed in full-on security gear.'

'Any idea how to get past him?' Gerald asked.

Sam shook his head. 'This hedge seems to go right round the farm, with razor wire all the way I'd reckon. Only way in or out is through the front gate, and past our new friend.'

The sound of a whinnying horse carried on the still night air.

Felicity raised her head and looked back the way they had come. She got to her feet and brushed herself down. 'Listen up, boys,' she said. 'I may have a plan.'

Gerald and Sam edged along the hedge line, as quiet as overly considerate mice. Gerald winced at every footfall as it squeaked into the snow. Cloaked in the shadow of the foliage at their backs, he and Sam took an age to advance to ten metres from the gate.

Gerald could just make out the dim outline of a pair of heavy metal gates, set between two large trees. Beyond, a pale light glowed in the window of a poky gatehouse. Gerald couldn't see any sign of the guard. He turned to Sam and gave him a quizzical look.

Sam shrugged.

Gerald checked his watch. He was about to crawl a little closer to the entrance when a sound came from back up the lane—the sound of a horse's hooves.

Gerald froze. He watched as the riderless horse approached, walking slowly down the middle of the laneway. It was a large grey with a heavy rug over its back. In the silver moonlight, it seemed to glow with a ghostly sheen. The horse let out a gentle whinny as it passed Sam and Gerald.

It ambled right up to the farm gate.

Then it stopped.

Seconds passed.

A giant of a man emerged from the shadows. His black fatigues blended into the night and it was only the rattle and clank of equipment dangling from his belt that confirmed he was a real person and not an apparition.

The horse bobbed its head and pawed the ground. The guard looked up and down the path. His hand rested on the butt of a pistol in a holster on his right hip.

'Where did you get loose from, eh?' The man inched forward. 'Who let you out on such a cold night?' The horse turned its head towards the man. The guard slowly raised his left hand and stroked its muzzle.

The horse blew two shots of steam from its nostrils and nuzzled up to the man's touch.

'That's a girl,' he said gently. 'Everything's all right.'

Then Felicity popped her head up from behind the horse's flank and yelled, 'Surprise!'

'Wha—?' The guard recoiled, shock plastered across his face.

Felicity swung up onto the horse's back. She dug her heels into its ribs and the beast reared onto its hind legs. The guard stumbled backwards, his arms spinning as he tried to regain balance. The horse neighed and lashed out with a front leg.

The hoof collected square on the guard's jaw, knocking his head back and sending him flying into the snow. Gerald and Sam scrambled out from the hedge and pounced.

The guard was out cold, laid out like a body in the morgue. Gerald grabbed the pair of handcuffs on the man's belt.

'Help me roll him over,' he said to Sam. Together, they strained to get the guard over onto his front. The handcuffs barely reached around his meaty wrists.

Felicity guided the horse between the trees and jumped down to help drag the guard into the gatehouse.

'At least it's not too cold in here,' Sam said with a grunt as they heaved the man through the door.

Gerald looked around the sparsely furnished room. There was a table with a two-way radio on it, a chair, a sink, and a bar heater struggling to hold back the cold. Gerald unclipped the man's belt and dragged it out from under him. He found a second pair of handcuffs and manacled one of the guard's ankles to a pipe under the sink.

'That should hold him for a bit,' Gerald said.

'Nice riding, Felicity,' Sam said. 'I would never have guessed you were hanging onto the other side of that horse.'

'Thanks. A little trick we used to play at pony club,' she replied.

Sam shook his head and looked from Gerald to Felicity. 'Flying lessons and horse riding. I've got to find me a better school.'

Gerald went through the guard's pockets. He handed a stun gun to Felicity and a truncheon to Sam. Then he pulled out the pistol from its holster and held it in his palm. They all stared down at it.

'Have you ever used one before?' Sam asked, his eyes raking over the sleek lines of the handgun.

'No.' Gerald swallowed. 'I'm not sure I want to.'

'What? No gun club at St Cuthbert's?'

Gerald stared at the pistol in his hand. 'Yeah, there is. I just haven't joined yet.'

'Then let's hope you don't need to use it,' Sam said. 'Come on. We need to find Ruby.'

Gerald stuffed the radio into his jacket and followed Sam and Felicity out into the night. He locked the gatehouse door as he left.

A broad path, bordered on either side by a line of trees, led up a slope towards the farmhouse.

'That's strange,' Felicity said. Her voice was barely louder than her footsteps. 'There's no light in any of the windows.'

Gerald squinted into the gloom. The building was more a cottage than a house. A thatched roof and white-washed walls. Two rooms wide at the front, with the door in the middle like a nose on a face. The windows were blank eyes. The only sign of life was smoke curling from a chimney at the back of the building.

'Someone is keeping that fire going,' Gerald said.

'And there'd be no point having man mountain on the front gate if no one was at home,' Sam said, nodding back towards the gatehouse.

'Let's sneak around the back,' Gerald said. He tightened his grip on the pistol.

They kept to the shadows and cut a path wide around the building. A cluster of trees at one end of the house provided some cover. Gerald motioned for Sam and Felicity to stay put, and he crawled across the frozen ground right up to the cottage. He pressed his back against the wall and glanced up. There was a window right above him. Gerald felt the weight of the gun in his hand. He rose up on his knees and peered inside.

It took a second for his eyes to adjust well enough to recognise a tiny farm kitchen: ancient timber benches, an old wood burning stove, a stone sink with a water pump beneath the window. But there was something odd about the scene. Something not quite right. It took a moment for Gerald to realise what it was. He ducked down and beckoned Sam and Felicity.

They scampered across and plopped down next to him.

'What is it?' Felicity whispered.

Gerald frowned before replying. 'I don't think anyone's here,' he said.

'What do you mean?' Sam said. 'What about the smoke from the chimney? What about the gorilla at the gate?'

'Follow me,' Gerald said. 'I'll show you.'

He crept along the wall until he reached a door. He tried the handle—it opened easily—and he ducked inside.

The kitchen smelled of neglect. Gerald ran a finger along a timber bench. It left a shiny trail in a layer of dust.

'There's nothing on the shelves,' he said to Sam and Felicity. 'No food, no packages. There's no fridge. There are cobwebs in the sink.' He scanned the room. 'This place hasn't been used in ages.'

Sam ducked through a doorway on the far side of the kitchen. 'Come and look at this,' he called.

Felicity and Gerald followed him into an empty room. There was no furniture, no pictures on the walls, no rug on the floorboards. The entire cottage consisted of just four rooms and they were all bare.

'It's like a ghost ship,' Felicity said as they completed a circuit of the house and returned to the kitchen. 'Like no one has lived here for a hundred years.'

'Do you have to use that word?' Sam shivered.

'What word?'

'Ghost.'

Gerald shook his head in frustration. 'I don't get it,' he said. 'Why the security if there's nothing here to guard.'

'Maybe there's another building on the property,' Felicity said. 'We should keep looking.'

Gerald leaned his back against a wall and slid to the floorboards. 'I just keep thinking about Ruby and how she—' He stopped mid-thought. A strange expression washed over his face.

'What is it?' Felicity asked him.

Gerald cocked his head to the side. 'My bum's warm,' he said.

Sam narrowed his eyes. 'Pardon me?'

'My bum's warm.' Gerald put his palms flat to the wooden floor. 'The whole floor is warm.' Then he jumped to his feet. 'The chimney!'

Sam still looked confused. 'What about the chimney?'

'There shouldn't be one,' Gerald said. 'Did you see a fireplace? There aren't any. It should be as cold as death in here.' He jumped to his feet and pulled open a pair of doors under the sink.

'What are you looking for?' Felicity said.

Gerald had a quick look inside the bare cupboard. 'Answers.'

Felicity and Sam exchanged puzzled looks and followed Gerald into the next room. He pulled open a broom cupboard and dropped to his knees to inspect the floor inside.

'Gerald?' Felicity said.

'The smoke from the chimney outside,' Gerald said, running his fingers around the edge of the walls. Then, to himself, 'Nothing here.' He darted into the next room. 'The heat under the floorboards must be coming from somewhere.' He looked around the space and shook his head. Then he went into the final room, which could at one stage in the house's history have been a bedroom. In the corner stood an ancient timber wardrobe. Gerald turned the handle and opened the door. His eyes lit up.

'Here we go,' he said.

'What is it?' Sam asked, looking over Gerald's shoulder.

Gerald knelt down and poked an index finger through a knothole in the wardrobe floor. He lifted clear a large square of timber sheeting. A burst of heat funnelled up through a square opening in the floor, as if he'd opened an oven door.

Gerald, Sam and Felicity peered down a narrow shaft that disappeared deep into the ground.

Chapter 33

Gerald stuffed the pistol into the waistband of his pants and lowered himself into the hole in the floor. They had agreed that there would be no more talking. And that they would not leave until they had found Ruby.

A metal ladder ran down the length of the shaft. Hand over hand, Gerald started the descent. Warmth radiated from the rungs. Gerald hated the cold as much as anyone, but he couldn't imagine why Brahe would need to have it so hot, especially the way he sweated.

Gerald glanced up to see Felicity and Sam following him. The shaft emptied out to a bare antechamber, carved into the island bedrock. Gerald jumped to the ground and unzipped his jacket. The heat was oppressive.

Sam and Felicity joined him. They were both perspiring. Sam wiped the sweat from his forehead and gave Gerald a 'what's this all about, then?' look.

Gerald shrugged, and pointed to a door in the far wall. There was a window in the top half. The three of them edged across to peek through.

A gasp escaped Felicity's lips.

On the other side of the door was a scene straight from a medieval torture chamber.

An enormous brick furnace, like a giant circular kiln, dominated the room. There were half a dozen arched doorways around its circumference. Flames licked its insides, painting the chamber blood red. A single chimneystack poked from the top and soared up and through the high vaulted ceiling.

Little wonder there was so much heat radiating up to the cottage above, Gerald thought. The only thing missing from the scene was a ring of horned demons fashioning horseshoes on hell-blackened anvils.

The chamber walls were lined with wooden pens, housing an array of animals: horses, cows, goats, pigs. It was like someone had sunk a barn into the mouth of a volcano.

Then Gerald saw them. Locked in an iron cage at the far end of the chamber.

Alisha.

Ox.

And...

Gerald couldn't help himself. He saw her face, pink from the heat. He broke his silence. 'Ruby.'

Without thinking, he pulled the door open and ran. It was a good twenty metres across to the cage but Gerald couldn't remember his feet touching the ground. He skidded up to the iron bars and thrust his arms through, wrapping them around his startled friend.

'Oh my gosh, Gerald.' Ruby's voice came out muffled through the folds of Gerald's jacket. 'Let me go.'

Gerald squeezed her harder. He was never going to let her go again.

Ruby pummelled punches onto Gerald's chest. 'Let. Me. Go!'

She pushed hard and finally broke free of his grasp.

Gerald stumbled back a step and was shocked by the look on Ruby's face. All colour had drained from her cheeks. 'What?' he said.

Ruby swallowed and pointed over Gerald's shoulder. 'Behind you,' she whispered.

Gerald was turning as the words left her mouth. His eyes filled with the sight of a coal shovel swinging fast at his head.

Gerald ducked. The shovel blade brushed the top of his hair as it whistled past. Pugly nearly smacked himself on the head with the follow-through. He swung again. Gerald threw himself backwards, avoiding a hit to the chin by millimetres.

Gerald sprawled across the floor, wriggling left then

right as Pugly rained blows down at him. Each time, the metal blade hit stone, striking sparks into the air. Gerald was vaguely aware of his name being shouted, of the rattling of iron bars. But all his attention was directed towards avoiding a fatal meeting with the back of the shovel.

He tried to scramble to his feet. But a hefty swing of the blade connected with his ankle. A searing pain bulleted up his calf as his legs were swept from under him. He landed heavily on his right shoulder. His eyes popped at a sharp *crack*.

Gerald knew in an instant—his collarbone had snapped. His left hand shot to the opposite shoulder as he rolled onto his back. Fire pulsed through his body. He looked up to see Brahe's man staring down at him, a glint of triumph in his eyes.

Gerald took in a huge breath. With the last of his strength he rolled to the right. Rockets of pain exploded in his eyes as he put weight onto his busted shoulder. His left hand ducked around to his waistband to grab for the pistol.

It wasn't there.

It must have fallen out during the struggle. Gerald rolled flat to the floor, spent.

His breath came in painful bursts. Pugly loomed above with the shovel poised over his shoulder like a batter at home plate. He tensed, about to take one final swing, when Felicity appeared behind him. She pressed the stun gun into Pugly's neck, and pulled the trigger.

The result was instantaneous. A crackle of electricity sent Pugly into a violent convulsion. He hit the floor like a sack of coal with a twitchy leg.

Felicity dropped to her knees at Gerald's side, placing a hand on his injured shoulder. He winced at the touch.

'Are we quite finished?' The voice was calm but assertive. Gerald turned his head. Tycho Brahe was standing by the furnace. He had the pistol, and he held it pressed into Sam's ribs.

Brahe's face was awash with sweat. He reached into his pocket and tossed a set of keys to Felicity. 'Open the cage,' he instructed. He shoved Sam towards Ruby, Ox and Alisha. 'I expect you have some catching up to do.'

Chapter 34

Gerald sat propped against the stone wall. His right arm was strapped across his chest in a makeshift sling fashioned from Sam's jumper. Ox, Alisha and Ruby had stripped down to T-shirts but were still perspiring in the heat. Felicity sat by Gerald's side, worry written on her face.

'We were grabbed by Brahe's men right after we escaped the avalanche,' Alisha said. She reached out and took Ox by the hand. 'Oswald and I were thrown into the back of a helicopter, and then into a private jet. We've been down in this hellhole for I don't know how many days. It's been stifling.'

'Oswald?' Gerald said, cocking an eye at his old school friend.

The pink in Ox's cheeks turned two shades brighter. 'Alisha doesn't like my nickname,' he mumbled. 'She thinks it's disrespectful.'

'Does she?' Sam said, raising his eyebrows. 'That's very considerate of her.'

Alisha shot Sam a filthy glare. 'Oh, grow up,' she said. 'You could learn a lot from Oswald. Maybe you should be concentrating on how to get out of here.'

Gerald suppressed a grin. Alisha was right, of course. But still—he looked at Alisha patting the back of Ox's hand. Alisha and Ox! Who would have thought?

'What is this place?' Felicity asked.

'We haven't seen him much,' Ox said, his voice low. He glanced over his shoulder. Brahe was bent over a workbench, fussing with a complicated arrangement of flasks and titration tubes. Pugly was hard at work, shovelling coal through one of the arched doorways, deep into the heart of the furnace. 'He comes and goes,' Ox said. 'But he seems to be working on a chemical creation of some sort.'

Felicity nodded. 'We think it's the universal remedy,' she said. 'A medicine that can cure everything.'

Alisha was taken aback. 'Cure everything? Surely that's a good thing,' she said. 'Why all this secrecy and kidnapping if he's making something that could help millions of people?'

Gerald tried to sit straighter. He winced at the movement. 'That's the problem,' he said. 'Felicity thinks the recipe calls for one special ingredient.' He paused, looking from Felicity to Alisha and then to Ruby. 'The heart of a young girl.'

Alisha rocked back. 'That's absurd!' she said. 'Why would anyone believe that?'

'Because it works.' Brahe's voice carried across to them from his workbench. 'And I am living proof.'

He swung around to face them. His face was soaked in perspiration. Despite the heat blasting from the furnace, his skin was wax pale.

Gerald was shocked at the change in Brahe since the first time he'd seen him, in the butterfly house at Jasper Mantle's estate in England. All the colour had leached from his face, as if his life force had drained away. In its place was a cadaverous pallor, as plain and lifeless as any slab of marble in the morgue.

'What do you mean?' Gerald said.

Brahe leaned on the bench, as if the act of breathing was an effort. He let loose a liquid cough.

'Oh yes,' Sam said. 'He's the picture of health.' Ruby shushed him.

'I mean, Mr Wilkins, that I know the secret of the universal remedy. I have denied death for four hundred years. And I will keep doing it, again and again.' Another burst of coughing wracked his chest.

Behind Brahe, Pugly kept feeding coal into the furnace. Fire and fumes belched from the six archways.

'He's a complete nutter,' Sam said. Ruby shushed him again.

Felicity rattled the bars of their cage. 'Are you saying you're the same Tycho Brahe that served in the court of King Rudolph? That's ridiculous.'

Brahe drew back his shoulders. 'I am Tycho Brahe,' he declared in a voice far stronger than his appearance suggested possible. 'I am the melder of mercury and lead. I am the creator of gold. I am the cartographer of stars and planets. I am Astrologer Royal to the court of King Rudolph II of Bohemia, Holy Roman Emperor and ruler of all the civilised peoples of Europe. I am his confidant, his alchemist, his adviser. And as possessor of the universal remedy, I am, by right, his successor.' His voice rose if he was addressing a rally of ten thousand, rather than six bedraggled kids and a barnful of farm animals.

Ruby dipped her head low. 'Is he seriously saying he's the king of Europe? Sam's right. He is a nutter.' This time, Gerald shushed Ruby. He had spotted a large knife on Brahe's workbench. It was best to keep the man talking.

'What about all those graves with your name on them?' Gerald said. 'The one in the church in Prague, and in the cemetery in Hadanka? Why would someone who has cheated death need two graves?'

Brahe stiffened and wiped an unsteady hand across his forehead. 'I am the possessor of the universal remedy,' he said. 'I have denied death for four centuries.'

Felicity rattled the bars again. 'If you've had that

remedy for four hundred years, why have you been running around Europe trying to find it again?'

'That's a good point,' Gerald said. 'If you're the real Tycho Brahe why do you need the Voynich Manuscript to get the recipe for your potion? Why go to all this trouble to decipher the code when you're supposedly the man who has it already?'

Alisha joined Felicity at the cage bars. 'Is that what you've been doing to the animals down here? Testing different recipes on them to see if they work? Is that what this place is? A test lab?' She turned to the others. 'You should see the number of dead animals that have been dragged out of here in the past few days.'

Brahe turned back to his equipment. He took a pinch of powder from a dish and threw it into a bubbling pot. A purple flash exploded from the surface.

'It is almost ready,' Brahe said. He picked up a ragged manuscript and consulted the top sheet. 'Just one item to go.' He reached for the knife on the benchtop.

Gerald's eyes grew wide. 'You can't do this,' he yelled. 'You can't take a life to lengthen your own. It's unthinkable.'

Brahe lifted the knife and held its broad silver blade to the light. 'Not at all,' he said. 'What do you think war is all about?'

'But that's not the same,' Gerald said. 'No one is threatening you. We're not trying to kill you.'

'If one of these girls dies, I live,' Brahe said. 'It's

completely rational.' Brahe took a step towards the cage. 'When I get the formula just right, I'll release the remedy to the world. I'll extend to all mankind the ability to cure all sickness. Cancer, dementia, diabetes—all cured. No one would lose a loved one again. Funerals and tears would be a thing of the past. I will be the ultimate doctor. The only doctor the world will ever need. Isn't that worth the sacrifice of one life—a life that will end one day anyway?'

A silence fell over the chamber. Even the animals in their stalls were quiet.

'Wouldn't you do that, Gerald? Give one life to help a million? Not to mention the time it gives. Imagine if the world's greatest scientists, artists and musicians could extend their careers by centuries. Imagine the advances that would deliver for all mankind. All from the gift of one child.'

Gerald stared at Brahe and the knife in his hand. He was clearly mad. But was there some sense in what he said? Was the loss of one to benefit the world a worthy sacrifice?

'This is insanity.' Ruby rushed up to the cage door, pushing Felicity and Alisha aside. 'Listen to what you're saying. You can't seriously believe all this rubbish about living forever. All this rot about Rudolph and his court.'

Brahe's face blanched. He strode up to the cage. 'Don't talk to me about Rudolph! What do you know of him?'

Ruby glared defiance. 'Rudolph?' she said. 'Didn't he have a very shiny nose?'

Brahe's eyes bulged with anger. In an instant he had the cage door unlocked and a hand wrapped around Ruby's wrist. He wrenched down, hard. Ruby screamed in pain. Brahe slashed out with the knife, forcing Sam, Ox, Alisha and Felicity to the back wall with Gerald. Before they could move again, Brahe had locked the door and was hauling Ruby across the floor.

Ruby's shrieks were joined by cries from inside the cage. Gerald and the others rushed the bars, trying to break free. The animals in their pens, sensing danger, raised a ruckus, a cacophony of barnyard bleating and braying.

Brahe didn't pause for a second. He dragged Ruby like a caveman with his conquest. She kicked and writhed but to no effect. Brahe tossed her onto a stainless-steel bench as if she was no more than a sack of onions.

Pugly strapped Ruby's arms and legs down with broad leather bands. She fought back but the binds held firm. She cried each time she moved her wrenched left wrist—sobs that seemed to urge her to greater resistance. But her efforts were futile.

'More heat.' Brahe turned to his assistant. 'The crucible must be kept at the right temperature to bring about the reaction.' A vat the size of a hot tub bubbled with molten metals and flux.

Pugly shovelled more coal into the furnace. The

temperature in the chamber rose ever higher.

Sam rushed the cage gate with his shoulder, rattling it on its hinges. Alisha and Felicity screamed for Brahe to stop. Ox and Gerald pounded on the lock plate. But nothing worked.

Brahe called out to Pugly. 'Keep them quiet,' he said. 'They're disturbing the other animals.'

Pugly dropped his shovel and crossed to the cage. He pointed the handgun in Gerald's face. The chamber was silent.

Drops of perspiration ran from Brahe's brow down his silver nose, and onto Ruby's face. She turned her cheek, trying to avoid the foul stream.

Brahe blinked the sweat from his eyes. 'I have so much to achieve, so much to do.'

Ruby eyed the blade in Brahe's hand and strained again at her bonds. 'Please don't,' she said. 'So do I.'

She was drenched in perspiration. Her clothes clung to her as if she'd been caught in a summer storm.

Brahe put a steel bowl at Ruby's side. 'I will make this as painless as possible,' he said. And raised the knife in the air.

Ruby arched her back, hauling at the straps.

Sweat washed across Brahe's face. He placed a hand on the collar of Ruby's T-shirt, and pulled.

The fabric tore.

The blade turned.

Brahe's nose shifted on his face. The sweat was

washing it loose. Ruby's good wrist, slick with perspiration, slipped its bonds.

The nose dropped free.

In a flash, Ruby snatched the lump of silver in mid-air, just centimetres from her face. Then, in a backhanded swipe, she wielded the pointed nose tip like a blunt weapon. It connected with Brahe's temple. The blow knocked him senseless and sent him sprawling across the steel bench.

By the cage, the sight of Brahe sliding towards the vat of bubbling metal caught Pugly by surprise. He turned his head for a second.

It was all Felicity needed.

She pulled Ruby's scarf from her pocket. Holding each end, she threw it over Pugly's head. She whipped the scarf tight, catching him around the throat and crashing him hard into the cage bars.

'Drop the gun,' Felicity whispered into his ear. Pugly's body convulsed, struggling for breath. 'Or I'll rip your head off.'

The gun clattered onto the stone floor.

Ruby was sitting up, unbuckling the straps at her feet. She looked across at Brahe, slumped on the edge of the bench. He was just centimetres from the lip of the bubbling crucible. The heat of the furnace was almost cooking them.

Ruby clambered onto her knees, bumping her wrist. She let out a cry of animal intensity. Her shirt was torn and her face was stained with sweat and grime. She shuffled over to where Brahe was lying. Her eyes were a blank mirror of intent. She reached out and peeled Brahe's fingers, one by one, from around the handle of the knife. And took the weapon into her own hand.

Gerald smacked Pugly over the back of his head. 'The keys,' he demanded. 'Where are the keys?'

The man's fingers clutched at the furled scarf that was pulled taut across his windpipe like a garrote. He could barely croak, 'Pocket.'

Ruby clutched the knife handle tight. She nursed her shattered left wrist in her lap. And she put the edge of the silver blade to Brahe's exposed throat.

'Ruby?'

Gerald crawled up onto the benchtop beside her— two friends, kneeling together as if at prayer. He looked at her flushed face, her hair plastered to her forehead. She didn't shift her gaze from the unconscious face of Tycho Brahe.

Again, she slid the blade across the soft skin beneath Brahe's beard, as if giving him a shave.

'Ruby?' Gerald said again.

'He was going to kill me.' Ruby spoke softly. Deliberately. 'He was going to slice me open and take my heart.'

'Ruby.' Gerald reached out and laid his hand on her arm. Her skin was on fire, burning with the intensity of the furnace. 'You can't kill him.'

Ruby turned the blade, moving the point onto a vein that ran the length of Brahe's neck. A bead of blood formed at its tip. 'Why not?' she said. 'Using his logic, if he dies, I live. That's what he said. That's how he justified what he was going to do.' Her eyes fixed on the red bubble as it expanded on Brahe's skin. 'Isn't that how everyone behaves, anyway? Who cares what happens to you as long as I'm okay. I'm the centre of the universe and the sun revolves around me.'

Gerald leaned in closer and put his arm around Ruby's shoulders. 'I thought the sun shone out of my backside.'

The edges of Ruby's mouth twitched up. 'Don't,' she said. 'Don't make me laugh.'

Gerald squeezed a little tighter. 'A very smart person once said to me that hurting someone, even an evil person, would make me no better than they were. Do you remember that?'

Ruby gave a tight nod. The confrontation with Sir Mason Green in the burial chamber under Beaconsfield seemed so long ago.

'I think the same applies here,' Gerald said.

Ruby twirled the blade on its point. The red bubble burst and trickled a thin trail into Brahe's collar. She pulled the knife away and tossed it into the crucible.

It landed with a splash of flame, then sank without a trace into the molten depths.

Chapter 35

When the Swedish police stormed the furnace room they found many things that surprised them.

Two men slumped in a locked cage.

A barnyard of animals.

A laboratory that looked like Frankenstein's workshop.

And six exhausted, sweating kids.

Detective Ericsson from Landskrona Police took some convincing of their story. 'Tycho Brahe?' he said. 'He's been dead for four hundred years.'

Gerald jerked his thumb towards the iron cage. 'Well you better tell him in there, because he's convinced he's the next king of Europe and that could put a damper on his coronation party.'

The police had arrived in force and were scouring the chamber. They located a large entrance on the far side and had started leading the animals up to the surface. Alisha and Ox helped Felicity with the horses.

Amongst all the activity, Gerald sat at Brahe's workbench with Detective Ericsson, trying to explain the inexplicable. Ruby leaned against the stainless-steel benchtop next to Gerald, fiddling with the rubber tube from a Bunsen burner.

'So, this man kidnapped your two friends in California and brought them here?'

'That's right,' Gerald said.

'Because he wanted to cut out a girl's heart to make a drug that would cure all diseases?'

'Precisely,' Ruby said.

'And he knew about this remedy because he is the famous Danish astronomer and alchemist Tycho Brahe who lived in Prague at the end of the sixteenth century?'

'That bit we're less clear on,' Gerald said. 'He certainly thinks he's Tycho Brahe. But that's not possible.' He looked the detective in the eye. 'Is it?'

The police officer flicked through his notebook. 'Of course not.'

Gerald looked uncertain. Ruby gave him an encouraging nod.

'There is this one thing that has us puzzled,' Gerald said. 'About him maybe being a ghost, or something.'

Detective Ericsson lifted his eyes. 'Yes?'

'In this church in Prague, where Brahe was supposedly buried all those years ago. There was an open grave with his name on the gravestone. And the grave was empty.' Gerald looked embarrassed asking the question. 'Isn't that a bit...strange?'

Ericsson raised an eyebrow. 'One of the Danish universities—Aarhus, I think it was—disinterred Brahe's body a short while ago.'

'Uh, disinterred?' Gerald said.

'Dug it up,' Ericsson said. 'Some research project investigating whether he died of natural causes or was poisoned.'

Ruby let out a short laugh. 'Does a busted bladder count as natural causes?'

'There have been stories that Brahe may have been poisoned with mercury,' Ericsson said. 'A little in his food over a period of time. He would have been in contact with mercury in his alchemy experiments so it would be a clever way for an assassin to kill him and get away undetected.'

'A patient assassin,' Ruby said.

'So Brahe's grave was empty because the body had been dug up by researchers?' Gerald said.

'That's right,' the policeman said. 'Not because he is what you might call a zombie.'

Gerald chuckled to himself. 'Sam will be disappointed.'

'What about the other grave in Hadanka?' Ruby said. 'That had Brahe's name on it as well.'

'I had one of my men make some calls about that. Tycho Brahe had many children. He named one of his sons after himself. Your friend broke into the grave of Tycho Brahe junior.'

'Believe me,' Gerald said. 'He's no friend of mine.'

'Who is he then?' Ruby asked. She glanced at the man who had nearly stolen her life. He sat haggard, and sweating, behind the bars.

'We'll find out,' Ericsson said. 'Even billionaires can't cover their tracks completely.'

Ruby winced as she moved her injured wrist. 'Detective, is there any way we can make a phone call? I'd really like to talk to my mum and dad.'

'Of course,' Ericsson said. 'From what you say they've been through a lot as well. I'll get my office to contact the FBI in Miami.'

Just then, Sam wandered over. 'Speaking of FBI,' he said, 'Gerald, I think you owe Special Agent de Bruin an apology.'

Gerald looked at Sam, confused. 'What do you mean?'

'About him not being with the FBI.'

'Sam, you're making no sense,' Ruby said. 'We haven't seen that de Bruin guy since Felicity cracked him over the head in Mason Green's apartment in San Francisco.'

'No,' Sam said. 'He's just over there.' He looked across to the iron cage where Brahe and Pugly still sat on the floor. 'At least, he was over there a minute ago. He came up and said hi—said he was part of this raid, helping out the Swedish police.'

Detective Ericsson looked at Sam stone-faced. 'We have had no assistance from the FBI or any agency,' he said. 'The only people on this mission are under my command. Are you saying there was someone else in here?'

'Sure,' Sam said. 'Special Agent de Bruin. He was asking where the Voynich Manuscript was. I pointed it out on the table over there.'

They all looked to the table.

There was no sign of de Bruin. Or the Voynich Manuscript.

Detective Ericsson was on his feet in a heartbeat, barking orders in Swedish. Policemen all around the chamber dropped what they were doing and ran to the exits.

Ericsson turned back to Sam. 'We will find him,' he said. 'And the manuscript. What name was he using?'

'It's de Bruin,' Sam said.

The detective nodded. 'As in bear?' he said.

'Huh?'

'De Bruin,' Ericsson said. 'It's an old Dutch term for bear.'

A light flicked on in Gerald's head. He couldn't believe it hadn't occurred to him until that moment. What an idiot. 'Just like Ursus, the bear,' he said.

Detective Ericsson looked at him, confused. 'What was that?'

Gerald ignored him and turned to Ruby and Sam. 'Ursus and de Bruin. They're the same person. They—he—was after the Voynich Manuscript the whole time.'

Ruby blinked at him. 'How can you be sure they're the same person?'

'There's the name for starters. And what's an FBI agent doing turning up at Mason Green's apartment by himself at night? He was looking for the manuscript.'

'Then why would he phone us and call himself Ursus?' Ruby said.

Gerald thought for a moment. 'If de Bruin wanted the manuscript he had to find Brahe. He must have known that Brahe would contact us to get the pendant. De Bruin couldn't have us going to the police—that would ruin everything. So he calls us, puts on a fake voice, and tells us to do everything Brahe wants. That way he can follow us to his precious manuscript.'

'So, who is this Ursus guy?' Sam said. 'And now that he's got the manuscript, is he going to try to cook up a universal remedy too?'

'I don't know,' Gerald said. 'Maybe there's more in that manuscript than just dodgy medicine.'

Detective Ericsson shook his head. 'I will need to hear everything you know about this de Bruin. And about this man calling himself Brahe.'

Sam gave a cheeky grin. 'That will be nose problem.'

Ruby let out a weary sigh.

Detective Ericsson looked at Sam like he was something stuck to the sole of his boot. 'That is snot funny,' he said.

It took Sam a moment to register what Ericsson had said, then he beamed at the detective.

'Oh, yes,' Ericsson said, cracking a thin smile. 'We Swedish have a sense of humour. We're not all Volvos, meatballs and flat-packed furniture, you know.'

Ruby shook her head and turned to Gerald. 'Of all the police in Sweden, we get the one that does nose jokes.'

Chapter 36

Gerald couldn't tell which was more comforting: the embrace he received from his parents when they all got back to London, or the quantity of food that Mrs Rutherford all but forced down his throat.

'You all look so thin,' the housekeeper said as she piled more steaming pastry packages of baked deliciousness onto the table. 'The terrible ordeal you've had to endure.'

'Thanks, Mrs R,' Sam said, helping himself to a pastie from a silver platter by his elbow. 'This should help us through it.'

Gerald and Vi and Eddie, the four Valentines, Felicity and the Colonel, Alisha and Mr Gupta, as well as Ox and his parents had all gathered in the formal dining room at Gerald's house in Chelsea, at his mother's insistence. Even in a time of crisis, there was no reason not to have a party.

Mr Fry even seemed pleased to be serving up the food.

There was a lot of excited chatter and laughter around the long table. The events of the Christmas-gone-wrong seemed so long ago. All of Vi's friends had returned home, with a new tale to tell at their drinks parties. And all the Wilkins staff had resumed their normal duties, with, at Gerald's insistence, a substantial Christmas bonus.

Vi raised her champagne glass and tapped it lightly with a spoon. 'If I could have your attention,' she trilled. She waited for the talk to die down. 'I would like to thank you all for coming along this evening. It has been a difficult start to the year,'—there were knowing nods and snorts of agreement—'but I have a few things I'd like to say.'

Gerald was seated next to Ruby and he leaned in close to her ear. 'I hope you don't need to go to the toilet,' he said. 'This could be a Brahe bladder moment.'

Ruby giggled into her serviette. 'Behave,' she said. 'You might miss something important.'

Gerald looked at Ruby curiously. What did she mean by that?

'My husband and I want to apologise for putting you all in such danger,' Vi said. She ignored the murmurs of dissent from around the table. 'But I am delighted that we have all come out the other end unscathed.' There was light applause. 'Gerald has told me all about that horrible man and his silly pursuit of some universal medicine. Honestly, why people can't just get on with living the life they've got rather than bemoaning the one they don't, they might surprise themselves and get more out of it.' Vi paused, as if surprised by her own statement.

'Well put, Mum,' Gerald said.

'Thank you, dear,' she said, taking a gulp of Dom Perignon. 'In fact, I had a call from the Swedish police this afternoon. They have finally identified who this Brahe man is.'

There was an excited murmur around the table. 'Really, Mrs Wilkins?' Ruby said. 'Who is he?'

'It turns out he is Tycho Brahe.' Vi took another generous swig.

The table responded as one. 'What?'

'That's his name,' Vi said. 'Some descendant of the original, apparently. He was born in Switzerland in 1956 and inherited the family fortune when he was quite young. Hence all the money and the spare time—a dangerous combination if ever there was one.'

'So he actually is Tycho Brahe,' Sam said. 'Just not the Tycho Brahe.'

'You sound disappointed,' Felicity said, giving him a wink. Gerald didn't miss that Sam's cheeks blushed pink.

'Apparently he became obsessed with his ancient

ancestor,' Vi said. 'He went a bit mad about it. He started believing that he was the original, even to the point of growing a beard and having his nose removed so he'd look just like him.'

'That's revolting,' Alisha said, recoiling. 'What type of doctor would do surgery like that?'

Vi tapped herself on the underside of the chin with the back of her fingers. 'You're too young yet, dear, but I can put you in touch with a dozen of them.' She quaffed a half-glass more of her champagne. 'Anyhoo, the poor man got so tied up in all this alchemy nonsense that he really believed he could turn lead into gold, and mercury into medicine. That's why he kept sweating so much, Gerald. Excess perspiration is a symptom of mercury poisoning.'

Ruby let out a sharp laugh. 'So the only reason he got sick was because of all the mercury he was handling trying to live forever. There's some irony for you.'

'No,' said Sam. 'She said it was mercury. Not irony.'

There was a long silence around the table.

Ruby shook her head. 'You are a loveable pea brain.'

The room erupted in laughter.

'I sort of feel sorry for Brahe,' Gerald said. 'He was trying to help people by finding the universal remedy.'

Ruby looked at Gerald, astonished. 'He was going to cut out my heart.'

Gerald shrugged. 'Well, apart from that, he seemed all right.'

Vi nibbled on a piece of asparagus and dabbed her fingers on her serviette. 'Well, he's getting medical treatment now, so he'll be on the mend soon enough. Then they can lock him in jail where he belongs.'

'Mrs Wilkins,' Alisha said from the far end of the table, 'did the police say anything about Sir Mason Green?'

'They still have no idea where he is. They're hoping to get some information from Brahe, but it seems members of the Billionaires' Club are pretty tight. He's not giving anything away.'

Gerald leaned in close to Ruby and whispered, 'Sounds like a good reason for me to join up.'

'What was that dear?' his mother asked.

Gerald sat upright in his seat. 'I was just saying it's a worry he's still on the loose.' Mason Green was never far from Gerald's thoughts. And he had the uneasy feeling that the chilling phone call in Prague would not be the last he would hear from him.

'Excuse me, Mrs Wilkins,' Alisha said. 'We haven't heard what happened to you after we got away from the chalet. Brahe said he didn't kidnap you.'

Vi drained her glass and waggled it in the general direction of Mr Fry. He glided across the floor to refill it. 'He didn't,' she said. 'We all spent the night locked in a drawing room at the chalet. We heard that terrible avalanche the next morning. Eddie and his pals broke the door down but there was no sign of the intruders. They'd all gone. Taken off. We were trying to get the phone to work to call for help when we heard a helicopter touch down. I thought it was the police. But it was another bunch of armed goons! Can you believe it?'

'So you were kidnapped, but by a different gang?' Ox said. 'Amazing.'

'I know,' Vi said. 'Their leader was very polite. I'll grant him that. Introduced himself as Mr Balu and told us we had to go with him. Something about everything having to be done in the right order.'

Gerald turned to Ruby. 'Does that sound like anyone we know?'

'You mean de Bruin?' she asked.

Gerald nodded. 'Someone who loves a process.'

Alisha raised her head. 'Mrs Wilkins, did you say his name was Balu?'

'That's right, dear.'

Alisha laughed. '*Balu*,' she said. 'It's Hindi for bear. Like in *The Jungle Book*.'

Gerald sat back in his chair. 'So Special Agent de Bruin is Ursus *and* Balu.'

Vi gave a frustrated ring of her glass again. 'I have no idea where we were taken. It was blindfolds all round for hours. Then we were left in a large dormitory with no windows. It must have been on the coast or an island because we could hear waves at night. Oh, Gerald, I've been meaning to tell you. You'll never guess who I saw there.'

'Was it Professor McElderry from the British Museum?'

Vi looked astonished. 'How on earth did you know that?'

'Educated guess,' Gerald said.

'The police are still looking for him, and all his academic friends,' Vi said. 'The morning we left, he and a bunch of others were left behind. We were blindfolded, put back on the helicopter, then into a van and finally dumped outside the FBI office in downtown Miami. Quite the most extraordinary thing.'

'So Brahe is under arrest, Green is on the loose, Ursus has the manuscript and no one knows where Professor McElderry is?' Gerald said. 'That's quite a Christmas.'

Vi leaned back and took a long breath. 'I'm sure everything will work out for your professor friend,' she said. 'But for us, it's time to move on, with a fresh new year ahead. And with that in mind, I have some pleasant news to announce. While Eddie and I were sitting around with not much to do, being kidnapped and all, we decided we needed to properly honour my dear Aunt Geraldine. So after long discussion with my husband, and indeed with Mr and Mrs Valentine, I am delighted to announce the establishment of the Geraldine Archer Memorial Scholarship.' Vi clapped her hands with enthusiasm.

Gerald leaned in close to Ruby. 'Why would she need to discuss that with your mum and dad?'

'Listen up,' Ruby said, the edges of her mouth twitching.

'And the inaugural recipients of the scholarship, I am delighted to say, are Ruby and Sam Valentine!' Vi launched into another burst of applause, joined in by the rest of the table.

Gerald blinked and looked to the Valentine twins. 'You what?'

Sam jumped up and clapped his hand on Gerald's sore shoulder, extracting a cry. 'It means, sunshine, that I'm coming to St Cuthbert's and Ruby is off to St Hilda's. We're coming to school with you!'

Gerald couldn't believe it. Ruby was grinning from ear to ear. Felicity was already around their side of the table bouncing with excitement and babbling about all the fun the four of them were going to have. Gerald couldn't tell whether Felicity was more excited about Ruby being a dorm mate or Sam being just down the road.

In the days since the events in the chamber under the farm on Ven, Gerald and Felicity's friendship evened out. Gerald would like to think that they'd spoken at length about their feelings and their mutual respect for each other. But it turned out they'd just grown less interested in each other's company. Which happens. And it was clear that Felicity was interested in getting to know Sam a bit better.

So that was that. No tears and no regrets. Simple.

The dinner party broke up and Gerald led the way to the games room, where Ox took control of the dartboard.

Sam teamed up with Felicity, who had a deadly eye with a sharpened weapon in her hand.

Gerald found himself sitting next to Alisha, who was taking idle interest in the score. 'So, you and Ox, eh?' Gerald said. 'Oswald, sorry.'

Alisha turned to him and fluttered her dark eyelashes. 'Gerald,' she said. 'You are a beautiful boy. And I love you like a brother. But you are such a child.'

Gerald sighed. 'Are you going to give me another lecture?'

'Yes, I am. You think just because Oswald and I were locked up together for a week that we must have become boyfriend and girlfriend, making goo-goo eyes at each other.'

Gerald shifted in his chair. 'No,' he said. 'Not at all.'

'Yes,' Alisha said. 'At all. Oswald and I are very close friends. We have gone through a terrible experience together and we provided enormous support for each other. I don't think I have ever felt closer to another person in my life. I trust Oswald. But that doesn't mean I want to cover him in kisses and write his last name after mine in the back of my schoolbooks, just to see how it looks.' Alisha patted him on the knee. 'Not everyone has to pair up, Gerald. Life isn't a game of Go Fish.'

Alisha stood up and went to join the game of darts, laughing at some joke Ox had made.

Gerald sat there, a little stunned by the conversation.

Ruby came over and settled beside him. They both wore slings, this time properly fitted by doctors.

Ruby nudged Gerald's good shoulder. 'How's your collarbone?'

'The doctor says I'll be in a sling for another few weeks. How about your wrist?'

'It should be right for hockey tryouts at St Hilda's,' she said. 'I can't wait. Felicity sounds like she runs the place.'

Gerald nudged Ruby back. 'You were mighty quiet about that whole scholarship thing.'

'Sorry.' She grinned again. 'Sam's beside himself. He wants to sign up for everything. Even flying lessons. Mum and Dad said it's a great opportunity and they're always on about not letting opportunity pass you by.'

Gerald nudged her again. 'Now that you mention opportunity.' He leaned in close to Ruby's lips. He could feel the warmth of her breath.

Ruby pulled back. 'Uh, yeah,' she said. 'I've been talking to Felicity and Alisha. We need to talk.'

For the second time that night, Gerald couldn't believe what he was hearing. 'What do you mean talk?' he said. 'What about the hug on Christmas Eve? All the hassle you've given me over Felicity? The look you gave me in the barn just before you set the place on fire? What was that all about?'

Ruby's cheeks went pink. 'Yeah, about that. Look, I was really confused. I thought you and Felicity were together forever and you didn't like me. I guess I lost the plot a bit.'

'Is that why you pushed Felicity and Alisha out of the way in the cage on Ven?' Gerald said. 'So Brahe would take you and not one of them.'

Ruby grinned sheepishly. 'Like I said, I lost the plot.'

'So what's changed now?' Gerald said. 'Felicity and I aren't together anymore.'

Ruby stood up. 'That doesn't mean that we have to pair up, Gerald,' she said. 'Life isn't some big game of Go Fish, you know.'

Gerald sat there dumbly. Ruby gave him a peck on the cheek and skipped over to join Felicity at the pinball machines.

Why was nothing ever straightforward?

Ox and Sam dropped onto the couch on either side of Gerald.

They stared at the girls, who were laughing at Felicity's hopeless pinball skills.

'How's it going?' Sam said to Gerald.

Gerald reached into his pocket and pulled out a small velvet box. He flipped open the lid—inside were the emerald earrings that Mrs Rutherford had found for him to give to Felicity for Christmas. He had planned to give them to Ruby. 'I started the Christmas holidays with two girlfriends,' Gerald said with a sharp snort. 'Now I don't have any.'

Sam nodded in sympathy. 'To lose one girlfriend is unfortunate. To lose two seems careless.'

Gerald snorted a laugh. 'Thank you, Lady Bracknell.'

Sam looked confused. 'Who?'

Gerald went to reply, then changed his mind.

'Girls, eh,' Ox said.

The three of them nodded their heads sagely.

'At least they talk to you now,' Gerald said, prodding Ox in the ribs.

'Yeah,' Ox said. 'There's some progress.'

By the time everyone was ready to go home, and the parents were rounding up coats and car keys, Gerald and Ruby were back on shoulder-nudging terms. She gave him a huge hug goodbye—or as huge as their broken wings would allow—and another peck on the cheek. This peck lasted longer than the first one.

'Flicka and I will see you two in Winchester for a movie on Friday night,' Ruby said to Gerald and Sam as she pulled on her coat. 'We can compare our first week at school.'

'Maybe we will,' Gerald said, loftily. 'We might get a better offer.'

Ruby scoffed. 'Ha! Like you could do better than us.'

Alisha hugged Ox goodbye, and Gerald couldn't help noticing the disappointment on Ox's face as they went their separate ways with their parents. Sam followed Francis and Alice Valentine towards their car, waving back at Gerald. 'See you at St Cuthbert's,' he called.

Ruby and Felicity hooked arms and danced down the front steps into the crisp London night.

Ruby pulled up and looked back to Gerald where he stood framed in the doorway.

'You be there on Friday night,' she instructed.

Gerald gave a small wave. 'I will.'

'Don't you lie to me,' Ruby said. 'Otherwise your nose will grow.'

Gerald laughed. 'A nose joke? Is that the best you can do?'

Ruby broke away from Felicity and skipped back to Gerald. She stood on the bottom step and rose up onto her toes. Gerald bowed down so they were on the same level.

'I'm inviting you to a movie,' Ruby said, her eyes sparkling. 'That snot to be sniffed at. A fun night out with nostrils attached. Don't blow this, Gerald. Who nose where it could lead?'

Then Ruby gave Gerald a cheeky grin, raced back to Felicity, and together they giggled their way to the waiting cars.

Gerald stood on the top step and waved after them. For the first time in his life, he was actually looking forward to the start of a school term.

Afterword

Tycho Brahe (1546–1601) was a Danish astronomer who shaped the way science is conducted to this day. His dedication to rigorous observation and measurement set a standard that has been the model for the scientific method for the past four hundred years.

He did lose his nose in a duel and replace it with a collection of silver ones. He was astronomer and astrologer to the court of King Rudolph II of Bohemia. He is buried in the Tyn Church in Prague. In 2010, his body was disinterred by academics from Aarhus University in Denmark as they sought to discover just how he died. Rumours still circulate that he was poisoned by his assistant who was hoping to gain possession of the volumes of data recording the movements of the moon and inner planets. This assistant was Johannes Kepler—now regarded as a giant in the field of astronomy and whose laws of planetary motion still rule the cosmos today.

On the tiny island of Ven, off the Swedish coast, there is a museum dedicated to the amazing life of the man with the silver nose. A statue of Tycho Brahe stands in the museum grounds, his head tilted to the sky, a timeless memorial to a great man of science.

Acknowledgments

Thanks to:

Mrs Huebner's fifth grade class from Sioux Central Community School in Sioux Rapids, Iowa, for detailed instructions on how to injure yourself on a snowmobile.

Stephanie Stepan, for help with Czech translations and for her limitless enthusiasm, patience and goodwill.

Nicola and Philip Seale, for expert tips on how to avoid a crash in a Cessna 185, and for refuge in their hangar.

As always, to Jane Pearson and her seemingly endless pencil.